CELESTIAL MAGIC

THE CELESTIAL MARKED SERIES: BOOK ONE

EMMA L. ADAMS

This book was written, produced and edited in the UK, where some spelling, grammar and word usage will vary from US English.

Copyright © 2017 Emma L. Adams
All rights reserved.

To be notified when Emma L. Adams's next novel is released and get a free prequel short story, *Celestial Hunted,* sign up to her author newsletter.

1

"I have a question," said the vampire, leaning on the bar next to me. "If you screw a celestial soldier, does that guarantee you a place in heaven?"

"No," I said, "but I can offer you a one-way ticket to hell if you take one more step." I lifted my hand to show the celestial mark on the underside of my wrist. It was shaped like an arrowhead, and his proximity—like any preternatural being—brought out a flash of white light underneath the tanned skin of my wrist. If I turned the power up to max, he'd probably go up in flames. The vamp's cocky grin slipped, and he quickly slunk away back to his mates on the other side of the bar.

I switched off the light and took another sip of my drink. On reflection, this wasn't the type of bar you went to if you preferred to avoid attention. Even if I hid my tattoo, my aura was visible to certain people—piercingly white, like the Divinity who'd given me the mark. It didn't fit with my cheap tank top and jeans, but I'd deliberately played down my appearance. The trouble with places like this is that if you're not one of them, they catch on pretty fast. Still, a job was a job, and my client had offered a reasonable bonus… if he ever showed up. I'd been here an hour and had burned through my patience when it came to rowdy vamps playing drinking games and knocking glasses over. Whoever thought vampires were a bunch of ancient stiffs had never been to the Royal Arms at Happy Hour.

Tapping my foot on the edge of the bar stool, I ordered another drink. As I did so, a man sidled over to me. I stiffened, ready to flip my wrist over and flash the mark again, but he sat without a word. His red-tinted eyes and the glowing undercurrent to his dusky skin indicated his vampire status. If the curved incisors visible when he opened his mouth weren't enough of a clue.

"Are you Devina Lawson?"

Ah, shit. The *client* was a vamp. I liked to avoid working for vamps, or warlocks, or weres… basically, anyone with preternatural abilities. But he'd seen my ad and apparently ignored the strong hints that I preferred to deal with humans who'd ended up in some magical dilemma or other. Not the people who were more likely to have *caused* a magical dilemma.

"Yes," I said. "I am. Are you Mr Evans?"

He'd called me this morning and asked for help catching a thief. No hints at anything weird. I should have known something was up when he'd suggested meeting in this preternaturally inclined bar. The vamps in the corner were about the least threatening group of bloodsuckers I'd ever seen, but if ever there was an opportunity to pounce on me and force me to kill someone again, this was it. Raucous laughter came from the corner, where one of the vamps had brought a keg filled with some sort of blood cocktail mixed with tequila. Good luck to the poor sod who had to clean the carpets afterwards.

"As I said, something valuable was stolen from me last

night," he said, in a raspy voice. He cast an irritated look at the vamps, who were now drunkenly singing along to Queen beside the old-fashioned jukebox and getting half the words wrong. Vampires looked ageless, but these ones were apparently stuck in student-aged party animal mode forever. You'd think they'd get bored eventually, not that I'd know. Celestials weren't immortal, and the Divinities' elite soldiers had no time for earthly pleasures like going to bars and having fun. Apparently.

"Stolen by whom, exactly?" I asked warily. I didn't generally turn down a job, but if it involved stepping into the middle of the vampires' ongoing feud with the warlocks, forget it. This dude looked too sensible to be involved with that, but I needed to get all the facts first.

"A demon."

Of course it would be. It was apparently that sort of night.

"A demon mugged you," I said, making it sound like I didn't believe him. If word made it back to the celestials that I was helping vampires out with anything, netherworld-related or not, then I could expect a stern phone call at the very least. It wasn't illegal, just a swift ticket to trouble. I might need the work, but there's a limit on how many risky cases you can take on before trouble starts snowballing around you and the next thing you know, there's a Grade Three demon on your tail. I'd like to avoid drawing the attention of anything big in the netherworld if I could help it.

"Yes," said the vampire. "Stole my wallet from my back pocket. Maybe four feet tall, and covered in scales."

"Oh." I released a breath. "A magpie demon. No problem."

Chthonian lizards—otherwise nicknamed 'magpie demons' because of their attraction to shiny objects like coins—were responsible for a fair proportion of crimes when amateur occultists summoned them into this world. It takes balls to rob a vampire, but they weren't particularly advanced on the common sense front either.

Problem: this wasn't their home dimension, and getting answers from a netherworlder would be a long way from a low-profile case. On the other hand, I could summon one in my sleep, and I needed the money.

"Are you certain?" he asked me. "I didn't know celestials dealt with demons."

So he did know what I was. It wasn't mentioned in my ad, so for some reason, the mark didn't bother him. Strange. Most vamps were at least wary of us, if not outright terrified. After all, the celestial soldiers were living proof of the Divinities' presence, even if the angel-like beings never set foot in this realm. Like the arch-demons, they had more important things to be getting on with. But like weres and warlocks, vamps were demonically aligned, and therefore distrusted us on principle. Or, occasionally, wanted to score with us.

"I don't 'deal' with demons," I informed him. "But banishing and killing them requires knowing how to summon them, too. If it was recently in this dimension, it can't have gone far."

"What level did you reach?" He eyed the celestial mark, the permanent tattoo the Divinity had put on me when they'd brought me back from the brink of death after a drunk driver had smashed into my parents' car when I was sixteen. Not a destiny I'd chosen, but one I'd been pushed into by the fates. I didn't detect any malice in his tone, and celestials had a kind of celebrity status in certain circles. Something clicked into place—he must be a new vamp, turned not long ago. No wonder he didn't hang out with the rest of them, or pick up the hints in my ad.

"Three," I told him. "I don't work for them anymore. I'm a freelancer."

"And it's just you?"

I gave him a false smile. "Yes, it is. Shall we get on with it, then?"

As I rose from my seat, one of the vamps vomited blood all over the carpet. I don't believe in signs, but it wasn't an auspicious way to begin our job.

As summoning demons in public places was frowned upon, to say the least, we had to find the nearest location away from prying eyes. Luckily, the pub had an alleyway for that very purpose, near the closed beer garden. Rain lashed the pavements, soaking my shoes. I needed a new pair, but hadn't been able to scrape together the cash. I'd been in a permanent state of financial crisis since I'd quit working for the celestials, and as this client had oh-so-helpfully reminded me, things weren't going particularly great at the moment.

The alleyway was cramped and smelled of a combination of piss and rain with a hint of brimstone. A poster peeled off the wall, one of many depicting the face of Faye Carruthers, the most notorious ex-celestial of all time. I might not have left the guild on the best of terms, but unlike her, at least I hadn't summoned a demon and killed a bunch of people on the way out. The brick was marked with dark sooty lines from warlock spells, suggesting I wasn't the only one who used the alley for nefarious means.

"Can you really find the exact demon who stole from me?" asked the vampire. "I thought there were hundreds of them."

"It'll be difficult," I said. "As I'm sure you're aware, summoning netherworlders isn't something my people often have reason to do."

He nodded along, falling for the act. I wasn't lying. If any of my former tutors knew how often I consulted the nether realms these days, they wouldn't be amused to say the least. But there was nowhere better to get netherworld gossip than from the mouths of minor demons, even if I couldn't find the one who'd robbed him.

I pushed up my sleeve to reveal the celestial mark, and muttered under my breath. The muttering wasn't necessary, but it sounded good, and I needed to scrape together some credibility.

Celestial light shone from the arrowhead on my wrist as I directed it at the wall. Crisscrossing lines formed a pentagram shape against the brick, which would keep the miniature demon caged. The glowing white edges burned out evil and sin, apparently.

I stepped back from the wall. "It's tuned into the creature's home dimension. Now we wait for someone to answer."

The vamp peered dubiously at the pentagram. "What if something stronger comes out?"

"It can't. The trap's only big enough to draw in smaller fiends, and besides, the bigger ones aren't interested. I'd need to offer them a worthwhile price." Like my immortal soul, for instance. The vampire stared at me in awe, while I pointedly watched the pentagram instead of giving him an opening to bombard me with questions.

Finally, a bald, horned head poked out of the pentagram.

"Hey, Dienes," I said. I spoke in lower Chthonic, the unofficial language of his home dimension.

The demon spat against the circle. "More of your tricks, celestial. You look like hell warmed over." He grinned at his own joke.

"Hilarious," I said. Come on, I didn't look that bad. Okay, my clothes had seen better days. And shoes. My hair had grown back somewhat after a moth demon had eaten holes in it, though I usually looked like I could use a nap. Maybe he had a point.

"What do you want this time?" he asked.

"I need to find someone." I glanced at the vampire. "A magpie demon recently committed a robbery, basically right here. Anyone take a little trip over into this dimension recently?"

"You're a real demon," said the vamp, sounding a little faint. "Are you—?"

"Don't ask the demon questions," I told him. "Not if you want to leave with your soul intact." Not that vamps had one, according to the celestials' doctrine. Same with demons and weres. Warlocks were more complicated. There was nothing like celestial training to make you into a total bore at parties.

"That's impossible," said the demon. "Magpies are impossible to track."

"You know them all by name and give them presents," I said. "You *told* me that. Also, there's your useful little ability. Find them."

He grinned. "Guilty. I'll find your fiend."

He disappeared, and the pentagram remained, five points of light burning against the dark brick wall.

The vamp opened and closed his mouth like a goldfish. "You *know* that demon? You can speak to him?"

"That's Dienes. He appears whenever I contact that dimension and has the ability to track demons by scent. Handy for jobs like this."

"You..." He stared at me. "You're a *celestial*, though. I thought the Divinities forbade you to ask demons for favours."

"Ex-celestial, technically. There's nothing that forbids us from *talking* to demons. If anything, we're encouraged to form contacts in the netherworld dimensions. At the level I was at, I was tracking high-ranked demons every few weeks. You need contacts to do that."

Of course, I wasn't supposed to *keep* those contacts now I'd left, but they didn't have to know.

"I need that wallet back," he said. "See, I kept a bloodstone in there."

I spun to face him. "You didn't mention that before."

"Didn't want the other vamps to hear."

I swore under my breath. Bloodstones. Magically charged objects in the hands of a demon were a disaster waiting to happen. Well, it'd make the demon easier to track if Dienes didn't find him, but the little bastards got high on human energy, and that's essentially what bloodstones were. A substitute for drinking human blood, if the vampires grew desperate.

"Is that… bad?" he asked uncertainly. "I keep it with me for emergencies."

"Probably not," I relented. "Unless the demon's passed it onto someone else. We don't want them getting a taste for humans. They come after us often enough already."

He glanced at me. "You… you aren't human, though, right?"

Great. Should have seen that one coming. "Yes, I'm human. Just with a few added bonuses."

Like not being able to hide. I'd wanted to go incognito when I'd quit the guild, but when you attract netherworlders like I do, it's only a matter of time before people start asking questions. So I didn't bother with a cover story. Really, I ought to have got out of the city altogether, but I'd left with no money, and besides, there was work here.

A scream came from the wall, and a pair of giant eyes pushed up against the pentagram's surface. "There he is," came Dienes's voice from behind the struggling creature. Its skin was scaly and wrinkled, like a lizard, but the size of a small cat.

The small demon screamed and flailed its tiny fists. "Celestial! Please, please don't burn me. I beg you."

"Give back what you stole and I won't have to." I loomed

over the pentagram, holding my arm at an angle to show the arrowhead symbol. White light clicked on.

The little demon wailed, throwing the wallet out of the pentagram, where it landed in a puddle at the vampire's feet.

I smiled. "That wasn't so hard, was it?"

The vampire bent and picked up the wallet, rifling through the contents. If the demon had taken a rush of energy from the bloodstone, it'd be hyper for a few hours, but wouldn't cause any lasting damage.

"Everything there?" I asked, and the vampire nodded. "Awesome. Bye bye, little demon."

The pentagram fizzled out as I muttered another nonsense phrase under my breath, switching out the light as I did so.

"He's gone?" asked the vampire.

I shrugged. "I can banish him to his home dimension, but it's not permanent. He'll be back in a few months. Maybe years. Depends if someone else decides to try an amateur summoning. "

His sharpened canines gleamed in the celestial light. "He shouldn't come back."

"Don't worry, he won't remember you by then." I approached him. "My fees?"

He handed me a fistful of notes. Score. Now I could replace my shoes. "Thanks. I'd watch out in future. Carrying bloodstones… well, carrying anything that might be used as a demonic prop can only lead to trouble."

He nodded. "Thank you, Devina."

I turned to make sure the demonic pentagram had thoroughly disappeared. By that point, I ought to have known the job had been too easy. And the netherworld wasn't finished with me yet.

Sidestepping the puddles, I was halfway out the alley when the mark on my wrist lit up again, a tingling sensation running from my palm to my elbow. Then a scream drifted over the rooftops.

That was a human scream.

I spun around and ran down the alley, which intersected with a narrow passage between the high fences of the neighbouring shops' back yards. This area attracted more preternaturally inclined people than most and my celestial mark reacted to anyone who wasn't human or celestial, but the brightness of the light indicated a demon of a high level. The sort that wasn't supposed to appear in this realm.

I exited the back alley and crossed the road as a second scream tore through the night. The smell of brimstone stung my nostrils, coating the back of my throat like ash.

A man lay huddled at an alleyway's end, writhing and screaming. White light flared up around his wrist, which bore the same mark as mine. *A celestial.* No demon showed itself. Just him, screaming as though tormented by terrible pain. I froze, grabbed his hand to stop him hurting himself, then dropped it as searing pain burned my palm.

He threw his head back, revealing burning holes where his eyes had been. White light filled the gaps, brighter than the light on his hand.

I couldn't move. Not even when movement came from behind me, and a number of figures appeared, white light shining from their wrists, pinning me under a spotlight. "Devina Lawson," said a male voice. "You're under arrest for attempted murder."

2

Did I mention I wasn't an example of a perfect celestial soldier? Maybe if I'd actually volunteered for the job, it'd be a different story. Ten years on, I didn't remember much of the crash that'd killed my parents, just waking up in a morgue with my fatal injuries miraculously cured and scaring the hell out of the hospital staff.

I'd spent the next year cursing the Divinities for sparing me and not my family. Not an auspicious way to begin my training. At sixteen, I'd hit the peak of my rebellious phase and had zero patience for following the rules of an organisation I'd never signed up for. What'd swayed me was that higher level celestials got to travel all over the world on assignments. So I'd stayed the course, and won my mentors' grudging admiration because I was damned good at killing demons. Half of them still cheered behind closed doors when I left. I'd bet they did, anyway.

But for all the trouble I'd caused, a murder accusation was a step too far. I returned the celestial soldiers' wary looks and accusing stares with the most intense *fuck off* expression I could conjure. They honestly thought I'd attacked one of them. At least they didn't point their weapons at me, though I spotted knives and stakes strapped to the legs of my captors, and doubtless more weapons inside their identical grey jackets. I'd bet the guild would have ordered everyone to dress in white if they could get away with it, but getting demon blood out of light-coloured fabric was a bloody nuisance.

Two soldiers flanked me on the walk back to the guild and into the office of Mr Gavin Spencer, my former supervisor. His long-suffering frown hadn't changed, though the wrinkles on his face had deepened. The celestial soldiers who survived to old age tended to end up in admin positions. He'd retired early after a demon had torn his leg clean off. His prosthetic leg tapped against the back of his oak desk as it always did when he was agitated. So, generally every time I wound up in his office. Like the others, he wore the celestials' official badge—a silver arrowhead—pinned to the front of his smart suit. He didn't wear their battle gear anymore, but his celestial mark still worked as well as it had before.

I planted myself in the seat opposite him. "Hi," I said. "It's been a while, Gav."

He didn't smile back. "Celestial Devina Lawson, we have substantial evidence that you were involved in a demonic attack on one of our soldiers."

"Since when did you call me by my full name? I thought we were friendlier than that, Gav." I folded my arms across my chest. "I didn't attack the guy. You seriously think I'm capable of that?"

"Capable? Certainly. You reached a high rank, and you might have been promoted to Grade Four if you'd stayed."

"Ouch," I said. "You must really think I've gone off the rails. Why would I kill one of you? I don't even know his name."

"That would be because Celestial Caleb Rogers signed up a year after you left. He's unlikely to survive the night."

I fidgeted, goose bumps prickling my arms. The kid's screams would haunt me for a long time. The fact that the attacker hadn't finished the job spoke of a brutality that went beyond most regular demons. And considering regular demons were evil little shits, I definitely wanted nothing to do with whatever the guild's new recruit had managed to get himself mixed up in.

"I don't know what you want me to say," I said to Gav. "You know perfectly well I can't have attacked him. I don't even know any demons who can kill someone like that."

"No, but you're well known to have been consorting with the netherworld in the last two years."

"Consorting?" I raised an eyebrow. "You mean making use of my skills to help people? Same as I did here, except on my own."

He cleared his throat. He'd known my last partner, Rory, almost as well as I had. He might have been our supervisor, but even he didn't know the truth of what'd gone down on my last mission two years ago. Not because I hadn't told the guild, but because they didn't believe my report. Perfectly obedient celestial soldiers didn't drop dead of their own accord, eyes burning as though imbued with the fires of hell.

"We both have very different ideas of what constitutes the best use of your skills, Devi," he said. "However, I think in this case, you have some knowledge which might be useful."

"Wait," I said. "You don't think I did it, then?"

"Mr Roth doesn't," he said, "and he has an offer to make you. Since you seem to make a living by summoning demons for questionable clients lately..."

Great. They *had* been watching me.

"...we thought you might be able to track the attacker."

"Not if I don't know where it was summoned, and how," I

said. "There were no marks in the alley where he was found. No signs of a summoning. The actual attack might have happened anywhere, right? I didn't get a close look before your people hauled me in for questioning."

"We do have people surveying the crime scene," he said. "However, we've never had a death quite like this before. Your area of expertise—"

"Usually, I know what I'm looking for," I told him. "Besides, I haven't worked for you in two years. The only demon I've seen lately is one of those magpies, and *they* aren't smart enough to have links with anything strong enough to attack a celestial."

He sighed. "Please consider it."

"I don't see what I can do that you can't," I said. "I'm not a detective. You're the experts here."

"And you were one of our best. From the moment you signed up as a novice, you were leagues ahead of the others."

"Excuse me?" I spluttered. "What about the time I used a homemade adhesive spell to glue your furniture to the ceiling? Or set off fireworks in the quadrangle?"

"You still killed more demons than half our novices. And this is a demon unlike any we've seen in this city before."

"But nobody's actually seen it," I said. "That's suspicious in itself. Stronger demons tend to draw attention." By slaughtering the locals and tearing buildings down, for instance. This case was a little too specific. Nobody targeted a celestial soldier by accident. But usually if a demon did so, they didn't live to tell the tale.

"Maybe it will," said Gav, "but I'd prefer not to have any more victims before we get to that stage."

"I don't have enough to work with here," I said. "If there was one clue, I might be able to figure out what we're dealing with. Possibly. You're the ones with the encyclopaedia of demons." I indicated the book on his desk with that exact title.

"You still have access to our archives."

I know. I use them more often than you'd think.

"Don't take this the wrong way," I said, "but I prefer to work alone now. The guild's better off without me. And I think you can handle this case without my help."

"It's a shame you've taken that stance, Devi. I hope you'll reconsider—"

An earth-shattering scream drowned out his words, guttural and almost inhuman.

I was on my feet before my brain quite caught up with my body's fight-or-flight response, ignoring Gavin's shout behind me as I collided with the door on the way out of the office. Further down the corridor, the nurse's office was open. Several others had gathered there, too, and all wore varying expressions of fear and disgust.

The injured celestial screamed again, writhing on the floor where he must have fallen from the bed. Two others tried to hold him down, but he kept screaming, and they let go as though burned.

"His skin's on fire!" one of them shouted, waving his hands. Smoke poured from his palms, like he'd pressed them to a red-hot surface. My stomach turned over.

The celestial sobbed, and guttural words came out of his mouth between screams—

"The netherworld will rise. You will burn, celestials."

His head fell to his chest. Smoke poured off his skin, which had turned red-raw. The pits where his eyes had been glowed, intensely bright as the light of heaven—or hell. Then the lights winked out, and he fell onto his back. The smoke dissipated. One of the celestials who'd tried to hold him down took a wary step forward.

"He's dead," said the celestial quietly.

Everyone looked at one another, and then pretended not to look at one another. A shocked hush permeated the building.

I swallowed bile, backing away, and hurried down the corridor to the exit.

Nobody stopped me.

———

The journey home was a blur. I hated taking the train at this time of night, and the smooth motion of tower blocks gliding past the windows did nothing to calm my nerves. My head rang with the sounds of screaming and guttural words, and a chillingly awful familiarity which usually revisited me only in my darkest nightmares. The fact that Gav—and Mr Roth, at that—had called on me for this case was like a twisted joke. After all, I was the only person at the guild who'd witnessed someone else die in the same way.

Death was a constant companion as a celestial soldier. The first lesson drilled into every new recruit was that demons would stop at nothing to bring our world to the same state of ruin as their netherworld dimensions, in which they'd killed every celestial in existence. In this particular dimension, the first celestials had gathered in the Middle East thousands of years ago, then spread worldwide as the demons did. Almost every culture had some kind of demon, and most had someone who fought against them, even if we didn't always agree on methods. Like other cities built by the celestials, Haven City boasted the lowest percentage of demon attacks in the UK, despite the high population of vampires and warlocks drawn to the magical energy present in the city. So what'd happened tonight was unusual at best. Small crimes like the magpie demon's robbery could slip by the guild's notice. Not turning someone into a human torch.

That's enough, Devi. I'd already backed out of the case. Even though I'd dealt with more demons than most celestials at my level, if they knew the truth—that I was likely the only person at the guild who'd actually been into a demon realm —I was more likely to end up with a ticket to jail than my old job back.

Some things weren't worth the risk.

I left the train at the closest station to my flat and walked the rest of the way. My flat wasn't too bad, considering my chronic lack of cash, but I missed having a car. The light in the ground floor room next to mine told me that my neighbour, Fiona, was still awake.

"You look like hell," she said through her open window.

"Not the first time I've heard that tonight." I scrubbed a hand through my hair. "Early night for me, I think."

"Your phone's been ringing for the last hour," she called to me in her crisp Irish accent, as I used my fob to open the door to the block.

I groaned. The guild had my old number. Figures. "Never mind. I'll deal with it."

"Want to talk?"

"Maybe tomorrow. It's just work stuff, not really what you'd be interested in." I didn't need to offload my problems on Fiona, who was thankfully a long way from preternaturally gifted. She was the ordinary friend I didn't deserve, and I planned to keep it that way.

"I'm interested." When I walked into the hallway, she pushed open her flat door. "There's another picture of you on DivinityWatch. Looks like it was taken tonight. I thought you were going to the pub, not a vampire bar."

She waved her phone in my face. Judging by the lighting and angle, a certain vampire had been responsible for the picture. The one who'd thought screwing me would save his immortal soul.

"Great," I said. "Just what I need—a vampire admirer. Or stalker."

"Need me to hit someone?"

"Nah, I'm good." Fiona was a brown belt in karate, but vampires could move faster than even celestials and were capable of snapping a man's neck with their hands. Also, this was hardly the first time someone had focused their attention on me. Most of us have a few hundred unflattering pictures floating around the Internet somewhere, thanks to the weird celebrity status some people bestowed on us. A picture was easier to ignore than a brutal murder. I handed Fiona her phone back, hoping photos of *that* didn't show up online.

"Why were you on that site, anyway?" I asked.

"Someone claimed to have seen a Divinity again."

I snorted. "Happens every other week." I should have guessed. Sites like DivinityWatch had been set up for people to upload pictures they claimed to be of true Divinities. Mostly they were celestials who'd gone out drinking and decided to create their own light displays in inappropriate places.

"You never know," said Fiona. "Not sure they'd want to read the comments on this photo, though…"

I sighed. "Let's see."

She turned the phone around to display the screen. "See? Looks pretty shiny."

"That," I said, "is a naked man covered in neon glow paint photographed through a filter. Amateur job."

"Dammit," said Fiona. "Oh well. Maybe I'll be the first to see one."

I'd already told her that I hadn't seen the Divinity who'd given me the mark, but she wouldn't drop the subject. It was a relatively harmless obsession, all things considered, so I left her to it. From what I'd heard from the celestials, everyone had a different description of receiving their mark. Considering I was agnostic, they'd probably thrown up their hands and said, "Let's just give her the Generic Strobe Light Experience." The Divinities didn't show themselves here, not when they had hundreds of celestial soldiers fighting their battles for them, which as far as I was concerned, meant they weren't here at all.

Fiona said, "By the way, one of the vampires commenting on that photo claims you dated one another."

I grimaced. "It was one date. I didn't know." Apparently my entire past wanted to revisit me tonight. "I'll get that photo removed. I've no idea why these people are so interested in my life."

If I'd been sensible, I'd have washed my hands of the celestials forever and taken on an ordinary mundane job when I'd left. But there's a reason demon hunters find it hard to retire, and after eight years as a celestial soldier, I'd had no training in anything else. Underage teenagers were better than me at serving cocktails, and I was pretty sure a toddler could operate a cash register better than I could. So I'd spent the last two years doing what I did best—wading deep into preternatural nonsense and ending up with vampires creeping on me.

"Because they know you're a badass," Fiona said. "You look like you could use some sleep, though."

"I get that a lot." I faked a yawn. "I'll go deal with whoever's calling me. See you tomorrow."

Once I was inside my flat, I tracked down my old phone and deleted every one of the messages. To add salt to the wounds, I'd forgotten I'd used a picture of Rory and me as the background image. The photo was from one of our last cases, where we'd managed to wrangle a couple of days on the beach out of the guild's budget to make up for the trouble the demon had caused us. Rory lay sprawled on the sand, sunburned in pink stripes. I remembered teasing him about it. Old Me grinned at the camera, looking startlingly young, skin tanned deeply from the beach. I looked more like my mum than I remembered, with the same curly hair flowing down my back. Pity I hadn't inherited her amazing cooking skills, though.

I'd lost touch with my other relatives after I'd joined the guild. Most higher-ranked celestials are 'gently' advised to break off contact, because of our high mortality rate and our penchant for attracting every demon within ten miles. Most of Mum's family lived in Greece, while Dad's were all the way over in Yorkshire. So I'd stuck around in Haven City, the closest to a home I'd had since that car accident. The guild was the centre of the universe for me, as it was for all of us. Cutting myself off from them had hurt more than I'd admitted to anyone, least of all myself.

I left the picture but deleted the rest of the voicemail messages, then sent a message to the administrator of DivinityWatch asking them to remove the photo of me. Then I switched my old phone off and shoved it into a pair of old socks at the bottom of my drawer.

After changing into my comfortable pyjamas, I collapsed into bed, seeing the celestial's dead eyes flash before me. I groaned, pressing the heels of my palms into my face. *Cut that out.*

My phone's ringtone blared. Someone had tracked down my new number. Wonderful. I let it ring out, shifting uncomfortably. My skin felt sticky with the residue of cold sweat. I rolled out of bed and trudged to the bathroom. I turned on the shower, then grimaced as cold water doused my outstretched hand. For a second, I daydreamed of luxury hotels and room service, private taxis and first class flights. The perks of being a Grade Three celestial soldier were fine indeed, if you didn't mind the demons. I bit my tongue as the water turned scorching hot, then freezing cold, then settled on a sort of equilibrium. I shouldn't be thinking about going back to the guild again. Those days were behind me, with good reason. Gav and Mr Roth had a dozen capable, qualified celestials to give the job to. They didn't need me.

He was new to the celestials. Barely a child. And the demons killed him. I breathed in and out, fists clenched tightly against the cracked tiles on the wall.

Blackness seeped between my knuckles, like blood.

I jerked back, my heart pounding. Not blood, but brimstone. Residue from the summoning, maybe, or from when I'd touched the body. Wait—my hands had burned when they touched him, but now no mark remained. Just brimstone. The only remaining trace of demonic fire.

The killer was demonic… and the celestials' all powerful demon detectors hadn't picked it up at all.

Damn. Maybe we were in more trouble than I'd thought.

The netherworld will rise. You will burn, celestials.

3

I gave up on sleep at dawn, figuring I'd go for a run to calm down my mind. I couldn't train with the celestials or afford a gym membership anymore, so running was my only outlet.

Tugging on a tank top and jogging trousers, I hesitated before sticking my phone in my pocket, set on silent mode. Gav's latest message—*if you change your mind, you know where to find me*—flashed onto the screen, but I shut it down.

I ran a few laps of the neighbourhood, then fell into autopilot mode, my thoughts steering back to last night. The screaming, the smoke pouring from the victim's skin, burning anyone who touched him. It was well known that some demons came from infernal dimensions, but I'd never heard of one that could make a *celestial* spontaneously catch fire from the inside out before. Of course, that was likely why nobody could solve the crime.

As soon as I tuned into the world again, I realised my pace had carried me right past the pub where I'd been last night. I stopped on the kerb, looking around. No sounds disturbed the early morning aside from a few birds. The celestials had surely searched the crime scene last night, but nobody was around at this hour.

I'm going to regret this.

I slipped into the alley, past the brimstone-covered wall where I'd summoned Dienes, and followed the same path as I had last night. My feet slipped in puddles, and water soaked through the underneath of my shoes. The rain would have washed away any evidence, no doubt.

I reached the wall, and halted. Sooty black marks ran in trails down the wall like inky tears from the rain, only forming words when I took a step back.

They will burn the sin from you, celestials. All will fall.

My throat went dry. The words hadn't been there before. So—had the killer been back, in the few hours since the celestials had last been here? I hadn't got a look at the wall before the celestials had unceremoniously dragged me off to their base for an interrogation, but surely someone who'd been back to see the crime scene would have taken note. Seriously weird.

It's impossible. Things like that don't happen, with no explanation. Not in a rational world, they didn't. Admittedly, working for the celestials required making allowances for levels of weird most people wouldn't take at face value, but a murder of one of their own? No wonder they were willing to contact even *me* to ask for help.

Dark trails ran down the wall. However the marks had got there, I'd bet my celestial sword the origins weren't human. Which meant the demon was still at large in this dimension. Any celestial could banish a demon, but solving a case like this required figuring out what type of demon it was, where it'd come from—and how it killed. Not to mention who'd summoned the damn thing in the first place. No ordinary amateur, that was for sure. Most demons couldn't damage someone without touching them. But the only residue that remained in the alley was on the walls. I brushed my thumb over the edge and sniffed. Yeah, definitely brimstone. It meant netherworld, but gave no more clues about its home dimension.

My phone buzzed in my pocket. Gav. He'd asked me to show him if I found anything.

I snapped a photo of the wall and sent it to him. He wouldn't berate me for going back to the scene of the crime—at least, I hoped not. He probably knew I would. I was still a celestial, whatever I'd been doing for the last two years. *Look,* I said. *I'm at the crime scene and these words appeared on the wall. They weren't there last night, right?*

I can't see anything, came the response.

My photo quality was less than ideal, so I sent him another, clearer, picture, with the message—*Ring any bells?*

Come in and we can talk.

I looked down at my feet. My shoes were soaked in water, but streaked with odd brown patches from the puddles I'd walked in… right next to the crime scene. *Wait.*

Demonic summonings left residue behind. I couldn't smell anything other than brimstone, but if any traces remained, I *did* have a contact who was an expert at sniffing out demons who'd decided to skip over into another dimension for a bit. The odds of the demon coming from the same realm I'd contacted last night were low, but I'd *spoken* to Dienes right before the killing. If anyone knew, it'd be him.

I put a fair amount of distance between myself and the murder site before I found another alley, where I used my celestial light to burn a pentagram onto the wall.

"Hey, Dienes," I said, as the little horned head appeared between the bright lines of the pentagram.

"Seven hells, what do you want this time?" He pouted at me. "I was sleeping."

"You don't do anything except sleep. You'll be fine. Besides, it's urgent."

"Ooh, well *that* changes everything." He crossed his arms and looked at me expectantly.

I didn't just keep contact with him because of his handy links with certain species of trouble-making demons. There wasn't a demon type he didn't know of, at least in theory. In his dimension, the bad demons had mostly died out in the war with the celestials, from what I'd gathered. But he was a more up-to-date source of knowledge than the celestials' archives.

"It's secret celestial business," I said. "I have a question. Would you be able to identify the demon this belongs to?" I pulled off my shoe, balancing on one foot, and showed him the ashy black substance on my heel.

He stared at the shoe without taking it. "What have you done this time?"

I steadied myself against the wall with one hand. "Someone died, Dienes. A celestial. And I found this at the murder scene. It's a demonic killing. It can't be anything else."

I was aware of the irony of questioning one of said untrustworthy demons for information on his bloodthirsty kin, but I was fairly sure he wasn't even from the same dimension as the killer. Dienes was a lesser demon, anyway. He'd only come to me in the first place because I'd accidentally opened a way into the wrong dimension and one of his kleptomaniac friends had swiped my purse.

Dienes's brow crinkled, then he withdrew. "Looks like ordinary mud to me. And brimstone can mean any dimension, or demonic species. You might want to be more specific."

Telling him the details would breach the celestials' confidentiality agreement... if I still worked for them. Which I didn't. "Fire demon," I said vaguely. "Higher than a Grade Two, with non-standard abilities."

"Non-standard?" he echoed. "If you mean a different ability to setting things on fire, that's kind of the definition of a fire demon."

I sighed. "Yeah, figures. Anything powerful crossed over from your dimension lately?"

"Not that I'm aware of." He sniffed. "You celestials make no sense. Someone was killed by a demon. Why do you need to know which? You kill them for a living."

"Er, to stop it happening again? Because the way he died was horrible and weird. His eyes were burned out, like he caught on fire from the inside. Have you ever heard of that before?"

"No," he said. "And I'd like to keep not hearing about it, thanks."

"Dienes." I narrowed my eyes. "Come on. Cooperate with me. You know as well as I do that a demon who slays celestials is bad news."

In his world, we didn't exist. Celestials and demons alike had perished in the war, leaving only minor demons and humans living alongside one another. It wasn't a bad outcome, all things considered, but I still preferred ours. We were a stable world, one in which the celestials had won the war centuries ago and the humans had been able to get on with building civilisation without demons rampaging around and ruining things. Of course, the humans in this dimension had done enough rampaging around and murdering and conquering one another anyway, but that was beside the point.

He peered outside the pentagram. "Did it happen here?"

"No. You really think I'd summon any demon at a murder scene? I thought that was demonic residue." I waved my shoe at him. "It was on the floor at the murder site. No mud there."

"And no traces of a summoning?"

I told him as succinctly as I could. When I reached the part with the screaming, he swore so loudly, I lost my balance on one leg and accidentally put my shoe-less foot in a puddle.

"What?" I said. "What did that mean?"

"One of the demonic dimensions is making a move in your realm."

"What's that supposed to mean? I didn't think you were interested in this world."

"I didn't say *I* was. The demons have one goal: wipe out all celestials. Your world is a difficult target because your ancestors wiped out the arch-demons long ago. Do you have any idea how few worlds reach that point? Most fall at some time or other."

All will fall. I shivered. "I learned that crap at school. *Celestials are the only thing standing between peace and destruction,* was what they told me. I might not have been a model pupil, but I'm damned good at killing any rogue demons. And that one's walked right onto my turf." I shoved my damp foot back into my equally damp shoe. "So I'm going to stop them. I'd just appreciate a bit of direction before I go poking my nose in."

"You should stay out of this," he said. "I thought you weren't a celestial, anyway. Not anymore. You told me. Several times, in fact."

"I'm not," I said. "Doesn't mean I want a demon killing the others without teaching it a lesson."

"You," he said, "really need a hobby."

He might have a point. And I'd sworn not to get involved. But I literally didn't have anything better to do today. Sometimes I wondered if he was as lonely as I was. Which was kind of pathetic. I was the one who'd cut off all contact with my fellow celestials when I'd left. It was easier than hearing Rory's name come up in every conversation, and the flood of guilt every time, knowing I'd failed to stop him dying. Because I hadn't been there.

And I might have caused it.

Why had I decided confiding in Dienes was a good idea? I'd scouted out the only clues. I'd go and see if Gav had made sense of the words at the crime scene yet.

And decide whether it was worth shackling myself to the guild again to stop a repeat of what'd happened to Rory.

———

The guild was oddly subdued for this hour in the morning. Usually, everyone was wide awake and ready to face the mountains of paperwork that followed any mission. A blanket of quietness lay over the nondescript red-brick building that lay behind a high spiked fence separating it from its neighbours. The layout was more like a school than a workplace, which made sense because it used to be the guild's academy for new recruits before the old guild was destroyed by a demon four years ago.

After I'd scanned my celestial mark, the glass doors opened automatically into the entrance hall, which was filled with people milling about and talking in hushed voices. I felt like I'd interrupted a funeral, and wished I'd sneaked in the back way when several people looked in my direction.

Nobody was more awake than Lydia, who skipped over to me and beamed.

"Devina!" she said delightedly. In the past, we'd exchanged few words other than 'hi', but she spoke that way to everyone. She was a poster example of a model celestial soldier, radiating goodness as bright as her blond highlights even when everyone else was panicking.

"Hey, Lydia," I responded.

"You're back!" she said, for all the world like we were in an emotional reunion at an airport, not a murder investigation. "It's so good to see you."

"Uh-huh." I sidestepped her and made my way across the lobby. Lydia and I had been in the same year during our novice training, and considering every time I'd heard her name it'd been in phrases like "you should be more like Lydia", I should perhaps have built up more of a sense of resentment than I had. But it was hard *not* to like someone who could also take off a demon's head from ten feet away. Right now, however, her cheerfulness was a grating contrast to the memories stirred up by my entrance here, and stopping for a chat would inevitably involve an unwelcome trip down memory lane.

"You know your shoe's wet, don't you?" she called after me.

"Yep," I muttered, turning left into the corridor.

I rapped on Gav's office door, moving aside as a group of novices ran by, exchanging theories about the murderer. Apparently, instead of keeping the case details casual so as not to freak everyone out, the guild leaders had opted to go down the "terrify all the novices with every gory detail" route.

"What's *she* doing here?" whispered one of them. "Thought she quit."

"Thought she killed Rory..." The male recruit trailed off as I glared daggers at him. "Nice to see you again, Devi."

Ugh. Samuel Groves. He still wore his novice badges, so he must be retaking first year yet again. Despite being several years older than the average recruit, he apparently hadn't outgrown his terrible mullet haircut. I'd had the unwelcome job of having him as a shadow on a demon hunting job and he'd nearly got me killed. And then asked me out.

"I see you haven't improved your personal hygiene, Sam," I said to him. "Or your taste in haircuts."

Laughter followed from the novices.

"So you're *the* Devina Lawson?" asked a blond novice of around twenty. "What're you doing here?"

"She's come to find your vamp boyfriend, Louise," said one of the others. "Told you you'd get into trouble."

"Quiet," she hissed. "She's here for the killer, right?"

"I'm here to help with the case," I told them. It was none of my business if she was really dating a vampire, but trying to impose a bunch of rules on people often led to them doing the opposite. This batch of novices, given their rainbow-coloured hair and outrageous outfits, seemed determined to flaunt every rule in the celestial handbook at once. When I'd been a novice ten years ago, we weren't even allowed to swear in class. I was glad they'd loosened up a little. Maybe I'd been a good—or bad—influence after all.

The door opened. "Devi," said Gav. "I'm glad you came in."

"You knew I was coming." I walked in after him, closed the office door behind me and scooted over to the desk, planting myself in the chair.

"Why are you dripping water everywhere?"

"Slipped in a puddle. What did you want to discuss?"

"The photo you sent me," he said. "The words… they weren't there at the crime scene last night. The killer must have been back in the early hours of the morning. Maybe to unsettle us."

"Apparently, it's working." I was glad he believed me, if just so I didn't feel like I was losing my mind. "So we have a message which apparently appeared from thin air, and someone who died without any trace of who actually did it… anything new?"

"We've examined the body, for a start," he said. "There's no doubt his death was demon-related, which means it's up to us to solve, not the police's magical affairs branch. It's also clear that the demon in question never physically touched the victim. The forensic evidence shows that, at least."

"Damn. Are you sure? I mean, he caught fire. That's not usually something that occurs without a prompt."

"It seems he caught fire from the inside out, by some kind of demonic magic we haven't seen before. Unfortunately, there's no evidence of what type of magic. It's not one any of us at the guild have ever encountered."

"Plus he's a celestial," I added. "Most minor spells wouldn't affect him. Vampire bites barely tingle, were bites never get infected... I can't even think of a demon we're vulnerable to."

Not that anyone, even the celestials, knew every demon in existence. But most of the time, for a demon to cause physical damage, the attacker had to be touching the victim, or at least be close by. That should narrow our options—in theory.

"Precisely," said Gav. "No footprints or other traces were found at the scene, human or otherwise. The peculiar thing is the lack of residue which would accompany a summoning. Brimstone, yes, but not where we'd have expected it to be. I can only assume that the demon in question wasn't summoned anywhere near the site of the actual murder."

"Damn. You're right." Come to think of it, demon attack sites usually carried a weird stench, too. I'd been too focused on the screaming celestial and the fact that I was being arrested to notice its absence.

"All the evidence suggests we're dealing with an unknown element," said Gav. "The forensic team is still at work, and the victim's family have been informed."

I nodded. "If I'm to get involved with this, what exactly

can I do? I've already been back to the scene of the crime. Nothing there. It's not the sort of place with CCTV cameras, either. Sure would help to know what the recruit was doing last night. Maybe he ran into the demon and it followed him."

"We're still piecing it together. But there are certainly ways of tracking down any new demons in the area." He spoke with a clear emphasis.

"You seriously want *me* to do it?"

"We're under-staffed," he said simply. "Half of the team doesn't have the authorisation to deal with demons higher than a Grade Three, which is what we're looking at here."

"And the rest are already out on cases, right?" Now I got it. All celestials ranked Grade Three or higher were dispersed around the world on demon cases. Very few remained here. Not only had the city been built by celestials, it was plain impossible for a powerful demon to hide somewhere like this. Or so I'd thought.

"Correct," he said in answer to my question. "Some of the higher council have expressed reservations about your presence here, but the fact is, we don't have enough people. Demons like our killer won't wait until our reserve team gets here to strike again."

"Okay. I'm the stand-in." Doubtless several top-ranked Grade Four soldiers would be on a first-class flight back to Haven City, but if the killer struck again before they landed, Mr Roth had decided to place *me* as the one responsible. Awesome.

"Not exactly. I want to offer you full access to the guild's resources again, if you'd like."

He opened a drawer in his desk and pulled out a metal wristband, engraved with an arrowhead symbol. Burn marks and scratches marked the surface. "You kept it?" I should have expected that degree of sentimentality from my former boss—they guy who'd had my back no matter how badly I screwed up—but I thought I'd pissed him off intensely when I'd turned my back and walked out.

The smell of brimstone drifted over, remaining from the last time I'd worn it when fighting demons. Gav looked at me expectantly. What did he expect me to do, smile and reminisce about old times? Even the smell of dead demon reminded me of Rory.

"Are you sure?" I asked instead of taking it. "It might have slipped your memory, but I caused more trouble than I solved."

"I'm certain this is the right decision. There'll always be a place for you here, Devi."

Not according to some people. I swallowed the bitter responses and took the cuff.

I slid the armband onto my wrist and rotated it until the arrowhead lined up with the mark underneath. Not only did it allow me to direct the celestial energy wherever I wanted to, it also marked a clear challenge to any demon I came across. Not to mention, it was snazzy.

"Here." He handed me a stack of papers. "Fill those out and drop them off at my office within the next day, if you'd prefer to help yourself to clothes and weapons first."

"Thanks." The level of paperwork was one thing I didn't miss, but the wristband wasn't the only perk of my newly restored status. My regular human clothes weren't equipped with sheaths for hiding daggers or padded sleeves to reduce the impact when a demon threw me into a wall. And I was a sucker for a pointy object which could do some damage. Silver stakes—mostly for vampires, but they worked well on some demons, too—and knives were the only weapons we were technically allowed as civilians, but it's harder to fight demons with a bread knife or a corkscrew.

Still, I couldn't quell the sinking feeling that we might as well be facing down a demon armed with only a paperclip. A novice dead, with no evidence beside a taunting message. And there were far too many gaping holes in the story as to how the victim had ended up where he had.

I looked up at Gav. "I'll drop the paperwork off later. When they're done questioning the novice's friends, can someone give me an update on what he was doing last night? It might be important."

"I will." He nodded. "I know detective work isn't your forte, but…"

"Killing demons is." I gave him a grim smile. "And tracking them. I'll need to use your lab."

4

I had no business even being near the lab, but in my time at the guild, I'd developed a recipe for a potion which enabled a person to see a demon's aura. No demon could hide what they were, even the ones who were masters of deceit. Really, it was annoying that celestials lower than Grade Four couldn't see auras while most demons could, but I didn't make the rules.

Half an hour and only two explosions later, I held a vial of a thick mucus-coloured liquid. It looked as appealing as drinking paint, but I'd used it before and was reasonably confident it wouldn't poison me. The ashy taste clung to my throat and made me choke uncontrollably, eyes watering. With this potion, not only could I see demons' auras, I could pinpoint their home dimension. Well, if I described their aura to Dienes, anyway.

The second thing I made was a demonic compass, which would pick up on any demon within a few miles, even if it was too far away for my celestial mark to react to it. That was the tricky bit. Certain substances reacted to demons, but if the source was too strong, they'd break. I settled for taking a standard wristband—the sort that lit up when there were demons nearby—and a magical compass I'd bought at the market, which pointed in the direction of any sort of spell. Then I pulled them both to pieces and made what amounted to a Frankenstein's monster-like hybrid of both. It'd still fall to bits if it encountered a powerful demon, but only when I was close enough to essentially be standing on top of it anyway. So, the compass would be obsolete.

Normally, I'd have gone to the spot where the victim was last seen alive, but it was pretty clear the last place our demon had been was back at the crime scene, whether it'd actually committed the murder there or not. However, using any kind of magic came at a cost, and if the demon had taken up residence in this dimension, it'd need to recharge at some point. If it'd expended a ton of energy burning someone from the inside out, it'd likely head for somewhere with a big crowd, and at this hour in the morning, that place was the train station, not five minutes away from the celestial guild's headquarters.

I attached my mutant of a homemade compass to a necklace and slipped it around my neck. At worst, I'd draw attention from every preternatural being in the area, but at least it felt like I was actually getting somewhere.

I looked up from clearing the table in the lab and found myself face to face with Louise, apparent dater of vampires.

She sniffed. "What *have* you been doing in here? Making brimstone soup?"

"Taking up a side career as a scientist," I said. "I'm guessing Gav sent you to update me?"

"Yeah." She wore a sour expression that suggested she did *not* appreciate being sent on errands. Much less after her fellow teammate had been killed. "Nobody knows how Caleb ended up in that alley. He got off work at five, went home, then went out for a drink on the high street. So how he ended up on the opposite side of town is bizarre. The people he was with said he left early. Apparently didn't make it home."

I frowned. "Just how far away, exactly?" I'd suspected the demon had hit him with a spell somewhere away from the crime scene, but now I thought about it, there was a limit on how far someone could walk while burning from the inside out. Unless the spell hadn't activated right away.

"Too far to have walked to the alley," said Louise. "Unless he ran. But there's no footage, and he'd have passed at least three train stations with cameras running on the way over. We *think* he climbed through people's gardens near that alley, but he wasn't a rule-breaker, and he'd have no reason to. He's —he was—smart."

"Smart people do less-than-smart things when they've been drinking," I said, but she was right… there was something fishy about how a celestial would end up alone in a back alley near an area frequented by vamps and other preternaturals in the first place. And if they did, they were more likely to get cornered by a horny vampire. Not catch on fire.

"They were questioning his celestial partner," she added. "We'll get to the bottom of this."

"By 'they'," I said slowly, "you mean the inspector's here. Don't you?"

Inspector Deacon had been the final straw which had caused me to quit, after refusing to accept my report on Rory's death and suggesting my carelessness was to blame for the whole thing. As someone who'd lost *his* former partner when the old guild burned down four years ago, you'd have thought that'd make him more empathetic to my situation. Instead, he'd turned into an even more uptight rule-stickler who commanded his Grade Four soldiers to unleash full force against any demon, even the most harmless ones.

Needless to say, we didn't get on well.

"Yes, he is. But anyway, if you want more information on the case, Caleb's partner is in the inspector's office right now."

"Because what you really need after learning your friend died horribly is an hour with Inspector Stick in the Mud."

"I know, right?" She grimaced. "Hope he didn't keep her for long. Anyway. Can you do me a favour and warn me if he's leaving his office? I'm meeting someone and I'd rather he didn't see me leave the guild."

"Okay. Aren't you on duty?"

"Nope. Everyone in Caleb's unit has been given the morning off."

"Sure," I said, with a shrug. "I planned to talk to his partner, if she's still around."

"She will be." Louise skirted around me into the lab. Perhaps it was paranoia, but I hung about an extra few seconds to watch her through the small glass window in the door. Apparently I suspected everyone these days.

A slender figure slipped through the door at the back of the lab, wearing a thick hooded coat that covered his entire body from head to toe, and a balaclava. *Vampire.* I made to pull out my weapon, then she ripped his balaclava off and threw herself on him with more force than a starved vampire faced with a horde of humans.

Looked like the novices were right about the vampire boyfriend. But why sneak him into the back door of the guild? Likely for the same reason as the stunts I'd pulled as a novice: because breaking the rules gave a thrill like few other things. Apparently it was worth risking the inspector noticing—and also risking the vampire in question dying a horrible, painful death if any daylight got into the room. Guess that was why she'd picked the window-less lab.

Speaking of whom. I backed away from the lab at the sound of a familiar voice carrying down the corridor. Inspector Deacon's voice was a dull monotone, the sort that fitted a robot more than a human, and that pretty much summed the guy up. I headed towards the noise, and found the man himself inside one of the offices, surrounded by novices who looked possibly more frightened than they'd looked at the prospect of being murdered by a demon. The inspector projected a level of authority far beyond his six-foot-tall frame, and despite being in his late forties and completely bald, he still had the muscles from his days hunting demons as a celestial soldier. One of the best. Too bad his sense of humour had retired from hunting before he did.

"Devina Lawson," he said. "What exactly are you doing here?"

"Hi," I said. "I've been asked to help with the case."

He narrowed his eyes at me. "This is an ongoing investigation. I'm in the middle of a questioning."

"What, all of them at once?" My gaze swept across the novices. "If you're going to play detective, maybe you should lock the door. Or hire some actual detectives."

"Your attitude clearly hasn't changed, Celestial Lawson."

"Why change a good thing? I've been told I need to hear the latest on how the victim came to be where he did."

"Apparently he figured out how to walk through walls," said one of the novices. "He walked three miles in approximately five minutes."

"Are you sure?" I asked. "Might the demon's magic have caused it?"

"Naturally," said the inspector. "There's no other possibility, and no reason to repeat all our information to you."

"I'm part of this investigation," I said, then addressed the novices. "Which of you was the victim's partner?"

"I was," said Sandra Yun, a girl I knew from the weeks I'd spent mentoring novices as one of the guild's annoying annual compulsory 'team-building' exercises. "That's the part I don't understand. The reason he left the pub early last night was because we were supposed to be on a mission today."

"What sort?"

"Bag and tag mission. Suspected rogue vampire. Two others caught the vamp instead."

"And might this vampire be connected to his death?" I asked dubiously. I didn't think so, somehow. Vampires were susceptible to bursting into flame in daylight under any circumstances. No demons necessary. The attack had happened at night, besides.

"Perhaps. We're still waiting for him to calm down. He's in the jail. But he's blood-crazed and can't string a sentence together. He was caught miles from the crime scene. He can't even sign his name."

I guess I can't see a blood-crazed vampire writing creepy text on the wall in brimstone, either. "Okay. Just checking. Vamps can't use magic, anyway."

"Maybe he has friends in low places," said another novice. "Netherworld-low."

"I got that," I said. "And I don't think so." Vamps didn't get on with demons, despite falling into the same untrustworthy category as other preternaturals. If they did, they wouldn't get into fights with warlocks so often.

Inspector Deacon glared at me. "If you're quite finished, Celestial Lawson, this meeting is over. What is that around your neck?"

I looked down. "Homemade demon detector."

He gave me a disapproving look. "Put it away. Your hazardous lab experiments shouldn't leave the building."

"Does he normally hold important meetings with the door open?" I asked the novices in a stage whisper on my way out. Nobody laughed. Guess the doom-and-gloom atmosphere had got to them. They weren't yet at the stage of cracking jokes over dead bodies like those of us who'd lasted longer in the field.

I turned to Sandra as I was leaving. "If you don't mind my asking, what was he like as a person?"

"He was… fine," she mumbled. "I mean, he worked hard. Top grades. No trouble with demons. He was barely qualified, for the Divinities' sake. I don't understand why they'd target him."

"Me neither," I said. "I'm sorry." There wasn't much more to say. I didn't do deathbed talks well—I'd barely lasted five minutes at Rory's funeral before slipping out the back door. He'd have understood, though. If the guild had listened to me, he'd have had a private funeral, not a public one shared with a half-dozen other celestials. All celestials who died in the field were buried in the guild's private cemetery here in Haven City.

Thinking of Rory's funeral didn't help my unease about this whole situation. But I had the demon detector, as ridiculous as it looked, and now I apparently had free reign to hunt for the killer.

Okay. Do your thing, demon detector.

I switched it on, and left the guild through the front doors, heading for the train station.

A pair of glass doors led into a wide open space dominated by a giant statue of an angel, which bathed the whole place in golden light. People gathered in front of the display boards, while others dragged suitcases between the many cafes and restaurants open even at this hour in the morning. I wove in and out of the crowd, searching for an aura that looked out of place. Most people's were muted. Only the preternaturally inclined were visible—and there were a few here, mostly warlocks. No vampires, for obvious reasons—aside from Louise's balaclava-wearing boyfriend, they tended to sleep during the day, sometimes in actual coffins. As for the handful of warlocks, they looked barely more awake than the humans did, and their auras were hardly visible. Maybe the demon was too scared of the angel statue to show itself here.

I boarded a train along a route I didn't normally travel by, taking me into the more preternaturally inclined part of town. The theory of the vampires' involvement was probably false, but demons were also drawn to their own kind, and there were an awful lot of warlocks living close by. Thanks to careful planning, they were housed in certain areas, with enough distance from the ordinary humans to stop complaints about being cornered by blood-starved vampires or woken in the early hours of the morning by warlock spells causing explosions.

Unfortunately, everyone seemed to be asleep, and the streets were almost deserted. *Right... it's a Saturday morning.* I worked whenever jobs came in, and the guild operated on a shift system, so I forgot most sane people were sleeping in or nursing hangovers.

Despite my own general lack of alertness, I'd walked for half an hour before realising I'd somehow wound up back at the pub I'd been at last night. The compass device around my neck glowed bright as a beacon.

Damn. Is there a demon here after all?

The pub wasn't open yet, so I slipped down the back alley. The glow intensified, pointing at the wall where I'd summoned Dienes.

"I *know* there are traces here." Two hours in the lab and the compass had led me back where I'd started. I might as well have walked around a steel building with a metal detector. What a waste of time.

At this rate, I'd have spent more time near the murder scene than the rest of the guild. Muttering a curse under my breath, I backtracked and circled the pub again. Maybe one of the vamps *did* know something, but they'd be asleep. I was contemplating breaking into the place to hunt for traces when the tracker lit up with a loud beep.

Demon. The trace was unmistakable, and easy for me to pinpoint. Right behind me. *Thanks for that, handy device.*

The neighbouring alley emerged into a street at a right angle to the one the pub sat on, and my mark was heading right this way. If I stayed out of sight, I could see my target. I fiddled with the band on my left wrist, wishing I didn't feel so rusty with my celestial powers. The beeping grew so loud, I buried the device in my armpit to muffle the noise. Maybe this wasn't such a good idea.

I reached the alley's mouth, and saw it, on the other side of the road. The demon was shaped like a tall broad-shouldered man. *Wait.* He wasn't a demon at all, but a warlock. Their auras sometimes looked similar, so it was an easy mistake to make… and a warlock could certainly be capable of burning someone's eyes out. Half demon, half human, they inherited their magic directly from their demon parent and could be just as powerful. My device had one big flaw I shouldn't have overlooked: it was drawn to anyone with demonic origins, not just pure demons.

The beeping grew louder, and the device began smoking. Battery overload. I wrenched it off and shoved the broken device into my pocket. To have caused such a reaction, the man in front of me must be stronger than any warlock I'd seen. *Definitely not my best idea.*

But he was too close to the murder scene for me to risk running for backup and losing him, and besides, I'd subdued warlocks alone before. They were as vulnerable as any demon to my celestial weapons.

I kept following at a distance, until he veered down a side alley parallel to the one in which I'd found Caleb dying last night.

No way. He just did my job for me.

I barely restrained a smile as I slipped into the alley behind him, and white light flared around my hand, striking the ground in front of him and leaving a sizzling hole. Five holes would create a trap to encase him. I fired a second bolt of light from the mark on my wrist. Then a third. Three points on a pentagram. The fourth shot from my hand, and he spun around, raising a hand. Lightning sparked between his fingertips, halting my steps.

"Celestial," he said. "What do you want?"

"You're standing on a murder site," I said, "and there's demonic traces over both you and the body. I'm sure I don't need to explain further."

His brow furrowed. He didn't look like your typical warlock. Half of them had horns or tails. He looked human. Strong jaw, chiselled cheekbones underneath dark golden eyes. His skin was deeply tanned. I'd have guessed he was from somewhere in the Mediterranean had he been human. As it was, I was pretty sure the dark red touch to his hair wasn't from regular hair dye, and the golden glint in his eyes wasn't from tinted lenses. His whole posture exuded *danger*, an electric sizzle in the air promised that when he attacked, I wouldn't like it. He'd melted my demon detector without even touching it.

I had the distinct impression I'd unwittingly ambushed someone not only stronger than any warlock I'd seen before, but also stronger than most *celestials* I'd met. But backing down wasn't an option.

"Going to confess?" I asked. "Or do I have to use this?" I switched on the light under my wrist.

He smiled. "You don't want to do that."

Tension gripped my shoulders, my body moving into a fight stance. "Tell me your name, warlock."

"The name's Nikolas Castor," he said. "You don't need to remember it."

Shadows closed around him, like a cloak, and when they cleared, the warlock was gone.

It took a second for my brain to clock that he'd disappeared. I took a step forwards. He didn't reappear. He'd opened a door into the netherworld—one of the demon dimensions—in two seconds flat, without a single prop.

"Well, shit," I said aloud. The celestial lights died out at a snap of my fingers, and still, the warlock didn't reappear. He really had gone.

I'd always thought of warlocks as living closer to the human realm than the demon one, and being mostly indifferent to their warmongering demon kin. I'd dealt with a few rogues in my time working for the celestials, but other than the occasional punch-up with vampires or weres, they were secretive and kept to themselves. We didn't bother them, and they didn't bother us.

Not so much anymore.

This was personal now. Mostly, it pissed me off that he'd slipped through my fingers. *You over-confident, cocky warlock. You'll be sorry you challenged me.*

I found myself smiling at what was left of the trap. This was what I'd missed about the job. Not that I'd ever in a million years admit so to Gav.

I'd find that warlock, and if he was the killer, I'd make him pay.

5

"A *warlock?*" asked Dienes later, when I summoned him into the alley wall, after switching off my half-formed trap.

"Yep." I gave him a description, with no embellishment. The guy had spoken English, so he definitely lived in this dimension, even if he apparently split his time with another one. "He also walked through a shadow and disappeared. Know any demons who can do that?"

He swore. "Shadow aligned. One of the demon-ruled dimensions. Don't mess with them."

"Too late. I need to know how to contact that dimension."

He groaned. "You would, wouldn't you? The netherworld dimensions are bad news."

"I don't care. He might be the killer, and if we take him out, we stop other celestials from dying."

He folded his arms. "I didn't think you cared about them."

"I care about people getting killed by a demon, Dienes. Or a warlock. Whichever it is, I want them caught and punished for their crimes."

"You're going to get *me* killed," he said. "I'm only a lesser demon."

"And my best source of information," I said in my most flattering tone. "If demons are moving in on this dimension, they'll reach you eventually. I seriously need to track this dude. His power broke my demon tracker."

"Your what?"

I pulled a broken piece of the tracker out of my pocket. "Homemade demon tracker. It almost worked, but he was too powerful. I need a list of the ingredients to set up a trap to drag him back into this dimension. He's not a full demon, so I won't need to go all-out."

He sighed. "You're determined to get yourself killed, aren't you? You can't catch a shadow demon using your celestial whatsit." He butted his head against the line of white light keeping him caged, and yelped as it singed his forehead. "You'll need a proper sturdy pentagram to keep him enclosed. And to summon him, you'll need goat's blood, a ton of brimstone—"

"By a pentagram," I said, "you mean a guild-made one, don't you?"

"Unless you know someone else who does custom-made demon traps."

No. The guild were the only ones authorised to make demon-summoning equipment, as he knew well. And the only pentagram I'd seen was in Gav's former office... which was, of course, where Inspector Deacon had been conducting his investigation. Oh, that was just bloody perfect.

"And," said Dienes, "you'll need something from the dimension itself."

I blinked. "Like what? The guy didn't drop anything."

"If he skipped dimensions, it's not possible to do that without leaving residue behind."

"Well, that means I'll have to do it here." I looked down at where he'd vanished. "If I spend any longer hanging out in alleys, people will think I'm the killer."

"That would be unfortunate. I do enjoy our conversations."

"You know, sometimes I do, too," I said. "Not sure what that says about me."

"You have good taste," he said, and disappeared.

I exhaled in a sigh. Wonderful. Just what my day needed—stealing from the very people who'd given me my old job back. Apparently my teenage rebellious days were back in full force.

Since the warlock had left no traces, I'd have to summon him here in this alley—without the celestials catching me. Since a certain inspector approached such things with the subtlety of a vampire on a blood craze, there was no way I'd tell him about the warlock until I knew for sure he was the killer. If the pentagram didn't work, no harm done. If so… I'd interrogated and killed demons before. A warlock would be no trouble.

Once again, I rode the train to the guild, wishing I'd asked for my guild-issued car back. Handing the keys over when I'd quit had been more difficult than signing away my demon-killing weapons. But the trains were quieter now the morning rush had died down, and I got there in record time. So far, so good.

I stopped at the lab first. It looked like Louise and her vamp boyfriend had run off, which was probably for the best. I slipped into the room and shoved as many ingredients as I could into my rucksack, in case things went wrong and I had to run. Then I went the long way around the campus-like structure, walking casually to avoid giving myself away. There were a handful of people about, but the crowds from earlier had dispersed. And the office was unlocked, probably because Gav figured I'd be back.

Naturally, as soon as I'd entered the room, footsteps carried down the corridor. I cursed under my breath, glad I'd taken stock of the room's layout when I'd been here before. The spacious desk had just enough room to hide underneath, even for a tall-ish woman. I ducked under the wooden surface as the door opened again.

"The timing doesn't add up," said Gav's voice. "He *couldn't* have reached the scene of the crime so quickly. It's not possible, even if someone got him in a car and drove him. I think you're appointing blame in the wrong direction, Inspector."

"That's not for you to decide."

The foul smell of one of the Inspector's cigarettes drifted overhead. I shoved my hand in my mouth to avoid coughing. Damn. I'd forgotten that slight detail about the murder.

The victim didn't end up in that alley because he walked there. Something took him there.

Like… a warlock who could skip through dimensions.

"Perhaps not," Gav said, "but the murder itself was likely not committed at the place where he died. Alerting the human authorities will only cause panic amongst the public."

Damn. One murder and he was already talking about letting the humans know? Just imagining what the tabloids would do with that information made me shudder. They were convinced we were waging an invisible war every minute of the day, and gleefully sought out any netherworld drama. Demons loved the attention. They'd be doing them a favour. I'd have hoped the inspector would know better, but apparently not.

A moment passed before the inspector said, "Was one of your novices treading in brimstone? It's on the carpet."

"Probably," said Gav, without missing a beat. "You know how novices can be. This is a mistake, Inspector. We can discuss the matter later. Maybe you should give orders to the novices. I think it'd help for them to have something to occupy their attention."

"Don't tell me how to do my job," said the inspector. "You're running close to overstepping your boundaries. Don't forget who's really in charge here."

"You, of course, Inspector."

I bit back a laugh. The inspector apparently didn't pick up on the sarcastic hint underneath Gav's tone, because seconds later, retreating footsteps sounded. *I owe you one, Gav.* I counted down from ten, then climbed out from underneath the desk and darted to the cabinet at the back of the room, where the gold-plated pentagram lay. I pulled out a lock pick and opened it, thanking the inspector for being so bloody hopeless when it came to security. In fairness, no non-celestial could actually step into the building, even through the back doors. And nobody but one of us would be able to operate the pentagram. Didn't mean I wanted it missing or damaged, but hopefully the summoning would go smoothly enough that I could return it in one piece. I'd talk to Gav in confidence later and explain what I'd been doing.

The pentagram—a bulky metal device carved with runes I couldn't read—wouldn't fit in my rucksack, so I shoved it up the back of my coat instead. *This wasn't your best idea, Devi.* Between the pentagram's points poking me in the spine and the added weight of my rucksack, I was out of breath and sweating by the time I'd boarded the train. I picked an empty carriage and did my best to avoid the occasional stares.

After disembarking at the stop nearest to the crime scene, I hurried out of the station as fast as possible. Luckily, nobody had shown up at the alley yet.

"This had better bloody work, Dienes," I muttered, when I'd finally got the damn pentagram set up. I pulled out the ingredients and scattered them into the centre, using my celestial light to ignite each of the five points.

As light filled the gap, it turned fluid, expanding to cover the ground and half the wall, too. I backed up, hoping nobody wandered past the mouth of the alley. The area where the warlock had vanished was entirely covered. Hopefully it'd be enough.

Seconds ticked by. Sweat trickled down the back of my neck, and the taste of brimstone coated the back of my throat. *Come on, warlock,* I thought.

The liquid-like surface of the light glimmered. Then, the shadows came.

6

Shadows filled the gap in the pentagram, from one point to the next, until I looked down into a mass of total darkness. I held up my left hand, ready to grab a weapon. If the trap had caught the wrong person, considering what Dienes had told me of that dimension, I'd be in trouble. *Or not. They can't escape the pentagram.* It was strong enough to hold a high level demon, after all.

The outline of a man appeared, arms held out as though to push against an invisible force. Furious words in a language I didn't know grated against my ears. And then he appeared properly, trapped between the points of the pentagram.

Damn. I'd actually got him.

"You again," Nikolas snarled. "Release me."

"Nope," I said. "You and I are going to have a little chat."

He glanced down at the point of the pentagram beside his foot. "You dared to trap me?"

"You're a murderer."

He looked me in the eyes. "So are you."

A shiver ran down my back. Sure, I knew what I was. And

what *he* was. But I hadn't got a close look at his aura before. Pinned in my trap, it was like a shadow, charcoal-black—cold, and ancient, and terrible. I might as well have stared in to the very depths of hell.

"You killed a novice celestial last night," I said to him. "Didn't you? How did you do it?"

"I have no idea what you're talking about." He stepped forwards, reaching out a hand to touch my face. "You're an interesting human."

Shit. He shouldn't be able to touch me. I recoiled from his ice-cold fingers. The pentagram was meant to contain him. How—?

I looked down, and froze. The pentagram's points had shifted towards me—surrounding me. Now *I* was the one trapped.

"How the hell did you—?"

His hand caressed my face again and the smell of brimstone washed over me, abruptly turning to something more appealing, warm and enticing. Damn. He was using a lure on me. Even celestials weren't immune, and with the trap caging my feet, I got the full blast of it. My eyes watered as though he'd sprayed perfume in my face, and all my senses flared up. My body fell still, even as I fought to move. The pentagram's magic had trapped me, immobilised me.

How? It's supposed to only work on demons.

His hand moved down my face to my shoulder, his gaze inches away as though searching for something invisible. He took my wrist and flipped it over—not the celestial hand, but the other one. Fear churned inside me, even as scorching heat followed the path of his fingertips. My blood responded to the lure, a primal longing stirring.

"Where is it," he growled, his lips close to my neck. "Where is your demon mark?"

He thinks I'm a demon.

The thought broke through the stupor of his lure, and I squeezed my eyes shut, fighting with all my strength. Holding my breath to avoid inhaling any more of that intoxicating scent, I clenched my left wrist and *pushed.*

The light split, and I broke free, slamming into him. The warlock hit the wall, and my fist collided with his. "Give me one good reason why I shouldn't burn the darkness out of you right now."

"Celestials." He laughed softly. "You think yourselves righteous purely because you hold the power of the divine in your hands. As though light could ever exist without the dark. You're marked, celestial. Maybe the mark isn't visible, but a demon has left its magic inside you. And when the celestials find out…" He trailed off suggestively.

He was lying. He must be. Demons made lying into an art form. He was screwing with my head, now the lure hadn't worked.

"How long did it take you to practise that line?" I asked. "Luckily for both of us, I don't give a crap what the other celestials think of me. Same as you."

Light suffused my palm, washing over him.

"You can't kill me," he said. "I'm the son of an archdemon, and even your celestial light will merely tickle. You can try it if you like."

Oh, boy. He was the offspring of a fallen angel, which made him virtually indestructible. If he was the killer, taking him out would be all but impossible. If not, he'd violated me with his magical ability, screwed with my head, and shoved me into my own trap. That was enough to earn an arrest, but I highly doubted he'd meekly agree to come with me to the celestial guild.

"Did you kill any celestials?" I asked in my most threatening voice.

"I told you," he said, "I didn't. And I'd advise you to leave this place before things get… uncomfortable."

"Sure, like I'm letting you go after what you did." His aura alone told me he was a cold-hearted killer. Who other than the offspring of a major demon could have committed such an awful murder? He was the perfect tool for the true arch-demons who wanted to take our world. I'd really screwed up. But come on, how was I supposed to know what he was? The chances were one in a million. I might as well have set up a trap for a mouse only for an escaped lion to wander into it instead.

Celestial light circled my wrist. "I didn't want to do this," I said. "Sorry. This might hurt a little."

The pentagram hummed, and a large furred shape leaped out of the air. Light spun from my fingers, catching the demon across the neck. As it died, its body vanished, back into the pentagram. I'd broken the barrier when I'd come out —but it was still tuned into the dimension I'd originally opened.

Nikolas turned to me with narrowed eyes. "That," he growled, "was what I was dealing with when you dragged me into this dimension. Now they have your scent, too. If I were you, I'd put that pentagram away."

Three more jumped through. Each biter demon was dog-sized and covered in fur, but the three sets of serrated teeth sort of took away their initial cute-and-cuddly appearance. I dived, grabbing for the pentagram to switch it off, but a demon's furry body collided with mine from the side. I landed on my feet, conjuring light to my hand. Light speared the demon between the eyes, and its body collapsed.

The warlock faced two more demons. Black lightning crackled from his fingertips, making the air tingle with static. I pushed my wristband down, exposing the gleaming celestial mark. He wasn't the only one with fancy tricks. Light spilled from my hand, forcing another of the demons to back away and giving me an opening to search out the switch that turned off the pentagram. That'd teach me to borrow a prop without looking up the instructions for shutting it down.

I found the switch. As one of the lights of the pentagram died, two fiends leaped out. Lightning shot from the warlock's hands, spearing one of the fiends through its spine and catching the second in the face. As their lives winked out, their bodies disappeared. Damn, he was fast. I hadn't known warlock magic worked so effectively against other demons.

The second light disappeared, and a larger beast leaped out of the remaining shadows. The size of a boar, it bristled all over with sharp spines. Light wasn't enough to take it down, which meant accessing my celestial weapon for the first time in almost two years. I hoped it remembered me.

With my left hand, I reached through the invisible film connecting all the dimensions of this realm. A gleaming white sword with gold trimming appeared in my hand. I grinned. Now this was more like it.

I brought the sword down in an arc, decapitating the beast in one stroke. When the light hit, its skin melted from its bones, its body slumping and folding in on itself as death pulled it back through the rift into its home world. Dropping to my knees, I turned off the pentagram's remaining lights. The warlock watched me, his dark aura etching his body in shadow.

I stood, raising my sword, light shimmering up to the hilt. "Still don't believe what I am? No demon could wield this."

Nikolas carried no weapons, but then, he *was* one. A force of nature. A fallen angel with a human's face, looking at me as coldly as he had the demons. I had no means of containing him if he turned on me.

"I admire your courage, celestial, but it's too late for you now," he said.

I rolled my eyes. "Sure, keep spewing your cryptic demon nonsense. I don't suppose you want to save me the effort and tell me how you trapped me in my own pentagram?"

"I'm delighted you asked." He moved closer, his warm breath caressing my cheek. "I told you already, if you remember. The pentagram is designed for demons. You are one, as far as your angelic trap is concerned."

You liar. I opened my mouth to tell him as much, and he brushed his lips down my neck, hitting me with another blast of dizzying power. I swayed on my feet, and by the time I'd caught my balance, he was gone.

I swore loudly. The demonic residue would remain, but the creatures themselves had disappeared back to their own dimension. So did my sword, which spent most of its time in a pocket dimension of sorts whenever I wasn't using it. The closest the celestials got to real magic. What the warlock had done was something else entirely. Not the lightning, but the fact that he'd pushed the pentagram on top of me. I picked it up, shaking loose brimstone out of the corners. He was the offspring of a fallen angel. Of course he'd lied to me.

And now I had to sneak the pentagram back into the guild without getting caught. Awesome. In fairness, the trap would have worked on any demon other than him. I should have looked up the shadow dimension in the celestial files first, but I had the sneaking suspicion that it was hidden behind a big red FORBIDDEN sign. Even Grade Threes weren't permitted to deal with full on arch-demon territory. And most people wouldn't run into one in their lifetime.

Sighing, I took out my phone and called Gav's number.

"Devi," he said. "I don't suppose you want to tell me where you are?"

"On my way back to the guild," I said. "Thought I had a

lead, but it turned out to be false. Anyway, is there a chance I can access part of the archives? It's not something I can get hold of on my phone."

"It depends what it is," he said, sounding a little wary.

"I'm looking for everything you have about fallen angels."

"What are you scheming this time?" he asked.

"Nothing. I'd rather speak to you in person, but yeah… any info would be great."

"I'll need to get permission from the Inspector, and he's in a rage because someone broke into the office and removed the guild's ceremonial pentagram. You wouldn't happen to know about that, would you?"

"Not at all. Er, by the way, can they work on anything other than demons? Like humans?"

"What?" He sighed. "You know the basics, Devi. Of course they don't. They're designed to react to demons only."

Then the warlock did it. He must have.

"Okay," I said. "Thanks." I hung up. It was a mistake. Definitely a mistake. There was no sense getting worked up over warlock mind games. Maybe he was the killer, maybe not. But he certainly knew something. He hadn't ended up at the murder scene by coincidence. Add in his comments about me, and there was no way I was letting him go without making an effort to get hold of him again.

I kicked damp mud over the alley floor, and used my celestial light to burn the parts of the wall and earth where the demon blood had landed. Our light burned out everything demonic, even blood. Nothing remained but brimstone. And…

The warlock's coat lay at the alley's side.

I stared for a second. Did he do that on purpose? Was he goading me? As if I'd miss the chance to pick up a prop. I wouldn't take it home with me, but he couldn't enter the guild without a celestial mark anyway. Plus, I could hide the pentagram under there rather than walk with it poking me in the spine.

Thanks for that, Nikolas.

A loud beeping issued from my own coat pocket. "You're a bit late," I told the demon detector. "Also, you're supposed to be broken." The detector must be sturdier than I'd realised. But maybe it'd zeroed in on the warlock again. If nothing else, my sword would work on him. He might not be able to die—and I wasn't the biggest fan of torture—but I needed answers.

Rory's tormented face flashed before my eyes and my hands clenched on the warlock's coat. It didn't smell of brimstone or smoke as I might have expected of a demon. It smelled sort of like his lure—an unidentifiable pleasant scent. I held it at arm's length in case it carried any residual effects. After the morning I'd had, the last thing I needed was to end up under a warlock's thrall.

My pocket beeped again. Loudly. It couldn't be reacting to the warlock's coat. Maybe he'd come back after all.

I half-ran down the street, following the beeping noise. Of all the times for the device to start doing what it was supposed to—it had to work *after* the warlock had got away. The way it was vibrating, I ought to be standing on top of the target. But nothing appeared. I ducked into an alley and checked the compass. It pointed straight ahead.

Then came a scream, high and loud. Human screaming.

Shit. Not again.

7

I picked up speed. The beeping continued in tandem with my quick footsteps, and the screaming didn't stop. I didn't know this neighbourhood well enough to take note of the route, but all I cared about was finding the person screaming. Even though part of me knew it was too late.

I saw the aura first. Blinding white, specked with dark spots amongst the blank auras of the crowd surrounding the screaming girl. She lay on the pavement, her cries already dying out. I moved closer, trying to see properly over the crowd. *Human witnesses. Not good.*

"She's on fire!" said one of the onlookers.

Burning. Like the first victim. And her aura was—wrong. Not a true demon's, or even a warlock's, but tainted.

The girl screamed again. "All… will… fall."

Her words died out, and her head hit the pavement as her body gave one final convulsion, then went still. Too still.

I stood, cold sweat gathering on my forehead. Just like that… she was dead. As though an impossibly powerful being had reached out a recriminating hand and touched her, burning the life out of her. The crowd shifted, revealing the victim's face. Louise.

What? She was at the guild. Her vampire boyfriend hadn't been involved, had he? Maybe he'd dissolved into ashes somewhere nearby. She must have been with him. It hadn't been long since I'd caught them in the lab...

"Move aside," said a quiet, authoritative voice.

My mouth dropped open as the warlock strode casually towards the crowd, sweeping a hand. Their expressions glazed over one at a time and they traipsed away. In seconds, we were alone.

"What the hell?" I stepped aside, away from him.

"I believe that's mine." He yanked the jacket from my hands.

"Didn't you leave it on purpose?" I wanted to check he hadn't mesmerised the crowd into walking into traffic or anything, but I didn't dare take my eyes off my adversary. "You did this."

"You know that I was with you up until a minute ago."

I waved a hand at the humans. "Look at what you did to them. You might have sent anyone else to kill on your behalf."

"I know nobody weak enough to be controlled who might have done this."

"Then you did it yourself, through a proxy, or—something." The timing was skewed, but this was the second murder scene he'd shown up at. "Even if not, how did you know she was here?"

"I felt it. I can sense a strong demonic presence."

"Like a walking demon detector."

He tilted his head. "I suppose I am. Does that explain how *you* got here so fast? One would almost think you're deflecting blame onto me to avoid admitting your own crimes."

"You think *I'm* the killer?" The bastard was screwing with my head on purpose. I had an alibi—and more to the point, I wasn't a demon.

He stepped close behind me. "I know what you did."

Those five words chilled my blood more than the sight of Louise's sprawling body did. *No. He can't know.* He reached out to touch me, and I threw the demonic detector in his face.

On reflection, it wasn't my smoothest move. The device bounced off his forehead, and its beeping intensified to a piercing noise too much like screaming. He caught it in his hand, brow furrowed. "This is your demon detector?"

"Yes, and it's going to explode." I lunged at him, snatching the device from his hand, and yanked out the battery, swearing when liquefied brimstone melted all over my hand.

"What did you do that for?" His tone carried a touch of both puzzlement and amusement.

"So it wouldn't explode on the crime scene," I pocketed the remains, sticking my battery-soaked hand into my pocket. Smooth, Devi. "You were saying?"

"I was saying that if that detector is anything to go by, you can't have had the subtlety to commit the crime."

"Well, fuck you too." I crouched down. I couldn't touch the body with either hand, demonic battery acid or not, but I didn't need to touch her to know that she'd been burned with some kind of demonic fire. Her eyes had melted in their sockets, and heaven only knew what the guild would find if they cut her open. I swallowed hard, trying to focus on the facts rather than the awfulness of her death—and the forbidding presence of the warlock behind me. There was no covering this up. People would start talking, speculating on what could bring the mighty celestials down so low.

"White-hot," Nikolas said. "Like the pits of hell itself."

"Is that where you took her?" I asked. "The first victim

was found miles from where he was supposed to be. You can use one dimension to move around the city, right?"

"Ah." He looked at me with piercing golden eyes. "I can't fault your reasoning, but you're wrong. If I step into the shadow realm from here, I appear in the same place geographically that overlaps with this city. It's not possible for me to move someone from one side of town to another in the space of a few seconds, even if I were to go in and out through the other realm. And as you might have guessed from those beasts which attacked us earlier, the shadow realm isn't the safest place to wander into without a plan."

Well, crap. Didn't mean he wasn't involved, but it still left the question of how the victims had ended up in completely the wrong place. The only possibility was that someone else was the killer, but that didn't mean he hadn't orchestrated it.

"Then why are you here?" I asked.

His gaze went to the body. "Why else? I'm here because these killings have the potential to affect a great deal more than a couple of celestials. And I find it interesting that *you're* here, because your file tells me you haven't been an active celestial in over two years."

I straightened up, still holding the pentagram in my right hand. "You read my files?"

"The celestial guild needs to keep its security under wraps."

"Nice try. That information's easily available to anyone with the tendency to poke their nose into someone else's business." Prick. I knew for a fact he couldn't know the guild's secrets, because the top-secret files were kept sealed even to most of us.

He stepped over the body so I was between him and the wall. "Doesn't it bother you, having to obey their rules? Wouldn't you rather act on your own account?"

I leaned away from him, even as the magnetic tug of his lure threatened to hit me again.

"Don't *touch* me," I spat, pulling my demonic battery acid-soaked hand out of my pocket. It'd turned an interesting shade of green. *Hope that isn't permanent.*

He didn't move. "I'm not the one you should be afraid of, celestial. By my estimate, the first celestial soldiers should be here shortly. And if you're found at the crime scene holding a demonic summoning pentagram..."

"Then they'll know I was here on business," I spoke loudly to cover the sound of my heart thundering in my ears. "Unlike you. If you were acting as a detective, you'd actually be looking around the crime scene. I think you're feeding on the energy here."

"I'm no lesser demon," said Nikolas, his tone somewhat disdainful. "I don't feed on human energy to live. This death was caused by someone who enjoys causing pain and has the powers to back it up. That person is not me, celestial, but I can guarantee I'll find answers sooner than the guild will. I'm afraid I'm going to have to offer you a choice. If you mention me to the inspector, they will not find me, but they *will* find their records scrubbed of every trace of their investigations into these killings. You don't want that, do you?"

"You can't threaten the celestials," I said. "They'll—"

"I already said I cannot be killed. Being arrested would be inconvenient, however, and I'd rather avoid that if at all possible."

"You have *got* to be kidding me. I can't lie to protect a warlock."

He took a step back. "You are one of us," he said. "Whether you believe it or not."

"Don't you *dare* run off—"

Bolts of light struck the ground on either side of me.

Shadows wrapped around my hand, and the pentagram disappeared. "Hey, you prick—"

"Celestial Devina Lawson," said a robotic voice. "Might I ask why you're shouting at nobody?"

Damn. The warlock was gone. Not only that, he'd snatched my pentagram. Though considering the look on Inspector Deacon's face already, his head would probably have exploded if he'd seen me standing here with a warlock, holding the guild's most valuable demonic summoning device.

"I'm looking into the crime scene." I indicated the body, which, unfortunately, was about ten metres away from me. Instead, it'd looked as though I'd been yelling at the wall.

"There was a warlock!" yelped a voice. Oh great. Why bring Bad Haircut Sammy to the crime scene? "I knew one of those preternaturals was involved. They all are."

"Way to leap to conclusions," I said. Typical. The inspector would pick the loudmouth who hated vamps and warlocks almost as much as they hated each other as his assistant. And something told me Nikolas *wasn't* the killer. He was a glaring obstacle in solving the crime—no denying that—but also a potential source of useful information.

If he didn't do as he'd promised and erase all the celestials' evidence.

———

Once again, I was frog-marched back to the guild. The celestials commandeered an entire train carriage to themselves, pushing every other passenger out of the way by sheer intimidation. Heaven knew what pictures of me would end up floating around DivinityWatch now.

Everyone stared even more when we actually reached the guild. Worse, my hand was still covered in battery acid which smelled of brimstone, and the pentagram's absence was even more glaringly obvious when I sat down in front of the desk in the main office. Nikolas had taken a powerful summoning device into a demonic dimension. I couldn't have screwed this up more thoroughly if I'd tried.

"What in seven hells were you playing at?" Inspector Deacon bellowed at me across the desk.

I fastened a glare on my face. "Your bunch of incompetent novices nearly skewered me."

"And I suppose the dozen reports about a warlock vanishing from your side are a coincidence?"

Shit. Apparently he'd seen, too. Not that there was ever any question of my obeying the warlock and keeping my mouth shut when he potentially had information and *did* have the pentagram.

"I was getting to that," I said. "I found the warlock near the first murder scene. Then I tracked him. He claimed not to have been involved. The second attack happened literally while we were talking. He couldn't have done it. The timing's all wrong."

"Demons of his sort would certainly be capable of killing in such a manner. If a warlock is making an assault on the guild, there will be consequences."

"All right." I threw up my hands. "Maybe calm down a little before declaring war on anyone? Have you even looked at the crime scene yet?"

"Why," he interrupted, "is your hand green?"

Oh. "My demonic detector fell to pieces."

"Demonic detector?"

"Handmade. Can I go and wash my hand? Melted brimstone is a bitch to clean up."

He sniffed. "Brimstone. You walked into the crime scene carrying this?"

"I was looking for any demonic traces." I pulled the

remains of the device from my pocket. "A demon of that level of power can't pull off a magical murder without needing to recharge. I figured if it was still in this dimension, it'd be feeding off a crowd. But this thing's faulty."

"It led you to the crime scene, though?"

"Too late," I said bitterly. "If you don't mind, I'd like to clean this crap off my hand and—"

"The next time you want to cover for a warlock, I'd advise you to remember they're nearly as far from human as pure demons are."

"Sure, whatever. You know warlocks supply all the guild's ingredients, don't you?" In fact, it'd likely been a warlock who'd made the pentagram. Warlocks might not be trustworthy, but they were half human, mortal, and an asset to the guild. I didn't trust Nikolas, but the number of demons summoned by non-magical humans outnumbered those summoned by warlocks twenty to one—and that was taking into consideration that warlocks were actually half demon. So, you'd think they'd have more cause than most to summon one. Then again, they also had more of a clue than humans just how dangerous demons were.

Instead of responding, the inspector asked, "What exactly did this warlock have to say for himself? Tell me everything you know about him."

"He's powerful." *Half arch-demon powerful, to be precise.* But I wanted to confide that particular detail to Gav or someone trustworthy, not someone who'd send the entire guild out with pitchforks if he had reason to. "He can use the shadows to cross over into another dimension, but he can't teleport. He couldn't have reached the victim in time to kill her. Also, he's not a fire demon." Having seen him fight, I didn't peg him for the type who enjoyed torture either. And again— why show up at the crime scene afterwards if he was the killer? Unless he'd vanished on purpose to confuse and terrify everyone, of course.

"These demon kin have skills beyond human comprehension," he said. "What exactly did he tell you?"

That I'm a demon, apparently. "He said he wasn't the killer. As I said, it doesn't add up. The demon has to be able to touch or at least see the victim to attack them. Even Grade Three or higher demons obey that rule."

He gave me a stern look. "You're correct, but that doesn't mean this warlock wasn't involved. Perhaps he had an accomplice."

"He's not a fire demon," I repeated. "And the aura around the victim didn't match his, like it would have if he'd used magic on her." I hadn't considered that part, but those dark spots on her aura weren't a sign of regular demon magic. I wasn't sure *what* they were. But they'd taken her body away.

"Is that all you got from questioning him? Why are you sure of his innocence?"

"It was a thorough interrogation."

That's one way of putting it. My skin still burned where he'd brushed his lips over it, searching for a mark that wasn't there. A mark this man should have been aware of, if it existed. And what about how the pentagram had trapped me?

Seven hells. If the inspector put me under interrogation, the guild's own angelic magic would turn on me if the warlock had told the truth. Besides, the real culprit might be getting away while we sat here bickering.

"Will you let me get on with the investigation now?" I asked. "I did nothing wrong. I had every reason to suspect the warlock was involved. Now, I don't believe he is."

"I believe you're hiding something," he growled. "You've been given entirely too much responsibility for someone who's known for flaunting the rules."

"Tell that to Gav or Mr Roth, not me," I said. "I'm doing my job. I'll thank your people not to *shoot at* me while I'm working."

"The light wouldn't have harmed you."

It would if I really did have demonic magic. Crap. I needed to find that bloody warlock again. But where did I even start looking for him?

"The only reason I'm letting you go," he added, "is because you're correct in saying that the victim was at the guild earlier. She was seen leaving alone, and therefore, the warlock you were with couldn't have been the one who initially caused her to move across the city. Unless, of course, I find proof you were lying."

Okay. Her vampire boyfriend must have left separately, then. "Have you questioned the people she was with? Wasn't she meant to be on a mission today?"

"We're still gathering the details," he said. "You, Celestial Lawson, should leave now, before you implicate yourself further. And I'd clean that brimstone off your hand too."

"Of course." I got to my feet, left the office, and made a beeline for the lab.

It took fifteen minutes of scrubbing to return my hand to normal, and the neon green demonic battery acid had left streaks all up my sleeve. I also disposed of the now-useless demon detector. Weird how it'd reacted to the attack even in its broken state. The way the warlock's power had set it off, though... even if I believed he wasn't the killer, he was definitely a world of trouble. As for what he'd said...

You're a demon. The pentagram reacted to you. Something was off, and once I'd eliminated all the other possibilities, it was entirely possible that was the only likely conclusion. But until I had confirmation from anywhere other than the mouth of a warlock, I'd put it in the back of my mind and get on with the job.

My first step: I needed to find an antidote to his lure ability, in case he used it on me again. Considering I planned to confront him over the pentagram the next time I saw him, I needed a way to protect myself. In the end, he hadn't tried to hurt me. But he was clearly dangerous, if not outright deluded. Problem was, I didn't know exactly how the lure worked. By touch? Or scent? He must have control over it, because he hadn't used it on me during our first encounter.

"What are you doing this time?" asked Gav, opening the door to the lab. "I thought the inspector told you to go home."

"I'm trying to brew a spell to counter a warlock who can... affect emotions."

"In what way?"

Ack. I really didn't want to have this conversation with my supervisor. Not to mention, the paralysis had been down to the pentagram, and I wouldn't be mentioning *that* to anyone.

"Someone who can touch you and make you feel whatever you want them to." That covered it, right?

He gave me a strange look. "You might need more information to go by than that."

"Not to worry. I've got it in hand."

"Well, try to stay out of the inspector's way."

Great. I'd been deposed within only hours of being rehired. Not that I'd expected the guild to want me to stick around for long, not now their backup had arrived. But the warlock was my responsibility. I'd found him, now I'd find out how he was connected to the case. If I could figure out his damn lure ability. If I did something obvious like removing my sense of smell, I was leaving myself wide open to being sneaked up on by any other demon. My senses were too valuable to mess with. And short of covering myself with a full suit of armour and gas mask, there was nothing I could do to stop him from touching me again, except maybe cover myself in something that warded him off. Or a weapon that activated if I was touched by unwanted hands.

I looked up and jumped out of my skin at the sight of someone standing behind me. "Damn, Clover. Don't scare me like that."

With vertical scars along her face courtesy of a saw-toothed water demon thirty years ago, Clover had refused any cosmetic surgery and instead let the wounds heal as they were. The result was that she terrified everyone she came across, including some demons, but had the mild manner more reminiscent of a friendly grandmother when she wasn't telling horrible stories of dismemberment to the novices. After retiring from the field, she'd spent her time perfecting the art of standing silently in corners and scaring the crap out of people. For some reason, she'd taken a shine to me when all my other tutors threw their hands up in despair.

"You've been spending a lot of time in here since you came back," she remarked.

She didn't ask why I'd come back. Or why I'd been gone for so long. I appreciated that.

"I'm in trouble," I told her.

She scratched her chin where two scars intersected. "How big?"

"Warlocks," I said.

She grunted. "Bad news, they are."

"Yeah, you could say that. I'm trying to brew up a way to counter a warlock's lure."

"Give him blisters," said Clover. "You know how to make a blister charm, right?"

"Blisters?" I snorted. "You mean the most basic charm would work on a high-level warlock? I thought they were immune."

"Surprisingly not. It's when you factor in demonic magic that problems arise. Basic spells are the key."

"Awesome." I started separating ingredients again. I'd make a pendant, hide it under my shirt, and if he touched me again… I smothered a laugh. I almost wanted him to try it. Full-body blister attack. It'd be worth the indignity of being overpowered again.

"What did this warlock do to you, exactly?" Clover enquired. "Is he a suspect?"

"Not exactly," I said. "But he did appear at both murder scenes. I know what it looks like, but from the reports, there's no way he could have killed that girl. Anyway, whether he's the killer or not, I need to find him again. He stole something important from me."

"It sounds like this warlock operates on his own clock. They all do. But if he wants to find you, he will. Set up your defence, and be ready."

I frowned at her. "You aren't going to tell me to leave it to the experts?"

"You are the expert. I told the inspector how many demonic cases you've solved. Between me and Gavin, you might just be able to get away for another day before someone realises the inspector's pentagram is missing."

Oh. "Believe me, I didn't know that would happen. I thought it could hold a warlock."

"It can, usually." She paused. "Be careful, Devi. Call me or Gavin if you need backup, but not the inspector. It's not good news he's here."

No kidding. But it lifted some of the weight from me to know I had at least one authority figure on my side.

"You're better without the celestials at your back, if you do decide to find him," she added.

Was she giving me permission to go rogue? I was halfway in that direction anyway, but the fact was, I needed the guild.

They held my weapons—and my freedom—in their hands. Like it or not. So I had to toe the line, as far as they could see, anyway. But that left me with some options.

And I really did need to find out if Nikolas was telling the truth.

8

A couple of hours later, I sat down at a cafe in the shopping centre to read over the files from the celestial archive I'd downloaded onto my phone. Specifically, the ones concerning warlocks, and their relationship with their demon kin. Gav had been true to his word and sent me everything he had on arch-demons, so I'd be prepared with at least some knowledge if I managed to track the warlock down. I also had the contact details of the local chief warlock, so calling him was next on my list.

It was a relief to get outside again. I remained on my guard, of course, but I'd had a hell of a day, and needed food and a caffeine fix. I ate my sandwich one-handed while skimming through Gav's notes on my phone. When I reached the part on arch-demons, it was about as useless as I'd expected. Arch-demons were princes of hell, fallen angels, all-powerful, et cetera. Nobody seemed to want to tell me *what* exactly made them so powerful, except that they were ageless and terrifying, and any world with an arch-demon still living in it wasn't a nice one for either humans or warlocks. As for warlocks, they were generally shunned by their arch-demon parents and kicked out into another dimension. I couldn't imagine anyone doing that to the warlock I'd met, but I couldn't really imagine an arch-demon either. I imagined most people who saw one didn't live long enough to remember it.

I turned my gaze back to the table and found Nikolas sitting in the vacant seat opposite me.

"Seven hells," I said.

"It's delightful to see you, too," he said. "I believe we got off on the wrong foot, and I'd like to offer you the opportunity to speak to the leader of the warlock community in this city."

"What?" I blinked. Where in hell had he materialised from?

He flashed me a smile, all white teeth. "You wished to speak to a warlock, did you not?"

"I never said that." Was I cracking up? I hadn't told anyone except Gav I planned to speak to the warlocks' leader, in order to find Nikolas himself. I must have looked away for too long, because even he wouldn't use his shadow power to appear in the middle of a public cafe. Right?

"You implied that you'd like to meet my contacts," said Nikolas. "So, I'm offering you the chance to meet with our leader. Oh, and you might need this." Something sharp bumped against my leg under the table. *The pentagram.* I grabbed its sharp edge firmly, tugging it from his hands.

"Why give it back?"

"I don't need it," he said simply. "And given its design, I highly doubt it originally belonged to you. We need to keep good relations with the guild."

"You do realise they suspect you, don't you?" I asked, moving the pentagram underneath my chair out of his reach. "You vanished in front of several witnesses. If you wanted to avoid suspicion, I doubt they'll forget easily."

He regarded me with a cool gaze. "Yes, I expect not. However, when we find the real criminal, that'll be irrelevant."

"Okay, is there a conversation I don't remember having with you?" I asked. "Because I thought we established that if the celestials found out about you, you were going to delete all their records."

"I believe I said that if *you* told the celestials about me, I'd do so. Given my investigation into the killings, I assumed we'd run into one another sooner or later. I have nothing to fear from them."

"Right." I shook my head. "So according to you, we're retracting the threats and pretending that never happened?"

Warlocks. It was sort of surprising that *he* wasn't their leader, given his level of power, but I kept forgetting he wasn't anywhere near human. He was someone who thought society's usual rules didn't apply to him. Never mind that I wasn't a model celestial: he acted like the whole world ought to step out of his way. The side of him I'd seen in battle attested to that. I should have told him to leave me alone. We were in a public place, for crying out loud. Though if anyone got suspicious, I suspected he could use his mind trick again and make them look away.

"I don't doubt you'll remember, celestial, but I have need of your assistance," said Nikolas. "The celestials were likely to suspect me sooner or later. What they won't find is any evidence connecting me to the crime, because there isn't any."

"You're that confident, huh. You know the inspector is in town, don't you?"

"Yes, I do. That's what prompted me to repair our arrangement."

I shifted the pentagram underneath the chair. "There is

no arrangement between us. I was trying to eat in peace before you intruded on my personal space."

"But you'd still like to meet our leader?" he asked.

"How did you even know that was my plan?" Could he read minds, on top of everything else? Warlocks had only one power, the files said. Bollocks.

"If you needed to find me, it'd be the logical response," he said. "In fact, I already told him about you, so you won't have to wait for a meeting. He wishes to speak to you tonight."

Suspicion flared. "About the killings?"

His eyes bored into me. "You know why."

"No." My hand clenched around my half-full coffee cup, and I suppressed the urge to throw it at him. "I'm not one of you."

"Then why are you avoiding telling the celestials about me, aside from the regrettable incident two years ago with your partner's death?"

My composure slid away. "Why the hell are you so interested in my life?"

I know what you did, he'd said. I should have known better than to give him the chance to explain himself. I ought to call the authorities right now—but given his shadow power, he'd vanish before they got here. And I wasn't a hundred percent certain the celestials could take him. He was so…unpredictable.

"You have your resources. I have mine."

No kidding. "You know the celestials think one of your people is the killer, right? You're the main suspect. Not me. See to your own issues before you start accusing me."

"My people?" he echoed. "The celestials are fools if they think to blame my fellow warlocks for these attacks, but if they want to challenge us, we will meet them with all our might." His tone was as matter-of-fact as though we were discussing the weather. Of course, he might be posturing, and it was none of my business whether he decided to start a war with the celestials or not, but I was supposed to be finding a killer, not playing head games with overconfident warlocks.

I pushed to my feet. "Right. If you don't mind, I'm going home. It might have escaped your attention, but you're not the supreme ruler of the universe, whoever your arch-demon parent is. So if you don't mind—"

His hand snagged my sleeve. I tensed, expecting him to set off the trap I wore around my neck, and almost wanting him to. If we caused a scene, maybe they'd actually catch him this time.

"Wouldn't you like to hear *my* theories about the deaths?" he enquired. "Let's assume we're both innocent. One might say someone's setting one or both of us up to take the fall. We've both been found near the murder scenes, and possess abilities which put our own innocence into question."

"Nobody's setting you up," I told him, putting down my boiling hot coffee cup before it burned my hand. "You walked to the crime scenes of your own free will."

"As did you."

"Because the celestials asked me to investigate."

"And the first night?"

I took a step away from him. "How the hell do you know?"

"I put two and two together. I know how the guild works."

"You shouldn't. See, this is why we suspect you," I said. "So a warlock definitely isn't the killer?"

"No. What committed those crimes is not of this world. I know every warlock in the city, and they don't agree with the demons' goal."

I arched a brow. "What, to kill us all?"

"To add this world to the list of realms they've ruined," he said. "They're counting on the celestials overreacting in their response."

"Tell that to the inspector. I did, and he wouldn't listen. Of course the demons want attention. They thrive on it. But do you really not know who has the ability to set someone on fire from the inside out?"

"No," he said, his mouth tightening at the corners. "Either this is an ability I've never heard of, or a clever demon has devised a new method of killing not seen before using resources already available. And if you wish to find answers, then the leader of the city's warlocks has generously offered to meet with you to discuss the case."

"Yeah, I got that part. But I can't trust you," I told him. "You know why."

"I suspected you'd say that," he said. "So I brought a friend."

A girl with magenta hair sidled up to the table. "Hey, Devina," she said.

"This," said Nikolas, "is my sister, Rachel."

I turned to face her. Unlike her brother, she showed no outwards signs of her demonic ability. She was maybe nineteen or so, with sun-kissed skin and vivid pink hair, and wore shorts and a strappy top as though it was beach weather, not a gloomy April morning.

"You're a shadow demon, too?" I asked.

"Nope," she said, with a grin. "I'm a chameleon. We're siblings by adoption. Meaning we adopted each other."

I hadn't thought of warlocks as having families. They seemed to live in a collective unit. Normally, their human parent didn't survive long after the trauma of giving birth to a half demon, or skipped town to avoid the demon who'd kidnapped them. And demons weren't exactly attentive parents.

"When you say chameleon," I said, "do you mean you can change your appearance?"

Her hair turned blue, then pink again. "Yep. Pretty neat, right? I can turn into any person, if I get a look at them. This isn't my real form, though. Niko says I'm not allowed to use it in public."

So she had the ability to blend into any crowd. And follow me around, making my demonic detector go off? Maybe. But she didn't seem capable of sneaking around in a stealthy manner. She vibrated with energy, bouncing on the balls of her feet. People were starting to stare.

I picked up what was left of my coffee. "I'll need you to swear on all the arch-demons that you aren't leading me into a trap if I do agree to meet with the chief warlock."

"Wouldn't swearing on the Divinities be more appropriate?" enquired Nikolas.

"Not for you."

He gave me a sly grin. "See, you're learning already."

"Don't think I'm caving to your every demand," I informed him. "I'm investigating a murder. Two, now. And you claim to know more than the guild does, so I'd like to know why that is. And why, if you know so much, you failed to stop the last attack."

His smile vanished. "Careful, celestial. I'm doing you a favour, but if you speak to Javos like you did to me, he's more likely to retaliate."

"Oh, don't be a spoilsport," said Rachel. "She's right—we *haven't* worked out who the killer is. But we have some ideas. Javos thinks you have some, too, and I think you're going to be interested to hear what he has to say."

"Look," I said. "I appreciate the help, but this is an ongoing investigation, and I'm not allowed to share every detail of our conclusions with strangers. Especially strangers with demonic ties. We'll all end up in jail if they find out I'm even considering meeting the warlocks' leader behind their backs. And if he—" I jerked my head in Nikolas's direction— "is really as powerful as he claims and manages get you both off the hook, guess who takes the fall?"

She looked from me to him, biting her lip. "Should have thought of that one, Niko."

He paused before saying, "Naturally, *if* you don't share our arrangement with the celestials, I would use my considerable power to… what was it you said, *get you off the hook,* as well."

I frowned. "You know that means I'm out of a job, right?"

"I thought you weren't working for them," said Rachel.

I glared at Nikolas. "Have you told her *everything* about me?"

"No," he said. "She's good at research herself. In fact, it was Rachel who pulled up the guild's archives on you. You've acquired quite the reputation."

I swore under my breath. "All right. Say I meet this warlock dude, and don't get caught. How do I know you're not setting me up to turn me into the next victim? I don't know the guy. I don't really know any of you."

"She has a point," said Rachel. "I've got it. I'll tell you Javos's weakness. I'm good at that." She leaned close to my ear. "If you play classical music at him, his demonic power totally switches off. It's funny. Sometimes I prank him by putting my iPod ear buds in his ears when he's asleep."

"Are you kidding me?"

"Nope," she said, grinning. "So if he attacks, turn up the music."

"This is weird," I said. "No offence."

"She's telling the truth," said Nikolas. "I'd advise you to avoid getting on his bad side, either way. So is that a yes?"

The guild just threatened to remove my newly reinstated job for meddling with warlocks. I could be worse than fired if I said yes —I'd get arrested. I shouldn't do it.

I needed answers. Before someone else died.

Screw it. "Yes, but only in daylight, in *this* realm. Nowhere else."

"The chief warlock lives in this city," said Nikolas. "He's agreed to meet you this evening at seven, at the Harpy's Nest on Prince Street. I hope you'll be there."

9

Three warlocks and an ex-celestial walk into a bar. This couldn't end badly at all.

Of course, one of those three was Rachel, who looked barely old enough to drink. I'd met Nikolas outside the Harpy's Nest, which was in the part of town where preternaturals mingled with regular humans.

"Devi!" Rachel shrieked, waving me over to the bar. She'd already ordered a lurid pink coloured cocktail, and perched on a stool so high her feet were a metre off the ground.

I sat down, too, with difficulty. These stools were apparently built for people seven feet or taller. Moving so that the bar somewhat hemmed me in, I ordered a drink, too. Nikolas sat on my other side.

As for the other patrons, they were... interesting. Unlike vamps and weres, who looked human at first glance, the clientele here was generally of the horned, scaly variety. I was glad I'd worn a jacket to hide the mark on my wrist.

The bartender was a young vampire with electric blue, spiky hair, who offered me three different types of blood cocktail, all of which I refused. At least he didn't seem to recognise me.

"So where's this… Javos?" I asked the others in an undertone.

"On his way," Rachel said, her hair changing to the same pink as the cocktail.

After they'd left the café earlier, I'd looked up chameleon demons in the guild's files. Rare as hell, and almost as deadly. Not from the shadow dimension, though admittedly, there wasn't much information available on the realm Nikolas claimed to be from. I knew most of the common demon types, but now I'd met two rarities in a short space of time and was about to meet a third. One who was feared by everyone, but was also apparently allergic to classical music. I'd downloaded some onto my phone, though this was the sort of place where you kept your valuables close at hand and your wits about you. The two warlocks sitting beside me at the bar were proof enough of that. As I looked up from my drink—Jack Daniels and coke, no dubious cocktails for me— two horned women with forked tails sauntered into the bar.

"Which species are they?" asked Niko, in an undertone.

"Succubus," I said confidently.

"And what is he?" He jerked his head in the direction of what looked like a cross between a large man and a rhinoceros.

"Half-rovak demon. Is this a quiz?"

"I'm determining the extent of your knowledge."

I sipped my drink. "Probably better than you think. We're required to know all the major demon types."

"No, you're required to know whatever the guild wants you to. No more."

His attitude was getting up my nose, and away from the threat of arrest, I was less inclined to let his bullshit slide. "You're one to criticise the guild, considering you're withholding vital details about the murder of two of their soldiers. I don't know what you're trying to achieve, either, considering I'm only working for them on this case. Nothing more."

"Then why did they give you access to your celestial weapons?"

"Because I might need them to kill a demon," I said. "Where is this dude, anyway?"

"He'll be here." He sipped his own drink, also neon-coloured. Somehow, I doubted it was a regular cocktail. Some warlock thing. They drew power from the essence of their own dimension, so I'd guess it was some sort of energy source. Why he needed it when he apparently hopped in and out of that dimension every five minutes, I had no idea. Maybe he was expecting a fight. Nobody gave me a second glance now I was at the bar. Perhaps here, they assumed you were a preternatural by default. There weren't any normal humans around that I could see.

The door opened and a bronze-skinned man with curling horns approached us. He looked like he'd stepped out of an illustration of Greek mythology. His huge arms could have wrapped around the front of a car and crushed it like cardboard. But sheer brute strength wasn't the terrifying thing about him. His eyes shone like molten lava, and his *aura* —bright orange, like the inside of a flame.

I raised an eyebrow at Nikolas. "Is this really the best place for a private meeting?" What with Javos's sheer size, he'd draw the eye of everyone in the bar.

"Nobody will hear us," he said confidently.

He must have hit them with that power of his. He could use it on other warlocks, too? I needed to reconsider my assumption that warlocks' power was in any way contained. Which, let's face it, didn't bode well for my investigation.

"You must be Devina," said Javos, planting himself on a

bar stool. Now I knew who they'd been built for. "Nikolas here tells me you're a former celestial."

"Does anyone here *not* know my entire history?" I remarked.

Instead of answering, he said, "I hear you're working on tracking a killer with unusual powers. Nikolas told me you have information for me."

"He said *you* had information to share with me," I said. "I was under the impression your people already knew everything I did, and then some. The killer was a demon, I'm told, but I can't identify the type."

He tilted his head. "You're the detective, right?"

"Not exactly. More of an independent consultant. I've never tracked a serial killer before, much less a demon one."

"I suppose you haven't," he said. "Who were the victims, and were they randomly chosen?"

I looked at Nikolas. "This is an ongoing case. If I share that information, the guild might take action against both of us. I'm looking at a jail sentence at the least."

"Is that so?" Javos summoned the bartender with one hand. The poor guy looked totally dazed, but filled up a glass with black liquid, apparently Javos's regular order. "The guild is about as useful as expected. But if you don't tell me, I can't help you."

"Prove you can," I said. "I don't think it's a secret that I don't trust anyone with demonic ties. I won't share valuable information."

"She won't," said Nikolas. "We'll have to find out the old-fashioned way. Luckily, I took the liberty of compiling a few notes on the victims. Both were new to the guild, for one thing. The first victim signed up a year ago."

"Hey—" I started indignantly, but he cut me off.

"Both had hardly any experience with demons at all, according to all records. And both disappeared with no witnesses and appeared in places which they couldn't have been without demonic assistance, according to witnesses who saw them shortly before the attacks."

"And their eyes burned out," added Rachel. "They burned alive, from the inside out. No marks on the bodies. It was demon fire, all right."

Apparently Nikolas had told her everything. Either he trusted all his fellow warlocks, or he just didn't give a crap about celestials. But then, why help me solve the crime at all?

Unless he wanted me for another purpose.

I know what you did.

"No marks on the bodies," said Javos. "No former connections with demons. The killer's targets appear to be easy ones without the ability to defend themselves against demonic intrusion."

"But not random," said Nikolas.

"Of course they're random," I said. "This is a demon with a grudge against the celestials, right? That means they'll pick the first target available. If they were trying to threaten the higher council or undermine our mission, they would have chosen someone stronger or in a position of authority."

"She raises a valid point," said Javos. "However, it's well known that celestials at Grade Two or higher are strong enough to kill most demons."

"Most low-grade demons," I corrected. "I thought we were dealing with a higher one. I mean, burning someone from the inside out isn't on most low-grade demons' skillsets. It's a unique one who's never been to this realm before, right?"

"She's better at this than you are," said Rachel, swirling her straw in her drink. "Yeah, it's got to be a new demon. But not an ignorant one. They know the celestials. They wouldn't have targeted you otherwise."

Nikolas nodded. He looked mildly annoyed. Maybe

because he hadn't expected me to take over the conversation. I'd probably rendered several of his notions invalid, too. But this was my job, whether I worked for the guild or not. The only difference was that they generally targeted non-magical humans, not us.

"I doubt the demon is ignorant," I said. "It'd need to be Grade Two or higher to wander around on its own, and Three or more to have a motive. The lower ranked ones stay away from celestials, and besides, none of them have the abilities our killer apparently does."

I couldn't believe I was talking about demons to a warlock. Several warlocks. Any of whom might be *related* to the killer. But none of them matched that ghastly aura I'd seen on the victims. And even though they might be scary, I couldn't see them skulking around murdering minor celestials when they had a real live Grade Three one right here and didn't seem to particularly care what I was. Okay, Javos was scrutinising me over his drink, but not my covered wrist.

I didn't know what to make of him. He seemed fairly mild-mannered for a legendary warlock the size of a tank, but no warlock had that sort of brute strength and never used it.

"Grade Three demons have one ability," said Nikolas. "Our killer apparently has two. Unless there are two working together, of course."

"I thought most demons were loners," I said. "You mean, one of them catapulted the victims onto the wrong side of the city, and the other burned their eyes out? I've never heard of either ability, but there's no way two higher demons with that sort of skill could work together for more than five minutes without one of them winding up dead."

No matter which dimension they came from, demons didn't get along even with other members of the same species. If it was a netherworld dimension, they worked for the arch-demon in charge or died. Only minor demons grouped together for their own survival. Unless their hatred of celestials had driven two of them to bond, but if that were true, it'd never happened before. Demon minds just didn't work that way.

Javos nodded slowly. "Yes. I believe we're dealing with a single individual. Whether they are using another demon in their plans, I can't say, but we should assume there's only one mastermind. The details of the victims appear to be random, however. The only connecting factor is the location… and possibly some other information about the victims that we aren't aware of yet." He gave me a piercing look. "Like their devotion to the cause, for instance."

"What does that mean?" I asked. "If the demon hates celestials, why would it matter how devoted they are? The outcome's the same."

"True," said Nikolas, "but the celestials are often quick to assign blame. I'm surprised it hasn't started already."

"I've no idea what you're talking about," I said. "Look, guys, it's been enlightening talking to you, but I was told you had more ideas. I get it, you hate the celestials. Beats me why you'd want to help solve their murders, to be honest."

"Because if a rogue demon is loose on my territory, I need to know about it," Javos said. "If someone is trying to incite a war between celestials and the preternaturally inclined, for instance, it might destroy our peace."

The celestials wouldn't do that. The words hovered on my tongue, but I knew they weren't true. Inspector Deacon proved that.

"It won't work," I told him. "They wouldn't put the city's safety in jeopardy over a lone demon."

"I suppose you know them better than I do," said Javos. "I

certainly hope they don't declare war. I've become fond of this dimension."

"Wait, you're not originally from here?" I asked.

He laughed softly. "The arch-demons aren't fond of their offspring… that seems to be a truth in every dimension in which they rule. We're too powerful to be controlled. They don't tolerate anyone who threatens their power. Either we submit to being their slaves, or we strike out alone."

"So you're what, in charge of every warlock here? Just this city?" It didn't surprise me that he was the son of an arch-demon, too.

"In this city, yes," he said. "It's been enlightening talking to you, Miss Lawson. I'd certainly like to chat further if either of us come up with any more ideas about this mystery demon of ours. And based on what Nikolas tells me, you'd be an asset working for us."

I choked on the sip of drink I'd just taken. "Working for you? I'm a celestial."

Javos and Nikolas exchanged looks I couldn't read. Anger buzzed through me. More and more, I felt like both sides wanted to push me around, and I wasn't having any of it. The case was a one-time incident. Even if I decided not to stay with the guild after the murders were solved, I sure as hell wouldn't be signing up to work with the warlocks. I could barely tolerate being near Nikolas as it was, and I thought the feeling was mutual.

"If you change your mind," said Javos, "you can find me here. I frequent this place most nights."

He climbed off the bar stool and strode towards the door, walking out into the night.

"Okay," I muttered. "I didn't know one person ruled over every warlock in the city. Figured you were mostly loners."

Actually, if I picked anyone as ruler of the warlocks, it

was Nikolas. Not that I'd be telling Javos, though. He was a scary bastard however powerful Nikolas was.

"We find it necessary to have someone in charge of maintaining peace," he said.

"So what do you even do for a living, except supply the celestials' weapons?" I asked. "Why do that, if you hate them?"

"I don't hate them," he said. "Some of them are quite interesting company."

Nice try. "You've been belittling me for being connected with them since we met, when you know full well I haven't worked for them for two years. And for the record, if you said any of that crap to any other celestial, they'd have locked you up."

"Then I'd better stay on your good side." His mouth curved in a grin. "By the way, you still haven't apologised for the murder accusation. Which I assume you're retracting, seeing as you're still here."

"You still haven't apologised for violating my personal space." He hadn't tried to touch me again, but I still wore my improvised trap around my neck, tucked into my cleavage.

He raised an eyebrow. "That's the part you focus on? Not how you wrenched me from one dimension to another and tried to trap me in a pentagram meant for a higher demon?"

Now he put it like that, the pentagram—which I'd returned to the guild in one piece—did sound kind of excessive. "You acted guilty." I glanced away from his piercing eyes. "All right, I'm sorry for suspecting you. And the pentagram. I didn't actually know I could trap a warlock in that."

"You couldn't. Not me, anyway. Few traps can hold me."

"I gathered." As for what he'd said afterwards… maybe it was the drink, but I wanted it cleared up, now. "What about the part where you said I had a demon's mark?"

"You do. Javos noticed it, too. Why do you think I invited you to speak to him? The others don't like celestials."

"Cut the bullshit," I said. "I was recruited as a celestial when I was a teenager—I know you've read my profile. The Divinities chose me. They hate demons. I can't be one of them."

"I never said you always belonged to a demon."

His voice was quiet, yet each word hit me like a stone. My chest tightened. "What the hell do you mean?" I asked. "I have a celestial's aura. I know because I've seen it."

"Auras." He gave a quiet laugh. "Not all demons have them."

Like the killer. No—the aura around the victims meant something, but he hadn't brought it up yet, so perhaps it wasn't worth noting. Wait, could warlocks even see auras?

I took another sip of my drink and then asked him.

"We can," he confirmed. "But they tend to look different to us than they do to others, like true demons."

"And celestials?" I asked.

"If you haven't seen your mark, I imagine so."

I gripped the bar stool with my free hand, looking at him in what I hoped was a calm manner. "Listen, mate, if you're screwing with me, I'm off this case. If not, then if you don't tell me what kind of demon I'm supposed to be, I'll use that pentagram to yank you into the nearest pond."

"Oh, how terrifying." He raised an eyebrow. "I can't answer because I don't know. You have a mark on your aura —unmistakably demonic in origin. But not a warlock's mark, and you're clearly human, despite your celestial nature. It's a mark I don't recognise, like one touched by a demon."

"Touched?" I echoed, my stomach lurching as though I was about to fall from much higher than a bar stool. "In what way? Like you did to me?"

"Not physically," he said. "Spiritually. It's your soul that's marked, Devi."

My soul. Even as a celestial, I didn't really believe I had one. I mean, sure, I was going somewhere after death, hopefully not a demonic dimension. But the Divinities alone knew that. Souls were corrupted by doing terrible things, none of which I'd done.

"How can that happen?" I didn't mean to speak aloud. It was none of his damn business, besides. He seemed to think the whole thing—murders included—was a joke.

"You're intriguing to me," he said, his eyes glittering. "How indeed. I don't know. It's rare for the demons to take an interest in a person, especially one sworn to defy them. Unless it's to do with why you left."

"I left because a demon killed my partner," I said. "And if anyone here has no soul, it's you."

I slid off the bar stool and made for the door, ignoring Rachel's stare. The oak doors swung open and a torrent of rain hit me full in the face. I hadn't thought to pack an umbrella. What a shit show. Demon marked? Me? I'd killed well over a hundred of them. And my soul couldn't be marked. I'd done my part for the army of heaven, however little gratitude I'd received in return. And I'd never done anything bad enough to put a stain on my soul.

Except walked into a demon's dimension, and came out alive.

My hands clenched. Just because I didn't know anyone else who'd done it, didn't mean I was damned. Losing Rory was bad enough, but I'd never seen who'd killed him. All I remembered was fire, burning in his eyes, burning in me.

Rain dashed against the pavement, soaking through my clothes. I stood for a moment, willing the rain to wash away the sensation of flames crawling over my skin. Rory's face flashed through my mind, replaced immediately with

Louise's. I'd spoken to her right before she'd died. If I'd known…

Celestial lights shone in the night, piercing the gloom in front of me. I took one step forwards, trying to see through the driving rain.

"You need to leave," said a voice, and shadows closed in around me, masking my view.

The rain stopped so abruptly, I froze. Everything stopped, and nothing remained behind but shadow so complete, even my celestial light didn't pierce the gloom. A hand found my arm, tugging on me, and I staggered away from Nikolas as the shadows melted away. Behind him was a sheer cliff face, ascending above our heads. Cold stone beneath our feet in the place of pavement. And instead of the driving rain, a bitter wind raised the hairs on my arms.

Because it wasn't raining here.

We weren't in Haven City anymore.

10

"What the *hell* did you do?" I gasped. Nikolas stood beside me, with Rachel just behind. Other than that, all I could see was the dark face of a rocky wall. Opposite was another cliff. We were in some kind of valley—a massive one. The looming surface of a full moon shone over the clifftops.

"Don't," warned Nikolas. "If you scream, you'll draw their attention."

"I'm not going to scream." Chills raced down my arms. I wasn't dressed appropriately for a cold night on an alien planet. The icy wind was nothing like the warm April rain at home. For the second time in my life, I'd been dragged into another dimension entirely.

He could kill me here and nobody would know.

I reached for my sleeve.

"I wouldn't," said Nikolas. "You'll draw attention. I brought you here because we were about to walk into a third crime scene. I assumed the celestials would be less lenient on us than last time."

My head spun, and metallic-tasting fear rose on my

tongue. "So you thought a dimension ruled by demons was safer?"

"Technically, it's not ruled by demons," he said. "Not arch-demons, anyway, though there's a provisional ruler. There are even humans here. You haven't entirely gone extinct."

"And have celestials?"

He didn't need to answer for me to guess. In this world, the celestials had failed in their quest to vanquish all demons, and had been destroyed in turn. If this area did overlap with the same place in the world we'd come from, then this ruined wasteland was all that remained of the Divinities' most important city in England. If it had ever existed in this world.

It was more than I'd expected from a night at a bar, that's all I can say. At least it wasn't raining here. That was the only upside.

Rachel winked at me. "Here we are. Dull, isn't it? I don't know why he likes it so much."

"I can't believe this," I said. "You pulled me into another dimension, without my permission."

"Feel free to go back." He waved a hand, and the air split along a shadowy crack, showing me a slither of pavement with people gathering outside the pub. A second later, it vanished.

"Wait, can we watch the crime scene from here?" I asked.

"Not without being seen or heard."

Damn. "But—someone else was attacked, right? How did you know?"

"I sensed the demon, but I didn't get the chance to look. The celestials were a minute from arresting both of us."

"I didn't even know you *could* bring someone else into this dimension."

All my suspicions flared up again. Some inter-dimensional crap must have been involved for the victims to move across the city in the space of a few seconds… but he'd been with me the whole time.

"Very few of us can cross dimensions without assistance," he said, "and even fewer of us can bring others along for the ride."

"All right, then." Like it or not, he was my only ticket back into my own dimension. "We'll walk away from the crime scene and cross over somewhere else. I'm not spending any longer than I have to in this place."

"That was the plan," he said, "but there's a group of biter demons behind us."

I swore. "You brought us into a dimension overrun by demons. What did you expect?"

"It's up to you. Walk quickly, or reappear on top of a crime scene."

I gave him the finger, pulled off my wristband, and walked. He followed immediately behind, with Rachel on our left. No signs of other humans disturbed the rocky waste-land, no monuments to their presence here at all. It was as though nobody had ever set foot here except us. Rocky ground, a few caves, high cliffs on either side, and the outline of a larger shape on the horizon, silhouetted against the unnaturally large moon. A castle, perhaps, with a number of spire-like towers piercing the sky.

Rachel hissed in alarm. "There's something coming."

I raised my arm in defence, and two medium-sized fiends jumped down the cliffs at us, shrieking delightedly. Biter demons were swarm hunters, which meant they'd come to find food for their pack. Oh, joy.

Still, they were lesser demons, and I'd bet they'd never messed with a celestial before. White light flared around my hand, a warning hint they didn't take. Several furred heads leaned forward, jaws unhinging to reveal three sets of serrated teeth each.

Light pierced the first demon to jump at me. Flesh melted off its teeth and a horrible stench poured out of the dying demon. Of course, when I killed demons here in their home realm, they stayed there, rotting away, rather than vanishing as they did back home.

Black lightning seared past me and struck down two more, but instead of running, the beasts surged forwards in a mass of fur. I called the celestial light, feeling my way to the sword. For a heartbeat, I was afraid it wouldn't work—that not being in my home dimension would cut off access to my weapons. But the Divinities were beyond one single dimension.

I whipped out the sword, which shone brighter than any celestial light, and swung it at the nearest demon. Its head bounced off the cliff, jaws agape.

In a surge, the demons leaped down to meet us. Rachel wielded twin knives, while lightning sparked from Nikolas's fingertips. But it was the celestial light that burned them, severing heads, melting flesh. The angel's fury rode through me, and I cut two beasts' throats in one, their heads bouncing down the cliffs.

A bellow split the sky. *And there's their leader.* As before, a larger, spiny demon led the swarm, watching the ongoing carnage from the top of the cliff, surrounded by a wall of smaller demons.

Time to die.

I climbed one-handed up the cliff, using my left hand to wield my sword and cut down any demon that dared to grab for me. As another demon's head bounced down the cliff, a clawed hand snatched the back of my still-wet coat, yanking me onto the cliff top.

The bigger demon and I faced off. Porcupine-like spines bristled from its body, its paw-like hands were tipped with deadly claws—but it was afraid to touch my sword. The blade sang, cutting down the line of defence, driving the demon to the cliff's edge.

"Celestial," it said in a guttural voice, speaking in Malthric, one of the demon languages. "You're supposed to be dead."

"You just can't keep me down," I said, and lunged.

With the blade active, my speed was beyond most humans. What I hadn't counted on was him jumping off the cliff's edge, leaving me to fall into empty air. I flipped over, catching the edge of a rock protruding over the valley. My blade hung from my other hand, lighting the gloom. I'd forgotten how fast the bastards could move.

Claws latched onto my leg, dangling me upside-down. The grinning face of the demon loomed from the shadows. He'd grabbed the cliff beneath me mid-jump, waiting to ambush me as I fell. The blood rushed to my head and I struggled, trying to get at the right angle to wriggle free. My sword swung wildly from my right hand, narrowly missing the demon.

Then he let go. I fell, fingers scraping the cliff side, and managed to slow my fall. The blade remained in my hand, probably more due to its magic than any skill on my part. It was weightless, made of pure celestial light, and would stay until the job was done.

And it will be.

As the creature kicked out, I caught its foot on the edge of my sword. While it was unbalanced, I thrust upwards, severing its leg. A terrible scream pierced the sky, and the demon tumbled past me, clawed arms flailing.

I let go of the cliff, launching myself at the beast. My blade sank into its chest, in mid-air, and celestial light flared around its body.

I landed hard, the beast cushioning my fall. Then I ascended the cliffs again, where the remaining biter demons milled around in confusion, looking for their fallen leader.

"Come and get me," I said, grinning at them.

They bolted. Yowling in fear, the remaining demons ran for the hills, leaving dust in their wake. I killed the stragglers, leaving their bodies to the scavengers, and leaped down the cliff again. The dust barely stirred as I landed in a crouch. Rachel stared at me in awe. "So that's what a celestial soldier really looks like?"

"That's what I am," I said, more to Nikolas than to her. I might think the guild was short-sighted at best, but I'd been reborn and remade to do this. No warlock would ever understand that. I hadn't missed Nikolas's eyes following the movement with fascination as I jumped down the cliff, but now, he wore a mildly irritated expression. I looked down. Crap. Not only had my bra slid down during the fight, rain water plastered my clothes to my body, and my top was totally see-through. Saying farewell to dignity, I tugged my clothes back into place. "I didn't dress for a fight on an alien planet."

"I told you *not* to draw attention," Nikolas said. "Every demon for miles around will have seen that fireworks display."

"Sorry for saving your neck." The adrenaline buzz died down, though my heart continued to pound. My sword had vanished back to its storage point between dimensions, as it did whenever I wasn't using it. "I'll leave you to become demon food next time. You knew this was coming."

"I didn't," he said. "There aren't usually so many, but when demonic activity occurs in one realm, it has a knock-on effect on the others. If this demonic killer is moving realms, even more so."

"You think the killer caused this?"

"Or the person who summoned it," he said. "There are

few with the knowledge and skill, and I would know if a fellow warlock did so. What's unusual is the lack of any traces. One would almost think the demon was summoned somewhere untrackable." He spoke with an emphasis I didn't understand—until his gaze dropped to my uncovered left wrist.

"What—you think a *celestial* did it? *Why?*"

"He who fights monsters..."

I blinked. "Nice job quoting Nietzsche. Fine. If you're so convinced, then why not ask me about *them*, rather than the victims?"

"Because there's nothing you know that I don't already," he said. "You've been on your own for two years, so if anyone has left or turned to demons in the interim, you wouldn't know yet."

"Yet," I said. "You want me to spy on them. That's what this is about."

Un-fucking-believable. Sure, there was a one percent chance he was right, but if so, why pile this on me now when he could have asked me upfront? I might not have believed him, but at least I wouldn't be stuck in a demon dimension, dependent on him to get me out.

I didn't like being this vulnerable. At all.

"You're grasping at straws," I said before he responded. "Accusing the people who hunt demons as their life's calling? You know what, let's save it. Get me out."

"I'm trying to work out where we are in relation to the city," he said, the shadows moving around him. "We crossed over on a main road, which isn't ideal. If we end up stuck in the middle of a wall, for instance, it'll be unpleasant." He began to walk, Rachel joining him. She'd put away her knives, but seemed tense, on edge in a way she hadn't back on Earth.

"Like you haven't done this a hundred times before." I

walked after them. "There's nobody at the guild who'd murder novices. Come on, you must know that's absurd. Why jeopardise their own mission?"

"Why indeed," he said. "It's rare for me to hear of a demon I don't know."

Oh. So that's why he wanted to solve this. He was after the challenge. As for his interest in *me*, I had no clue. Nor should it matter. We needed to get out of this dimension and back to a world where people like me still existed, before my celestial light drew every demon on the planet. Nikolas's demon side might belong here, but I sure as hell didn't. In the pause after he spoke, silence slithered in, quieter than I'd heard in a long time. The sort of quietness of a place with nobody around for miles—but the castle, and the dead demon bodies heaped behind us, proved that wasn't the case. Rather than tranquillity, the silence spoke of dangers, of stealthy killers which crept up behind you and casually took your life. I kept my celestial light switched on even at the risk of attracting more demons. I'd much rather see them coming.

"What happened here?" I asked Nikolas. "The demons won, of course, but—you said your arch-demon parent wasn't here."

"He abandoned this realm long ago," he said. "The celestials lost the war, but most of the demons were wiped out in the process. He'd be ruling over a wasteland. He got bored. Babylon was a ruin when he left."

"Babylon?" I said dubiously. "This is what this realm's called? Wait, *how* old are you?"

He glanced over his shoulder at me. "I turn thirty this year. Any particular reason?"

"Babylon in our realm was… ancient. Also, I'd like to know if I flashed my tits at an old man."

He laughed, to my surprise. "You're not like the other

celestials. And warlocks aren't immortal, not even the children of arch-demons."

"Just hard to kill, huh." I looked up, frowning at the spiky shape of the turreted castle silhouetted against the unnaturally large full moon. "What's that for, anyway?"

"That's my home."

My jaw dropped. "You're kidding. The castle is yours?"

"Not mine, exactly," he said. "And we can't go up there. The way's blocked by creatures which wouldn't like that I brought a celestial here."

"No," said a voice. "We certainly wouldn't."

A human-shaped figure appeared from the shadows. As tall as Nikolas himself, he towered over Rachel and me. His dark red hair gleamed in the full moonlight, and he was clothed in black. His gaze slid over to Nikolas. "What now, consorting with celestials?"

"Just taking a shortcut, little brother."

Wait. No way—*now* I saw the resemblance. The arrogance. And the power. That, and the pitch-dark aura. I should have noticed that part before.

He tilted his head. "I saw that light a mile away. You're playing a dangerous game."

"I don't doubt you think so," said Nikolas, "but we're not here for fun. If you don't mind—"

The second warlock stepped forward. His shadow stretched behind him, splayed against the cliffs, and split into two identical warlock-sized shadows. Each one divided again into two more. *Shit. He has shadow magic, too.* The four shadows became eight, closing in around us. I stiffened as a shadowy hand touched my shoulder.

"Get off me," I snarled, waving my celestial light.

The real warlock laughed. He stood unmoving in front of us, but his shadows seemed to have a mind of their own. *Illusions. They can't be real.*

Nikolas took a step towards him. "Leave us," he commanded.

"I don't think so," said the warlock. "The celestial girl and I are going to have some fun."

"Are we hell—" My words were cut off as a shadowy arm grabbed me on either side. Sure felt solid to me. Crap.

"Let's see how well she copes with this," he said.

The shadows closed in, blocking off my sight. I couldn't see Nikolas or Rachel anymore, nor much of anything else, either. My celestial light should have lit up the dark—but it didn't.

"Let me go, you bastard," I shouted into the dark.

Soft laughter answered. "I wonder if you can fight without the light of your Divinity."

A shadowy hand squeezed my throat, cutting off my breath. I struggled, kicking out, as he lifted me off the ground. I couldn't tell whether it was the warlock or one of his shadows, but damn, it *felt* real. And I was in trouble if the blasted light didn't turn back on. *Come on. Burn him out. He's a demon.*

I gripped my left hand with my right, wildly aiming above my head. I might not be able to see the light, but no demon could switch it off altogether.

Sure enough, the pressure on my neck lifted, and I spun around. The faintest light shone in the dark, outlining a man-shaped shadow.

Laughter rang around me. "Let's see you fight all of them off, celestial."

The shadows closed in.

11

I raised my left hand. A sizzling noise sounded when my celestial light struck something solid, but the shadows prevented me from seeing my own hands, and a solid punch landed on my cheek. Jerking my head out of reach, I pivoted.

"Show yourself, you coward," I growled, aiming a punch with my celestial hand in the vague direction of the shadow. My hand sailed through thin air, and I damn near overbalanced. Where the others were, I hadn't a clue. I might not even be in the same dimension. Maybe that was why I couldn't reach my sword. From the humming sensation in my left arm, the light was definitely switched on, but apparently the shadows blocked even the light of the Divinities.

Falling into a defensive stance, I struck out at the shadows. The shadow hit back with a heavy blow that sent me flying back into a hard surface. *The cliff?* Was the real world still out there? I reached back with my right hand, feeling my way along its surface. Its solidness grounded me, steadied my rising panic. I'd reached the limit of the little shadow world he'd created.

Now to break the spell.

I jumped back and sprung, using the cliff face to launch myself into the air as though attacking a flying demon. Closing my eyes, I reached for the sword.

This time, a familiar weight settled in my hands. The blade sliced the air, and the shadows fell away like thin cardboard as I opened my eyes to see the warlock shadow-clones had gone, leaving only him.

The warlock faced me with a similar piercing look to his brother's. "Effective. How did you guess you hadn't left this dimension?"

"The cliff."

"Ah." He nodded. "I'll keep that in—"

I punched him in the jaw. He ducked, not fast enough, but his jaw was like iron. I yelped, my celestial magic not quite shielding my hand from the pain.

With a snarl, he grabbed my wrist.

White smoke poured from my skin and he let go with a loud curse. Backing away from me, he waved his hand around, giving me a glimpse of the impressive batch of bright purple blisters rapidly spreading from his hand to his wrist.

Black lightning sizzled past, striking him in the forehead. He fell back without a sound, mouth open in surprise.

I spun to face Nikolas. "You killed him?"

"He'll get over it," said Nikolas, with a scowl. "Are you okay? Zadok's shadows are designed to shut everyone else out. He has far too much free time on his hands."

"Huh? Yeah, I'm fine. He's a prick." I stepped away from his prone body. "What was that in aid of?"

"He's never played with a celestial before. I didn't think he'd be roaming around at this hour."

"Hmm." He looked pretty dead, a smoking hole in the middle of his forehead, but if he was a blood relation of

Nikolas, he must have an arch-demon's invulnerability. "So you two have a weird Cain and Abel thing going on?"

"You might say that. *What* did you do to his hand?"

From the way the blisters continued to climb up both his hands, he was apparently alive, after all. "I put a little defence charm on. So—he uses shadow magic, too. Can he cross between realms?"

"Thankfully not," he said. "What you witnessed was his main power—summoning up a shadow trap, populated by shades of his own making, and locking you inside it."

"Tell me those are the only powers he has. I thought all warlocks had only one."

"Most do," he said. "Luckily for the humans."

And the celestials. "So when you said there was a provisional ruler of this realm, you meant *him?*"

"Technically, he only rules this part of the wasteland. I suppose he couldn't resist testing a celestial. You handled him better than I expected."

"I'm so flattered that I met your incredibly low expectations. By the way, thank you," I said.

He blinked. "For what?"

"You're the reason I was wearing that blister trap in the first place. In case you're thinking of trying your little mind-trick on me again."

"Oh." His mouth curved in amusement. "I got under your skin that much?"

"I don't like being manipulated," I told him. "And by the way, I'm still wearing it, in case you need a warning to keep your paws off me. He'll be covered in blisters from head to toe when he wakes up."

"Then we'd better hope we don't have to come here again anytime soon." His eyes glittered. "I should warn the others."

He stepped around his brother's body, summoning shadows of his own. The air split and he peered through, shaking his head. "People will ask questions if we appear in the middle of the locked shopping centre at night." He began to walk on through the canyon, leaving his brother behind.

"And that's worse than demons?" I asked, one step behind him.

"According to him it is," said Rachel. "We're law-abiding, honest members of the public as far as your realm is concerned."

"Apart from how he keeps jumping into this dimension whenever he wants to avoid something or make a quick exit," I added, breaking into a jog. I wasn't out of shape, but damn, he moved fast. "Slow down."

"Don't bother," said Rachel. "He doesn't want to leave any traces of us near Zad, when he wakes up."

"I thought he couldn't cross dimensions."

"He can't, but Niko always wants to be certain."

My feet hammered against the rocky ground, and he still showed no signs of stopping. "Does he normally bring people into this dimension without their permission?" I asked Rachel.

"No. I think you've caused us more trouble than any human we've met."

"Awesome."

Nikolas finally slowed, and I did too, trying not to show how out of breath I was. Really good job I hadn't worn heels, though I'd probably shredded the soles of my nicest boots.

"There you are," he said. "I was beginning to worry I'd left you behind."

"Maybe you should have thought of that before you took off like a bat out of hell."

He looked highly amused at my word usage. I gave him a look. "I don't see what the fuss over us not being near your brother is, anyway."

"I don't know how fast he'll regenerate this time," he said.

"Might be hours, might be a couple of minutes. You'll be top of his hit list after what you did to him."

"Great. I really needed a new nemesis. At least I know my defence works, if another one of you decides to screw with me."

"I wouldn't assume you've got our measure so easily, celestial."

"You never said it wouldn't work on you," I added.

"No," he said. "I suppose I didn't."

He stepped close to me, power radiating out of the dark aura unfurling around him. I swallowed, my throat dry, as his gaze darted to my still see-through top. Was he seriously checking me out?

"Are you done bickering?" Rachel wanted to know. "Because I'd like to get home today."

"Me, too," I said. "I take it we're far enough away by now."

"Let's find out." A shadow split the air, and he peered through. "Not the best location, but this'll do."

"What do you mean?"

Instead of answering, he raised a hand. Shadows folded around the three of us. I tensed, but they disappeared a second later, and a torrent of rain instantly drenched me. Brushing my wet hair out of my eyes, I stood on tip-toe to get my bearings. "King Street, huh." We'd walked further than I'd thought. At least I knew how to get home from here.

"Aren't you going to thank me?" Nikolas looked at me expectantly, apparently oblivious to the rainfall. This time, when his gaze dropped to my chest, I knew it wasn't an acci-dent. And despite the trap keeping him from touching me, my neck flushed with heat under his stare.

"Sure," I said, pointedly keeping my gaze on his face. "It was fun. Nice change of scenery."

"Babylon has its moments," he said, apparently still

waiting for me to say something. What, I didn't know. "Will you be able to get home?"

The invitation was unmistakable. Normally, I'd say yes without a thought. Had he been a normal human man who hadn't snatched me into another dimension without my permission. I could only imagine Fiona's expression if I walked to my flat with a warlock. And if the celestials found out about any of this, there'd be no forgiveness. From here on out, I was as guilty in their eyes as he was.

I wouldn't tell them. Not even Gav. Our killer was still at large, and had claimed three victims in the space of a day. If we let things go on as they were, the inspector would take up permanent residence in the city. And if the way he and his fanatics talked about warlocks and vampires was anything to go by, there'd be full-on war by the week's end. Whatever Nikolas wanted from me, nothing was more important than catching our demon killer.

I peeled my gaze away from him. "I'll be fine. Try not to run into any celestials on the way home."

———

The next day dawned cold and grey. After I'd reached home —thankfully without meeting any celestials—I'd found Fiona in hysterics. By now, the latest murder was all over the news, and she'd been convinced I'd been caught up in it. I'd reassured her I was okay, warned her not to go near the celestials, and most definitely did *not* tell her about Nikolas, Javos, or our little excursion into another dimension.

Perhaps it was a bad idea to go into the guild the next morning, but I needed to know what had really gone down last night. So I rode the train there first thing the following day. As it was a Sunday, the trains were infrequent but quieter. Once at the guild I scanned my way in, and nearly collided with Inspector Deacon in the entryway.

"What are you doing here, Devina?" he snarled.

"I work here. There was another death?" I asked, careful to balance just the right amount of concern and surprise in my voice.

He wasn't fooled. "Don't pretend not to know."

Someone was in a mood today. "I just got in." Not exactly a lie, and they'd never guess where I'd been last night. A world away, literally. Leaping into demonic dimensions wasn't against the rules, technically, because they didn't think anyone would be reckless enough to try it. I didn't want to be the first to find out what the punishment would be.

"Were you out drinking last night?" he asked, looming closer to me. Not quite as intimidating as a warlock, but enough to put me on the defensive.

"Huh? No. I had a quiet night in. The victim was found near the high street, right?"

"Correct," he said. "To be precise, in an area frequented by warlocks, vampires, weres, and other demon kin."

"Same circumstances as before?"

He folded his arms across his chest. "Celestial Lawson, I think you should leave and cease to investigate this case."

"What's the issue?" I asked. "I was rehired by the celestials to help out, and I didn't even see the last victim."

"Have you been with those warlocks since yesterday?" he enquired. "We don't need the aid of unreliable individuals known for consorting with netherworlders."

"Whoa there," I said. "What exactly is your problem with me? No, I haven't seen any warlocks since yesterday." Technically true, because it'd been before midnight when I'd gone home after my round-trip to the shadow realm. "Who is the victim?"

"Celestial Helen Roberts," said Gav from behind the inspector. "She died at the scene. Inspector, I'd like Devina to come with me."

Thanks, Gav.

"Don't think I haven't seen you covering for her," he said. "If you're not careful, you'll find yourself on probation."

"That won't be necessary," Gav said.

Shaking my head, I followed him. "What's with him today?"

"Three murders in the space of twenty-four hours," he said, leading me into the office. "It's never happened before. Certainly not here. People are talking, the newspapers have got hold of it… it's been a disaster."

Given the huge bags under his eyes and his sallow complexion, I figured he'd taken the brunt of the backlash himself. He sank into his chair, his prosthetic leg clunking against the desk.

"I figured, but I'm here to help, not cause trouble."

"The inspector doesn't see it that way." He exhaled heavily. "I didn't know he'd pin all the suspicions on you. You weren't in town last night, were you?"

"What's it to him if I was?" I shot at him, anger sparking. "He knows I'm not capable of killing someone like that. And if he thinks I'm in league with warlocks, he can talk to their leader about it. They're not the killers."

Not even Nikolas's brother. Neither of their magic matched the aura I'd seen on the victims. White, with dark spots, almost as though corrupted from the inside.

"Devi," he said warningly. "I'd sincerely advise you to avoid associating with any netherworlders at all for the duration of this investigation."

"Assuming I'm even allowed to stay," I said. "What if the netherworlders have the answers? They know demons. Possibly better than our archives." I mean, the information on arch-demons was locked away. Nikolas had one for a parent. That fact alone made him a valuable asset. And for all that he'd yanked me into another dimension last night, he *had* saved me from being caught at a third crime scene. And returned the pentagram.

Hmm.

"The warlocks are fast becoming the main suspects," said Gav. "Mostly because if a new demon was on the loose, it would have attacked at least one regular human by now. The only place it could possibly blend in is amongst other nether-worlders."

"Assuming it's even permanently in this dimension," I said.

"What does that mean?"

I shrugged. I might trust him, but I wouldn't confide every detail of last night's excursion to anyone, not while I was the guild's suspect. "Some demons can cross through dimensions."

"Like that warlock."

I sighed inwardly. "He's from the shadow realm. His aura doesn't match the victims'. I used some of that aura-seeing potion yesterday, but it's probably worn off by now. The victims' auras… I don't know how to describe it. They were sort of… spotted. Like patches of darkness were spreading across them. I've never seen an aura that wasn't one colour, so I don't know what it is."

His brow crinkled. "Patches? If they were killed by a demon, their aura would remain the same colour. It should have."

Unless they were corrupted.

You wear a demon's mark.

A chill broke out on my arms. "Can a person be marked by a demon without knowing it?"

His puzzled expression remained in place. "No. I mean,

theoretically… people have summoned demons without knowing what they were doing, but they have to agree to have a mark put on them. You think the victims were contacted by a demon?"

"They must have been," I said. "Wait—the last victim. Was she anywhere near the crime scene originally?"

His gaze met mine. "No," he said. "She was at home. Her flatmate confirmed it."

"Shit," I muttered. "So they're really the same."

"They all appeared in a place they couldn't have been," he said. "Whether that was the same magic which killed them remains to be seen."

"No clues?" I asked. "None at all? Same manner of death and everything? They were all novices, right?"

"Yes," he said. "Not the same age, though. Louise was almost a Grade Two. And there was something odd about her case. A dead vampire was found near her house several hours later. It appeared that he'd walked into the sun of his own accord."

My heart lurched. Had he killed himself over her death, or had someone else? "Is his body here? I mean, what's left of it?"

That sounded insensitive, but some vampires turned to ash when they died.

"The vampire's leader took his remains back, as is custom," he said. "Why?"

"Looking for any connections," I said. "Three celestials and a vampire dead in the space of a day. All from bursting into flames… technically. I mean, vampires catch on fire if they look too closely at a light bulb." *Quiet, Devi.*

Gav gave me a long-suffering look. "It's none of my business what novices do in their free time, but I did hear the rumours. Vampire venom, thankfully, doesn't work on celestials."

"I know that." I'd dated one myself back in my rebellious phase. When I'd broken every rule…

They will burn the sin out of you.

My hand clenched beside the seat. Maybe someone did want the celestials to fall. But honestly, if I were an arch-demon wanting to conquer the world, I'd come up with something more dramatic than killing a few novice celestials. However the others were reacting, it was nothing compared to the wars that had ravaged worlds like the one I'd been to last night. But no matter how many times I told myself that the celestials had more sense than to go to war over a single lone demon, a sick, cold feeling remained inside me.

I couldn't tell him my theory. Gav might put up with a ton of crap from me, but he believed in the celestials, and he believed in our mission. I wouldn't find answers here. No… the warlocks were the only ones who might know the truth.

Even if Nikolas had implied the celestials might be involved deeper than we knew.

"Is anyone here acting weird?" I asked, not at all subtly. "I mean, the inspector's heading the investigation, and he's taking issue with me acting alone. I take it everyone involved is meant to report in to him, and not to… er, meet with contacts alone."

"Devi," he said. "Don't speak to the warlocks."

"That's not what I meant," I said heatedly. "And for the record, I got more information from five minutes with the warlocks than I did from years working here."

"Warlocks cannot be trusted. According to our doctrine, they're aligned with hell."

"Okay, that's *enough*," I snapped. "Good lord, pull your heads out your arses for one second and imagine I'm right. You hired me. I have contacts. You didn't say I couldn't use them."

I was so screwed. I couldn't believe I was taking the word

of a warlock, but I never did trust that the celestials had our best interests at heart. Their goal was winning the war against demons. Which meant one of them summoning an arch-demon was about as unlikely as Inspector Deacon suddenly developing a personality. But if anyone other than the warlocks had the know-how on summoning a powerful demon, it was the celestials. Their knowledge was purely theoretical, but the warlock was right—they *did* hide a lot of things from their recruits. If someone had gone dark, it might go unnoticed. Of course, they lacked a motive for randomly murdering novices, but it couldn't hurt to have a poke around and see if anyone was up to no good.

In a detective show, the good guys being the murderers would be an obvious conclusion. Here, it'd take some logical stretching to figure out how anyone here would begin justifying the murder of innocents, but demons were the definition of corruption. Bringing the celestials down from the inside would be the perfect revenge on us for killing so many of them.

"Devi," said Gav quietly. "Please, please don't aggravate the inspector. He's one mistake away from putting you in a cell for the duration of this investigation."

"Then I'll go," I said. Do as Clover suggested, and strike out on my own. It was how I worked best, after all.

I figured I'd leave via the lab to see if they'd got in any new stock of rare ingredients. Instead, I found two staff members in conversation, including Mr Roth—former leader of this very guild, before the inspector had stepped in.

"Celestial Lawson," he said. "What are you doing in here?"

I gave him a false smile. "Working on the case. I keep my props in here." I aimed for the stores, checking for anything out of place on the shelves. It didn't look like anything demonic had been removed since yesterday, but I double-checked just in case. Of course, the main prop was the pentagram—the only device big enough to hold a high-ranked demon.

Suspicion flared, unexpectedly. The inspector had claimed that very office as his own. There'd be irony in *him* being the bad guy, but he was an obvious choice, however unlikely it was that high-ranked demons were even interested in talking to him. He was a total bore even by celestial standards. Besides, if he'd used the pentagram recently for summoning a demon, I'd have seen the residue when I'd used it myself.

"Er, Mr Roth?" I asked. "Has the inspector been in here at all?"

"No, he hasn't," said the leader of the guild. "He's been run off his feet all day—and all night, too. We all have."

I nodded. "Just curious. I wondered—can I see the last body? I'm still on the investigation."

Mr Roth shook his head. "The inspector would need to authorise it."

"You hired me," I said.

"I did, when I was the leader of this guild," said Mr Roth. "Unfortunately, Inspector Deacon now takes that title, and he's the acting authority until the crimes are solved."

Bullshit. I bit my tongue. I should have seen this coming. The inspector was too power-mad to resist the chance to grab even more authority over the city, but his new position also made him the centre of attention. Surely he wouldn't be able to sneak off and talk to demons without someone taking note of his absence. So much for that theory. Guess I didn't get to hit the guy over the head with a pentagram after all.

"Okay, I'm off, then," I said. "Good luck with the investigation."

Without seeing the body, I couldn't be certain the death had transpired exactly the same as the others did. But I hadn't been to the crime scene yet. The inspector hadn't said

I couldn't. And for all our inter-dimensional adventures, I still didn't have Nikolas's phone number. If he had one, considering he apparently lived in a castle when he wasn't in this realm.

I shouldn't want to talk to him. He had no reason to help me solve the murders, aside from apparent curiosity and the drive to clear his own name, and I still wasn't absolutely certain another warlock wasn't involved. If the conflict did come to war, I'd have to stand by the celestials. Demon mark or not, that was where I belonged. We'd been set against one another from the moment the Divinity had chosen me. And if I lost sight of that mission, I'd lose myself.

Even if part of me had been lost ever since I'd watched Rory die.

Thankfully, it'd stopped raining by the time I departed the train station at the high street. Everything had a grey, washed-out look. I couldn't help thinking of the wasteland that lay here, in another world. A world in ruin. Like so many others. Dienes's world, too. Even if I'd grudgingly accepted that not all warlocks were pure evil, the idea of demons wreaking havoc on this realm didn't exactly fill me with confidence. I needed to disconnect myself from the warlocks as soon as possible. Solve the crime, and then disappear from the inspector's sight before I got locked in a cell.

That was what a sensible person would do, anyway. But sensible people didn't wind up working with warlocks in the first place—let alone walking to my third murder site within the last two days.

The corner of the street was cordoned off with police tape. A brief scan from a distance didn't give me any information. With the body gone, all that remained were ashes, washed away by the rain. This was a public place. No wonder there'd been an uproar. What I needed was a witness to question. The streets hadn't been deserted last night, and there'd been a large number of people going in and out of the pub. But it was closed at this time, with blinds over the windows like a vampire's den in daylight.

The normal-looking pub on the opposite corner was open, however. I strode casually inside and peered into the gloom. Nobody was around except for a disinterested-looking barman slowly polishing a glass. He spotted me right away—not hard, because there were no customers. And he was definitely human.

"Hi." I walked over to him. "I'm Devina, and I'm investigating the murder that occurred outside your pub last night."

"Celestial." His gaze darted to my wrist, which was covered. He'd guessed what I was anyway, then. I often wondered how people could tell. Maybe it was how I walked.

"Yeah. I'd like to know if you or any of your customers witnessed the girl's death."

He looked at me strangely. "A dozen people saw, at least. It's all over the news. Caught on camera and everything."

Why hadn't I thought of that? Well, to be fair, demons were tricky to catch on camera anyway. I should have asked Fiona if there'd been any new videos on DivinityWatch. *Amateur move, Devi.*

I pulled out my phone and ran a search, immediately finding two videos of the street outside, already with tens of thousands of views. What better way to get attention than to upload a video of someone being brutally murdered by a demon.

"Are you at least going to buy something?" the barman asked.

"Sure, I'll get a coke," I said absently, pressing play.

The person filming had been leaving the bar next to this one, I knew from the angle, and must have hit the record button almost instantly after the victim had appeared. Jumbled voices filled the background, and the camera's focus zeroed in on a woman surrounded by a crowd, screaming. I quickly turned the volume down, but the sound wormed into my head, brought me out in shivers. There were words in the screams, but too indistinct to hear them.

The camera holder moved closer, pushing through the crowd, and the woman's sightless, burning eyes stared directly at me. Then she slumped against the wall, her screams dying to a faint whimpering. A couple of people tried to help her but dropped their hands. Then the video cut out.

I found another, but like the first, the person had started filming after she'd appeared—however *that* had happened. I couldn't see people's auras on camera either, for some reason. But I'd bet it was the same as the others. White patched with darkness, like a shadowy infection. A demon's mark.

After last night, I'd almost be inclined to blame Nikolas's brother, but he didn't have the ability to skip through dimensions or set people on fire. No... someone, human or warlock, had summoned the demon. But a human had nothing to gain from a demonic war. Not even a celestial.

Bracing myself, I replayed the first video, this time with the sound on.

"They're coming!" screamed the victim. *"They're coming to burn the sin out of you. All will fall—"*

This time when I looked up and saw Nikolas sitting next to me. I didn't jump. Much.

"Little early for drinking, isn't it?" he asked.

I rolled my eyes at him, my hand shaking as I closed the video tab down. "It's just a coke. I suppose your being here is a coincidence, right?"

"I don't think it's wise for you to be here," he said in a low voice, too quiet for the bartender to hear.

"I'm still on this case, whatever they say," I said. "Two videos of the murder last night, but no actual clues."

"Videos?" He arched a brow. "This is entertainment to the humans?"

"It'd be evidence in any normal crime. Anyway, this one was the same as the last two."

"Who was the victim?"

"Another novice," I said. "Same method of killing. I need to talk to an actual witness to find out how she appeared from thin air, but I think if anyone had seen the demon itself, there'd be more stories floating around social media." I'd skimmed through the trending topics, and every one of them said the victim had appeared from nowhere.

"There were no witnesses to the victim's disappearance before she ended up here?" he asked.

"None," I said. "That's a common theme, too. The demon seems to have caught all three of them alone. Which is probably why the celestials are so on edge. The only person *not* under watch is me, but considering the inspector wouldn't give a shit if anything happened to me anyway—" I broke off as the bartender approached, but a glazed look entered his eyes and he walked away. "Nice," I said to Nikolas. "Do you do that frequently? Can many demons use the same trick? Like your brother?"

"My brother, thankfully, doesn't have that ability," he said. "And if he was the killer, I'd have found a more permanent way to disable him yesterday."

So he'd guessed my suspicion. "All right. I had to check. And by the way, your celestial idea doesn't pan out. Everyone's accounted for, and the inspector has everyone under watch to avoid any more attacks. Including himself. Not to mention that pentagram is the only device they have at the guild which can hold a high-ranked demon, and nobody had used it recently when I borrowed it."

He looked at me calmly. "Yes, I guessed as much myself. But I suspect that there are areas of the guild you aren't allowed in, correct?"

"You're right." I'd thought over my options last night, and all of them came back to the same point. The celestials might not be behind the murders, but they *did* have information they refused to let anyone get their hands on. Such as the movement in demonic dimensions. I couldn't be the only person who contacted the netherworld on a regular basis. "First, I've got a question. That castle is yours, isn't it?"

He blinked. "What? In Babylon? Of course."

"And you're allowed to walk in and out of there anytime you like, right?"

"Naturally." He sounded a little wary. I'd officially weirded out the warlock. Awesome.

"The celestials have helpfully shut me out of their investigation," I said. "I could break in, but I can't be bothered dealing with their security. That castle of yours overlaps with the guild. I looked it up."

He went still. "Yes, it does. But even though it's mine, I'm not the only person living in the castle. There are others."

"Your brother."

"One of the towers is his. It's not him I'm concerned about. Your celestial light will draw any demon nearby, if you use it."

"And if I didn't? If I took a shortcut through your dimension, sneaked into the morgue to see the body, and—" I stopped. "If you're right, and it is one of them who's the killer. I can't think of a better way to sneak into their top-secret room." The west wing was only open to higher celestials, and contained the library with information on forbidden higher demons... and arch-demons.

"It might be possible," Nikolas said. "I do know precisely where this city overlaps with the shadow realm, but it's still risky for me to take you there. The demonic dimension is not there to use as a shortcut. There's a reason there are so few of us with this power."

"Yeah, I suppose we can't have the world overrun with people hopping between dimensions. Anyway, I never asked if *you* had any more ideas. I can't be the only one. What about your amazing warlock powers of deduction? Or do you really think one of the celestials has gone dark?"

"I don't know." His brows drew together. "What else do the victims have in common? I'm beginning to believe that someone wanted to do more than stir up the celestials. Killing multiple victims in a short space of time suggests a purpose. If they weren't using magic to kill, I'd suggest the purpose was to feed on or harness their life energy."

"But if they used magic to kill the victims, they need to recharge," I said. "Which throws that theory out. Unless there's a demon who doesn't get tired from using powerful magic or need to recharge."

"High-ranked demons," he said. "That part, I'd guessed. However, that doesn't explain how they choose their victims. They're targeting younger, new recruits."

"I guess it has to do with them being easier to target," I said. "They don't have the training to fight Grade Three or higher demons."

"Or their influence."

I frowned. "What, recruiting them to the dark side? You think the *victims* were the ones working with the demon doing this?"

"No, but they're more susceptible to being recruited."

"Not necessarily," I said. "Training level doesn't affect intelligence, for one thing." Just look at Inspector Wilfully Ignorant.

"I suppose not." He looked at me. "So you wish to sneak into the castle tonight. Hoping to get a peek at my room?"

"I suppose it's painted in the fiery colours of hell."

His expression went stony.

"It's a joke," I said. "But you can definitely take me there?"

"There's one thing I'd like from you in return," he said.

"Yes?" *Oh, boy.* I knew there was a reason he'd caved in so easily.

"An arch-demon experienced in putting marks on humans recognised your name when I spoke to him," he said. "He wants to see you."

"What?" I said blankly. "Did you say *arch-demon?*"

"Yes, I did."

"Okay, you've lost it." I shook my head at him. "I met with Javos. I met your lunatic brother and nearly died in the process. I am *not* talking to one of the leaders of hell. They want me dead."

"One of them gave you their mark," said Nikolas. "I can't say I know which, but Themedes might know."

"*Gave* me their mark?" I echoed, my heart sinking. "Can you see my aura? Is that how you know?"

"Why?"

"Just a thought." I swallowed. I didn't want to think about what I'd done to draw their attention… but if it was true, then maybe the reason they'd killed Rory and not me… was because I was already damned.

"I told you, auras look different to us," he said. "We're not viewing them through the same lens as a celestial. To you, ours look dark and shadowy. Not to us."

"But what does it *look* like?" My voice rose, brittle and sharp, and he raised an eyebrow.

"Bright blue, like the other celestials'," he said. "Humans show up as pale grey, usually."

"What did the victim's aura look like to you?" I struggled

to keep my tone even. My pulse raced, my heart rate picking up.

"The same as yours, but with traces of magic," he said. "It's difficult for me to describe it, and all demon magic tends to produce the same aura effect. Not all warlocks have the same aura, either, but I'm sure we look similar to you."

"Not you. Yours looks… pitch black. Your brother's the same."

"Shadow demons." He nodded. "But you mentioned the victims. I'm guessing you see all celestials' auras as white, correct?"

"Yeah," I said. "The victims', though—the one I saw had these dark patches in her aura. Like something was eating away at her."

"Magic," he said. "A demon's subtle magic, perhaps."

"Not—a mark? Like whatever it is you think I have?"

He frowned. "No. What *you* have is latent demonic magic, but I can't say which type. And it's not like the magic that killed the novices."

My shoulders slumped. "Are you sure?"

"Positive. Will you consider meeting with Themedes? He'll know what type of demon magic you have."

"And he'll know about this." I raised my left hand. "It's not like I can hide it. Arch-demons are kind of my ultimate nemesis."

"Technically, their nemeses are the Divinities. I doubt they care much for individual celestials. And if one of them marked you, they saw your potential."

"Potential for what?" I shoved my stool back from the bar. "Look, I don't know how things work on Planet Warlock, but demons generally want to tear me into bloody pieces, not put a mark on me. Unless they plan on using me as a bargaining chip with the Divinities in their war."

"What would give you that idea?"

"Stories." I shrugged. "The sort of thing they tell novices as a warning not to meddle with demons. They put a mark on your soul and steal it. The thing is, it's total nonsense. Our souls are already claimed by the Divinities, so we're no use to demons. As for arch-demons, they can crush a thousand of us like ants. They don't need us as bargaining chips, and to be honest, I doubt the Divinities would care about sacrificing us for the cause, anyway."

"Precisely," he said. "The part about the Divinities, at least —you're their soldiers, so I doubt they care about your individual lives. If a demon claimed one of you, I doubt they'd notice."

"I think you missed the part where our souls are already claimed," I said. "Normal humans can be possessed or influenced by powerful demons. We can't. We're immune."

"You're not immune to all demons."

"You do realise that's not going to make me more likely to want to meet this arch-demon of yours, don't you? I don't particularly want to get torn to pieces in an alternate dimension. I quite like this one."

"You won't be torn to pieces," he said. "If I were you, I'd be curious about why one of them marked you to begin with."

I don't know. Maybe it was a taunt, or a reward for killing so many of them.

Or because of Rory.

"I've killed demons for nearly ten years," I said. "This makes no sense. None. And are you sure this guy isn't the killer? I'd bet arch-demons are perfectly capable of lighting someone on fire from the inside out."

"Oh, he's capable of it," said Nikolas. "But he can't move between dimensions, and is hardly capable of using his magic, let alone answering a summons. He's dying, Devina."

"What?" I stared at him. "Aren't arch-demons immortal?"

"No, just ageless. They can die. This one has lived for

many, many thousands of years. He knew my father. He's the only surviving arch-demon in Pandemonium."

What? Pandemonium was Dienes's realm. "But I thought there weren't any left in that dimension."

"He doesn't count," said Nikolas. "His power wouldn't register on the same level as even a demigod like me or my brother. You're far stronger than he is."

"But—" I spluttered. "Did you say demigod? I thought you were a warlock."

"It's the technical term for anyone with an arch-demon as a parent." He shrugged. "Think of us as the upgraded form of regular warlocks."

"Because that's not cocky at all. Look, how are we even supposed to travel to meet this demon? I thought you could only use your power to go to the shadow realm."

"There's one exception," he said. "Summoning. He plans to summon me to his side. All I need to do is give the word that I'm bringing you with me."

"Yeah… no." I shook my head. An arch-demon wanting to meet me after a monster with powerful magic had murdered my former colleagues was a major red flag if I ever saw one.

"I can promise you won't come to harm, as long as I'm there," said Nikolas. "I offered to take you through my own realm to help you in your investigation, and in return, you'll get to learn about your demon magic. Seems a fair trade. You never know—you might find you like being one of us."

"I'm *not* one of you," I said. "Never. I'm not signing over my soul, or whatever it is you want me to do. That wasn't part of our deal, Nikolas. I'm not getting an arch-demon involved with my life. No way."

His jaw tightened. If I didn't know better, I'd say he looked almost insulted at my outburst. "If you change your mind, my offer stands open."

"Wait." Shit, this was a mistake and a half. But if he was

right—if I could find out what'd really happened to me, and by extension, the victims—then I might be able to solve the murders without needing to sneak into the guild. If anyone knew the comings-and-goings of all things demonic, it was an arch-demon.

Assuming he wasn't the killer.

Despite every shred of my better judgement telling me this was a terrible idea, there I was, walking with Nikolas through warlock territory in search of a suitable place to answer an arch-demon's summons.

"How does this work?" I asked. "It's not your dimension, right? So if this demon wants us to come and see him, how do we get out?"

"I'm going to set up a portal," he said. "A true one, not a dimension hole. That means he can take us to wherever he chooses on the other side, and then send us back—but obviously, he's completely in control of that. Kind of like when you used the pentagram on me."

I grimaced. "You're going to hold that against me forever, aren't you?"

"Just stating a fact," he said. "The power always rests with the person controlling the summoning—and in the case of an arch-demon, even one whose power is low, they always have control. It's what makes the idea of summoning an arch-demon impossible to contemplate. We'd know if one had been anywhere near this dimension, for instance."

A not-so-subtle way to remind me that Nikolas thought the arch-demon was innocent. Sure, as innocent as a Prince of Hell. He might not be the killer, but he was old as sin and evil enough to fall from heaven. Of course, I'd considered the possibility of a similar demon's involvement, but he was right—there was no way to summon one inconspicuously.

Nikolas took me through a warren of roads lined with brick houses, some with the windows boarded up. Vampire nests, most likely.

"By the way," I said to him, "a vampire was found near the second victim's house. Dead, in sunlight. They were dating."

"Any reason I needed to know that?"

"Evidence," I said. "I admit it, I'm jumping on any clue possible, but I suppose none of it will matter if the arch-demon of Pandemonium decides to skin me alive."

"He won't harm you as long as I'm there," said Nikolas.

I jumped at the sound of a loud bang from the nearest house. "What was that?"

"Warlock spells. Nothing to worry about."

Oh yeah. We were in the thick of preternatural territory. Flashes and bangs indicated spell use, and the smell of sulphur and brimstone made my eyes water.

"Has nobody here heard of air freshener?" I coughed.

"It wouldn't do any good. Brimstone is too potent. We'll stop here." He halted in the mouth of an alley with a high fence on one side and the brick facade of a large house on the other.

"Do you live somewhere here?" I asked. "I mean, when you're not in the castle."

"I do, but I'm not opening the portal near my house." He put a hand in his jacket pocket and started pulling out handfuls of herbs and small bottles containing what looked like powdered rock.

"What's that?" I asked, indicating a bright power. "I know the other ingredients, but that's a new one."

"You really do know demon summonings." There was an approving note to his voice. "Like you know demon languages. I'm assuming you're still fluent in High Chthonian."

"Only you would find that impressive rather than disturbing. Yes, I am, but I've contacted that dimension before, and never used… whatever that is."

"Demonglass," he said. "Powdered. It forms a connection between here and the arch-demon's palace."

"Palace. Of course."

"By the way," he said, "you should address him as 'sir', or 'Arch-demon Themedes'. Like one of his subjects."

"And are you absolutely certain he won't smite me on the spot for being a celestial?"

"I wouldn't take you with me if I wasn't."

Black lightning crackled from his hands, burning the shape of a pentagram into the ground. He tossed the ingredients into the centre, finishing with the demonglass.

Liquid-like shadows spread across the surface, swiftly turning bright red. A voice rumbled through me—*"WHAT DO YOU WANT?"*

"You summoned us," said Nikolas.

Mother of all demons. Pure, raw fear rooted me to the spot. No way in seven hells did I want to see the owner of that voice.

"THEN COME," said the voice.

The pentagram lurched towards us, as though it contained a life of its own, and orange flames sprang up. Burning fire, too bright to look at. So close I expected to feel the heat searing my bare skin, charring my clothes and turning my body to ashes. I raised a hand to shield my eyes, and the fire vanished.

The brick alley wall had been replaced by smooth obsidian stone, and the smell of flaming brimstone faded. I blinked the sting from my eyes and looked down. Stone lay beneath my feet. Slowly, I swivelled away from the wall. We appeared to have landed on a balcony above a city, with sand-coloured roofs undulating like hills and valleys as far as the eye could see. We must be miles off the ground. *Seven hells.*

"This is the city of Pandemonium," said Nikolas. "He brought us directly to the palace."

"Nice of him." I dragged my gaze away from the view as Nikolas opened a sliding glass door next to the obsidian pillar I'd landed in front of. The mechanism was surprisingly modern-looking, though now I thought about it, I hadn't gleaned a *lot* from Dienes about what this world was actually like to live in. Just all the species of demon—except the one we were about to meet. Weird how Dienes hadn't mentioned him, but arch-demons scared the crap out of their subjects at the best of times. And apparently he was less powerful than me. *Hmm.*

Our footsteps echoed on polished obsidian flagstones, while clear pillars climbed to the ceiling, reflecting golden light through the high windows. And between two such pillars was an ornate gold throne. I'd expected either a human-like being or a horned demon squatting on a pile of human skeletons. The arch-demon, however, was built more along the lines of Javos—huge, muscled, maybe seven feet tall, with leathery wings folded against his back. He looked up, and his aura hit me like a freight train. Blood red. Flaming. Terrifying.

My throat dried up. The potion that enabled me to see auras had worn off. For me to be able to see his hinted at the level of power he contained—too much to hide behind an acceptable facade. He swept long, tangled dark hair from his tanned face, and stared at me with golden eyes of pure flame. Even though I knew all arch-demons must look the same, I couldn't help thinking of the murder victims, how they'd burned. How I'd burned when I'd come here.

He's going to kill me. And if he'd asked for me, knew who I was…

Fire blazed around him, an aura of darkened light outlining his wings with jagged edges. A fallen angel, cast down into hell, the Divinities alone knew how many centuries ago. I swallowed, not daring to look away in case he raised a hand to smite me.

"Why," he rumbled, "is a celestial here?" He spoke in High Chthonic, the more refined version of the language Dienes and other lesser demons spoke.

Somehow, I found my voice. "You asked for me, Sir," I said. "I'm Devina. From Earth. Ring any bells?"

"And why would I ask for you?"

I couldn't look away to see if Nikolas had my back, but he'd *said* the arch-demon wouldn't harm me as long as he was present. The reality was, though, I'd been too confident in my own ability to kill demons. The guy in front of me hardly fell into the same category. It was like staring at a force of nature—an earthquake, a tidal wave, a torrent of pure wrath contained in an almost human-sized form.

Nikolas had said he was powerless. I'd hate to think of his idea of a normally-powered arch-demon, because this guy was fucking intense.

"It was your idea," I said. "Nikolas told me I have a demon's mark, and you sent for me because you can tell what it is."

"A warrior of light?" he said. "I would remember if I marked one of you."

My heart sank. "You asked for me."

"Perhaps I was wrong." He tilted his head. "You don't look

familiar to me, but I've seen a great many of your kind in my time."

He'd killed people. Armies of them, even. What the hell was I doing here?

"I'm marked," I said. "Apparently. By a demon, maybe an arch-demon. Considering I don't remember how it happened or who did it, I figured you might know."

Even beneath my fear, the old guilt rose—and the fear that I'd done something terrible on that world when I'd killed the demon. Something that had killed my partner and not me. But to be marked, when I'd never touched or even seen the demon responsible… it was impossible.

"No," he said. "I can't say I do, human."

"Can I go, then?" I asked. Screw my so-called demon mark—I didn't want to spend a moment longer in his terri-fying presence. "If you can't tell me who marked me, or who's killing the celestials in my realm—"

"Let them burn," he growled. "Let them all die, every last one."

"You know?" I asked, my words half-buried in a clap of thunder as he rose from his throne. "You know who's killing them?"

"*I* killed them," he roared. "Every last one of them. This realm is purged of the light, forever."

He means the celestials in this realm. My mouth tasted of ash. "And not people from my realm? Have you—"

Flames exploded into life before me, leaping to the high ceiling, boxing me in.

"Hey!" I shouted, panicking. Dammit, where the hell had Nikolas disappeared to? *That's what I get for trusting the word of a warlock.*

The flames circled me, masking the arch-demon from view. A face appeared in the smoke, forming into the semblance of a man. Human-shaped, with long flaming wings.

"I get to play with a celestial?" said the fiery demon.

"Who the hell are you?" I took a step back, but a wall of flames roared behind, and the heat at my back indicated I was surrounded. Nikolas had gone. The traitorous bastard had left me here in a realm I couldn't get out of. And apparently the arch-demon had a personal servant he'd sent to kill me.

The fire demon raised a hand. The smell of ash and charred fabric reached my nostrils, and heat surged from my feet to my ankles. My shoes. He'd burned them off. So much for kicking the shit out of him. I stepped back, my bare feet sticking to the smooth floor, and reached into the dimension between.

My sword appeared in time to deflect a flaming hand. The winged man had appeared before me faster than anything should have the right to move. Celestial light poured from my blade, sending him staggering back.

"Get away," I coughed.

Heat choked my lungs. Demon fire. If I dropped my guard, it'd creep in and burn the skin from my bones. I'd be a pile of ashes in seconds.

I kept my blade high, surrounded by a shimmering wave of celestial light. A temporary shield against the flames. The fire demon flickered in and out of existence, camouflaged in the flames. Powerful—higher demon level, for sure. But my blade was designed to burn demons. Even ones who wielded a fire of their own.

I swung my blade, colliding with the edge of a fiery sword. The two of them burned, and the demon's broke first, shattering into fiery shards. He snarled, the flames shrinking a little as he formed another sword of flame. *So he does have a limit.* I'd fought demons like him before. He'd burn himself out before he burned me. I'd make sure of it.

Blade hit blade, white fire burned against orange. He swept low, singing my jeans. Pain stung my thighs, but I sliced viciously upwards, and dark blood splattered the flagstones. He might be fire, but he could still bleed. Wrath radiated from his very being, and he reformed his weapon, bringing it down like an axe.

I dodged to the side, dropped to a crouch, and brought the celestial blade to the hilt in his chest. Flames burst around the wound, only to be extinguished. I twisted the blade, and he collapsed, the flames disappearing. His body crumpled in on itself, leaving nothing behind but ashes.

I stepped back, my knees stinging, the taste of ash on my tongue. "I won," I said to the arch-demon. "Now let me go."

"No." The huge being rose from his throne. His looming muscled form towered over me, wings splayed, casting dark shadows across the flagstones and the ashy remains of the demon I'd killed. "Give me one reason why I shouldn't send you to hell, mortal."

Fire raged in his eyes, a thousand times worse than the lesser demon he'd sent at me. This was the sort of power that toppled armies and boiled the waters of oceans.

"One of your people marked me," I said. "For whatever reason, you chose me. And you called me here to talk to me. If you look at my aura, you should be able to see the—"

"Mark. You *do* wear a mark." He sank heavily back onto his throne. "That means your soul is bound to another demon, and I cannot harm you."

You might have checked before you nearly killed me, you bastard.

"And?" I said warily. "What does it mean? Do I have magic?"

"Magic?" His body surged with flame. "You call this magic?"

I call it fucking scary. Demon mark or not, every inch of me rebelled against the terror projected by the flaming damnation in his eyes.

"I was an angel, once," he said. "Did you know? I commanded legions of foolish apes like you, against the armies of hell. You all died. All of you."

"Wait. You commanded celestials?" Of course… arch-demons were fallen angels, former Divinities. So it stood to reason that he'd have once been on the opposite side of the celestial war. Nikolas hadn't mentioned that tiny little detail when he'd brought me here.

"Of course I did," he crowed. "They were so devoted. Pity for them."

Ice wormed through my chest. He'd led armies of people like me to the death. I should attack him, turn him to ash like I'd done to the other demon.

"Why?" I asked. "Why fall? What's the point?"

"You fight on the wrong side, celestial. As a demon, however… we could offer you much more."

"I'm *not* a demon," I said. "I've spent years training with the celestials. A Divinity raised me from the *dead.*"

"Oh, you're one of those?" He laughed, a terrible laugh like crackling flames. "Assuming you survive long enough to see the truth of our war, you'll find that the battlefield looks no different no matter which side you stand on. I regret nothing of my choices, so don't stand there and look upon me with your righteous justice, celestial. You're one step from being damned yourself."

"Because one of you *marked* me. Why would you do that?"

"If I had to guess, you went into hell, young celestial," he said. "You went to hell, and you didn't come back the same way."

How does he know?

I stepped away from him. The ashy remains of the other demon's fire stuck to the soles of my feet, and as I glanced down for a split second, I glimpsed my reflection. My aura burned, black as night.

No. It's a trick. A demon trick.

I glanced up, at the pillar at my side. Whiteness outlined my body, but my right hand was laced with a dark shadow like a glove. As though hypnotised, I stepped towards it, raising my right hand. My reflection did the same. Her hand met mine, and where it should have met smooth marble, hot ash burned my palm.

I yelped and snatched my hand away. The pillar went transparent, revealing burning ash in the shape of a… pentagram. Wait. I knew that pentagram.

"You can't hide from me, celestial!"

Flames roared across the floor, consuming everything in their path. I raised my marked hand—not the one holding the blade, but the one with the burned palm, and pressed it to the clear glass again. Flames seared it, and the pillar vanished as I fell forwards—through nothingness.

My knees hit the alley floor, sending a shock of pain through my nerves. I staggered upright, colliding with Nikolas. "Devina!" His eyes widened. "What happened?"

"What happened is you jumped ship." I punched him in the chest with my free hand.

To my surprise, he hissed and stepped back. "What's that on your hand?"

A black arrowhead marked my right wrist, in the same spot as the celestial mark on my left, but pointing the opposite way. "Oh shit."

"Your demon mark," he said. "It's manifested. What did he do to you?"

"First his pet fire demon nearly torched me, then he gloated about murdering celestials for a bit before trying to kill me." Adrenaline pumped through my blood, my body shaking so much I had to lean against the wall to catch my balance. "I got the impression he wasn't exactly… stable."

"Neither are your shoes."

I looked down. There wasn't much left of my boots. *That*

was almost me. Hellfire and ash.

"But you didn't say how you escaped," Nikolas said. "I've been trying to get through the pentagram, but he sealed it off. You shouldn't have been able to come through it."

I held up my palm, and the mark, which burned dark as the aura on my reflection. "The pillar was made of this reflective stuff. When I touched it, I fell through it and ended up back here."

"The mark." He grabbed my wrist. Instinctively, I hit out at him. He dodged smoothly, apparently reluctant to get hit with magical blisters. I'd bet they wouldn't have worked on the arch-demon.

"Get it off," I told him. "Seriously. If the celestials see the mark—I'm dead."

"I think the celestials are the least of your problems." He examined the remains of the pentagram at our feet. "But I'm very curious as to how you got out. Not all of us can cross dimensions."

"Wait. You mean… I can move between this realm and that one? Like you can with your home dimension?"

"Apparently," he said. "But you need a material to work with. Mine is shadows. You mentioned you touched the pillar… it must have been made of demonglass. Like this." He nudged the pentagram with his foot, stirring up glittering fragments. "The portal was already set up, which must have helped."

I raised my hand to my chest, where my heart beat like it was trying to escape. "But—it's absurd. Sure, *you* can travel between dimensions, but you're the son of an arch-demon. I'm not even a warlock. And if Themedes didn't do it, who did?"

"I have no idea," he said. "Perhaps another demon you've interacted with told him."

Dienes? No way—he was a lesser demon. Not everyone

got to speak to an arch-demon. But that dimension was connected with the murders. I was certain of it.

"That's it, then," I said. "I'm out of a job, I'm marked by an arch-demon, and another one of the bastards destroyed my bloody shoes." The shoes were the least of my problems, but walking home barefoot was the peak of the shittest day in the history of shit days.

"I can help with the shoes," he said, looking me up and down. "It's lucky that's all you lost, considering the arch-demon's power."

"Sorry to deprive you of another strip tease." I folded my arms, feeling oddly vulnerable under his gaze despite my— thankfully—fully clothed state. "Also, it wasn't the arch-demon who blasted me with fire, but his whiny little pet."

"His son, I'd guess," said Nikolas. "Did he give any clues about who might have marked you?"

"Nope," I said. "He's definitely the first arch-demon I've seen or spoken to, as far as I'm aware. And if anyone's capable of killing celestials without even being in the same dimension, it's him."

"I don't doubt your reasoning, but he can't move between dimensions. He could only summon us there because he knows my name. Besides, he has no interest in destroying the celestials in *this* dimension. His power will expire by the year's end."

"Sure as hell didn't seem like it to me." I took another step, grimacing when a stone poked my bare foot.

"I offered to replace those shoes," he said. "If you come with me, my place isn't far from here."

I sighed. "Hell, why not. Knowing you, you've got a bunch of pet demons camping out in your attic."

"Not quite," he said, reaching to take my hand, apparently to help me walk out of the glass-covered alley. "Your defences are somewhat inconvenient."

"Yeah, but at least I'm not drooling in the corner while you and your warlock buddies play tag with my soul."

I trod around the pieces of broken rock to find some smooth ground to stand on.

"Why are you celestials so fixated on the soul?" he asked. "Your soul doesn't belong to the demons, whatever mark you wear. The same with the Divinities."

"There's a difference there," I said. "The arch-demon definitely said my soul is bound to the one who marked me."

"He meant in the sense that your demon magic comes from the one who marked you," he said. "Like your celestial power is on loan from the Divinities."

"Except I've never seen a Divinity." I gritted my teeth as I trod on another rock. "I've no more idea why they chose me than why the demons did."

As we reached the end of the row of houses, he lifted a loose fence panel, beckoning me after him.

"We're trespassing now?" I raised an eyebrow.

"Not at all. This is my house."

"Seriously?" I ducked under the panel, wet grass sliding under my bare feet. The small square lawn was unremarkable, and so was the brick house in front of us. It might have been any ordinary home. Nikolas strode to the back door and unlocked it. I darted across the gravel path as quickly as possible. Inside was a dark, neat kitchen, and I sank into a chair with relief. "Ow. Bloody fire demon." My jeans were shredded at the knees, but the pain didn't suggest the burns were serious.

"Which demon?" he asked.

"A guy made entirely out of fire. I stabbed him with my blade and killed him." I yanked off the remains of my boots, and began picking gravel out of my feet.

"Killed… ah. No. Azurial is a demigod, and he'll be pissed, but alive. The children of arch-demons don't die easily."

"So he's like you?"

"Not in the slightest," he said. "In terms of power level, though—yes. Azurial is Themedes's most trusted assistant. I'm surprised you survived, though I doubt he's faced a celestial before."

"Nope, because Themedes himself killed all of them," I said. "He was in charge of their army, and he intentionally led them to their deaths. You didn't want to mention that before I met him?"

"I didn't think you'd agree to meet with him if I did, and I thought he was the one who put the mark on you. Some demons mark as part of ownership, some don't, but it's rare for a human to end up with a mark and not remember how it got there."

I gritted my teeth, pulling a particularly sharp piece of stone from my foot. "You still suspect me, don't you? When we first met, you all but said you were happy to watch the celestials punish me for my supposed crimes. I'm a little lost on why you're helping me, to be honest."

"At the time, I thought you'd intentionally asked another demon to mark you," he said. "As I spoke to you, however, it became clear that you're not aligned with a rival demon. I wouldn't have taken you into my dimension if you were. But that doesn't mean you've told me everything."

"I thought you were an expert on my history."

I didn't want to talk about Rory, or my suspicion that whatever had triggered his death had been what'd marked me. It wasn't relevant, and besides, there was no proof. And I hadn't lied. I'd never seen an arch-demon besides the one I'd met today, and I'd be seeing his face in my nightmares.

Nikolas opened a cupboard. "There's burn medicine in there, for your knees. I'll get the shoes. Oh, and don't touch the books," he added, retreating from the room.

Naturally, once I'd removed the last stone from my foot

and applied a layer of burn cream to my knees, the first thing I did was look for whatever books he meant. It came as a surprise to find his house was fairly ordinary. I mean, the guy had a castle in his home dimension, and after the palace I'd just been in, I was expecting something more… netherworld. Instead, plain wooden furnishings and neat shelves contained what looked like the entire contents of a chemist specialising in all things demonic. Jars and bottles of bright powders lined the shelf, while the one above contained a row of ancient-looking books, some engraved with runes. I stood on tip-toe to get a closer look, running my finger along the shelf. I could read a little of some demon languages, but not much.

Footsteps announced Nikolas's return. "Why am I not surprised you didn't do as you're asked?"

"The last thing you told me to do was to jump into an arch-demon's palace," I said. "These are…"

"Not connected with the case, before you ask. They're from my home dimension. I don't keep valuables in the castle. The reason I asked you not to touch them is because that defensive spell of yours will mess with the bindings."

"Fair enough. They look pretty valuable."

"Yes, but your guild has copies of every one of them."

I hadn't known that, but I didn't want another argument about the celestials. Considering how the dimensions where the celestials lost the war had turned out, I knew how things would end up if they were destroyed. I doubted he'd like it much, either.

He held up a pair of plain running shoes. "These are Rachel's. They might be a little loose, but they'll do."

"Suppose they will." I took them from him. "You and the arch-demon dude have a history, don't you?"

"In a manner of speaking. He and my father fell at roughly the same time."

"By fell, I assume you don't mean literally." I sat down at the table again to put on the new shoes. "So you don't think it's a coincidence that he invited us into his dimension right after you noticed my demon mark—and right after someone with fire magic killed a bunch of celestials?"

Nikolas seated himself opposite me. "A new demon's mark and several murders committed by another unknown demon certainly stirred my suspicions at first," he said. "But there's no proof. And no demon I've met from that dimension has the ability the killer apparently does."

"Seemed fiery enough to me." I shuddered. "As for the mark, I don't know when it happened. It might have been years ago."

"Perhaps," he said thoughtfully. "But you said all the people who've been targeted are novices, correct?"

"Yeah, they were. I need to look at the latest victim to get a full picture. But it fits. Our arch-demon put a mark on a novice, and for whatever reason, it backfired."

"That'd work if an arch-demon was able to access this dimension, but they aren't," said Nikolas. "As I said, Themedes can't call on just anyone, and you saw how much work I had to put into the pentagram to allow us to travel there."

"Damn." There went that idea. Didn't mean he was innocent, but someone else must be calling the shots.

"So theoretically, could someone else have made a link with that dimension?"

"I'd know if they had. Or Javos would know. Very little escapes his attention. And no demonglass has left my possession since before the first murder. You also need something *from* that dimension, and an energy source to fuel the portal while it's active."

"Celestial light works," I admitted. "That's what I do, when I summon demons."

"Search the guild tonight," he said. "If you see any suspicious signs, we'll pursue them."

Irritation prickled at me. "Do you always just assume your theories are correct as a given?"

"I'm rarely wrong."

I snorted. "I know you don't like the celestials. But considering how fast the killer moves, pursuing false leads might lead to more victims. This arch-demon lead was a dead end. And I'm not sure about our demon marked theory, either. None of the victims had demonic tattoos—that I saw, anyway. Or demonic auras."

But if the novices were dying because of a demon's mark, why hadn't I? I actively summoned demons and I'd done worse. Unless my punishment had been to watch my best friend die in front of me. But realistically, dozens of demons held a grudge against me. Past experience and paranoia conspired to drive me to the wrong conclusions. The arch-demon had provided no clues at all about the murders. He hadn't even known my name.

Nikolas's stare was a little too penetrating. "What are you thinking?" he asked.

I shrugged. "I'm a warrior of heaven, not a demon's slave. And I'm not exactly keen on being a pawn, to be honest, even if we do catch the killer."

"You're not a demon's slave. Not if you don't want to be. The mark offers you a choice. One I'd wager your Divinity did not."

I gave him a glare. "If not for the Divinities, I'd be dead. No demon mark can reverse that. And whoever marked me didn't give me the choice, either."

He didn't respond for a moment. "Perhaps not, but it can't happen for no reason. We'll need to look into the extent of your ability."

"You mean, you and Javos." I frowned. "Wait. You said I'm

not marked by anyone in the dimension we just went in. Then how could I travel home? You can only travel between your home dimension and this one."

"That's the usual rule." He eyed me thoughtfully. "This is an irregular case in every way."

"No kidding," I said. "How'd you discover yours, then?"

"I've answered a lot of your questions already," he said. "You do realise we don't hand out our secrets to every celestial? I'm trusting you not to share them with the guild."

"You seriously think I'd do that?" Hurt crept into my voice. "You've read my records. You know how many times they overreacted and punished me for the slightest thing."

"Yes, I do." His mouth twitched. "The superglue prank the year you joined the guild was a particularly inspired one. How long did it take to glue four hundred chairs together?"

"Less time than you'd think," I said, unable to suppress a grin at the memory. The six months of detention that followed had been entirely worth it. "But I'm not a snitch, and I didn't even tell them your name."

"I'm beginning to see why the inspector's so determined to keep you out of the way," he said. "All right. I'll answer your question if you answer one of mine."

"Deal. You know almost everything about me anyway." Except one thing. My shoulders automatically tensed.

"How did you die?"

Some of the tension left my body. "I died in a car accident. My parents were killed, too. It was over fast. One second I was there, the next I couldn't see anything but this light. Then I woke up in the morgue. Scared the hell out of the doctors. I mean, my body had completely regenerated. Horrific internal injuries, totally gone. It was a literal miracle. Only this was different." I waved my left hand. "The mark. Of course, once they saw it, the doctors knew what'd happened. They sent me to the academy for the celestials, and the rest is history."

"It is indeed." He studied me, his brows close together. "To answer your question, I discovered my ability the first time I went into the shadow realm."

I waited, but he didn't elaborate. "You evaded on purpose. That's no answer."

"To tell you the full story would involve betraying secrets that aren't mine," he said.

"Then I have another question. What exactly does a Divinity have to do to turn into an arch-demon?"

He raised an eyebrow. "Why the sudden interest?"

"Just curious. Fallen means they did something awful, but the Divinities do some pretty terrible things on the battlefield. So what makes them turn?"

"Usually it means they pissed off someone important. Most are ancient—they all are. After all, this war has been raging longer than you or I have been alive." He paused. "You have a new idea, don't you?"

"Not really." More a hunch, and my instincts hadn't been great lately. "I'm wondering who hands out divine judgement."

"I thought that was your job."

Now I'm not so sure. But if the Divinities *were* watching this realm, I'd bet they wouldn't be pleased at the notion of a demon marking their celestials. None of my theories explained why I'd been singled out, nor the novices. They weren't powerful bargaining chips. But souls were currency, as far as both heaven and hell were concerned. And if these deaths pointed to movement in the netherworld, who knew what the demons were planning?

Rachel's shoes pinched my toes as I stood. "I'm going home."

"Very well. Are you certain you wish to break into the guild tonight?"

Nope. "Not if it involves any arch-demons you haven't told me about."

"There are no arch-demons there," he said. "This time, at least, I can promise that I won't leave you behind, if that's what concerns you."

"Honestly," I said, "at this point I think I'd take a second round with the arch-demon over what Inspector Deacon will do to me when he sees the mark."

And I was starting to suspect that a demon owning my soul was nothing compared to owing my freedom to a warlock. He might have stopped accusing me of being a demon's willing mark, but it was too easy to forget it was in his interests to gain my trust, to make me believe I had a better chance of keeping my freedom if I sided with him—and the demons. He knew too much about my disdain for the celestials to be a reliable neutral force when it came to the decision I had to inevitably make.

I had two choices: submit and let him sign me up with the warlocks, or keep him around for the duration of the investigation, using his ability whenever convenient. In other words, be as much of a manipulator as the average warlock.

Nikolas reached a hand across the table, stopping just short of touching my right hand. "I'd suggest covering it up."

His fingertips ghosted over the mark, raising goosebumps on my arms. No blisters appeared on his hands so he hadn't actually touched me, but my heart rate picked up anyway. "No, I planned to waltz into the guild waving my hand in the air and dance on the tables, obviously." I didn't move my hand. Not because I particularly wanted to see his evenly tanned skin break out in purple blisters, but because I swore I felt the demon mark tingle with the undercurrent of the lightning he carried in his hands. A hint of power I might have myself. If I let the warlocks train me. If I gave up my celestial mark and stepped off the ledge into the unknown, without any idea what waited below.

Nikolas removed his hand without touching me, but the spark remained in the air, along with the question. His gaze was too knowing. He'd figured out the drift of my thoughts without me needing to speak a word. My heartbeat pulsed in my ears. A warning, or an invitation to jump.

"If it's any consolation," he said, his voice dropping to a low purr, "the netherworld isn't all bad."

I made the mistake of breathing in, and the earthy scent of brimstone washed over my senses. Licking my dry lips, I snatched my hand away from the table. "That's for me to decide." Somehow, my voice came out steadily, though as far as my racing pulse was concerned, I'd already jumped off the ledge and was in full-on freefall. Being so close to him was too much. I didn't even know if he was using his lure or not.

You're in deep, Devi. Get out, now.

"Then I leave the choice to you." His steady gaze didn't waver.

I pushed away from the table, looking away. "I'm going home," I said. "If we're breaking into the guild tonight, I need to be ready."

"Of course. The front door's that way."

He remained behind me at every step. I buried my shaking hands in my pocket, the demon mark still tingling. *Oh, no. I'm not ready to part with my celestial sword just yet.*

Nikolas kept too many secrets. Being a warlock, that wasn't a surprise, but the fact that he knew my entire history put us on an uneven playing field. I wouldn't forget that. And I needed to get away from him before he realised the extent of the power he held over me.

And just how close I was to stepping off that ledge.

"Hey! Devil!" Fiona leaned out of her window, her eyes widening as she took in my appearance. I'd stare too if I found her covered in dusted brimstone with the wrong-sized shoes and singed patterns on her jeans. "What happened to you? I've been trying to reach you for hours."

Guess my phone hadn't worked in the demon dimension. "Sorry, I turned my phone off while I was working. The guild's super busy."

"I hoped you were busy, not dead." She rested her elbows on the window ledge. "Seriously. You're worrying me. Don't switch your phone off when there's a serial killer on the loose, even if you *are* more badass than every demon in the city."

"Sorry," I said. I couldn't say I wouldn't do it again, not when I'd be back in the shadow realm tonight.

"So does the guild have any new theories? I take it they don't, if they sent you home."

"I'm pretty much suspended from the investigation," I admitted. "The inspector's being a dick. He's the one making all these terrifying statements, by the way, so if there's any fearmongering bullshit in the newspapers, it's on him."

"Haven't read the papers, but there's a ton of theories on the internet. Also, the DivinityWatch site crashed. People flooded it with videos of that girl's death."

"Vultures," I muttered. "I mean, it's not like the humans can actually help us solve this, but they can try not to stir up hysteria."

"It's sort of hard to keep it quiet when it happens in a public place like last night," said Fiona. "If you ask me, you've got a killer who loves attention. Surprised they haven't been caught on camera yet."

"Maybe because the killer isn't actually here."

Or is amongst the celestials. Not one of them, but something else. A force moving through their ranks, targeting them. Marking them. I wouldn't tell her about the demon mark I wore on my right wrist, like a brand. She deserved to be kept out of my crackpot life, especially with everything crashing about my ears.

Fiona blinked at me. "Not here? How does that work? Can a demon snap its fingers and kill someone on the other side of the world?"

"Probably not," I said. "I mean, not to my knowledge. The celestials are the experts on that sort of thing."

She eyed me, gaze lingering on my singed clothes. "You're talking about them like you aren't one of them. Please don't say you're trying to tackle this demon alone."

"It's not the first time I've done it."

"Devi." She crossed her arms. "I can't pretend I know what it's like to be chosen for a holy mission, but working alone against a serial killer is a good way to end up dead. If everyone in the city's saying these murders aren't normal, you know shit's got real. I don't want you to die."

"Nor me, believe me. It'll be fine. I just have one more

thing I need to do tonight." If the guild caught me, I'd be a fugitive. If they didn't but I *did* discover evidence of collusion with demons, it was likely to have the same outcome. And if I got caught, it'd cement my reputation as the guilty party even before they saw my demon mark. But whether the same demon had marked me or not, I owed it to the victims to at least try. "Then we'll have a girls' night in, with terrible movies. Okay?"

"Deal," she said.

When I closed my flat door behind me, I checked my phone and found I also had a missed call from Clover. Now the media's glare covered the guild, I doubted another murder had happened, but a cold feeling grew inside me as her phone rang with nobody answering. I breathed out when she finally picked up. "Hey. Clover, are you okay?"

"You're alive." She sounded like she spoke from somewhere crowded. "Good. I can't talk for long. The inspector will find out."

"Are you at the guild?"

"The inspector has requested that everyone, retired celestials included, is to step up and aid the guild in their fight against evil. Unfortunately for them, I was injured in my first battle with the netherworlders, so I'm on bed rest."

"Er—what? You retired years ago. *What* attacked you?"

"The inspector's word is law." She gave a short laugh. "I'm fine. I tripped chasing a thieving demon. Nothing related to the murders."

"Nobody else has been attacked?" I asked. "It's been nearly a full day since the last one."

"No. It might be a sign that the demon has exhausted its magic—or that it's planning something bigger. Either way, the guild will be ready."

"Ready to kill its retired members," I muttered. "He really

has lost his mind. I don't suppose they're any closer to finding the killer?"

"No," she said. "As I suspected, however, there's been a certain vocal minority insisting that the warlocks must be involved, as they're the closest to true demons in this realm."

I groaned. "It's not them."

"And you'd know?"

"I would." I didn't elaborate. I trusted her, but if the guild was resorting to extreme methods, I wouldn't strike interrogating their own allies off the list. I'd prefer to keep myself out of the line of fire as long as possible.

"Careful," she said softly. "The inspector doesn't accept excuses, even from our own."

"You knew they'd kick me off the case," I said to her. "Didn't you? What was the point in giving me back my magic only to try to take it off me five minutes later?"

"That's why I argued against them rehiring you, Devi. I knew they'd try to bind you to the guild, and they have no room for flexibility. Now the inspector's powers have strengthened, he can wield authority over every celestial who enters the city."

"What's the point?" I asked. "We're looking for a murderer. There's no point in sending the city into a mass panic."

"It's not one murderer that concerns them, Devi. The inspector thinks that these deaths indicate hell making a move against this realm."

That's what I'm afraid of. "Hell has been moving against us forever," I said. "No excuse to turn into total despots."

"Inspector Deacon has been waiting for this opportunity, Devi, ever since the demons attacked the old guild headquarters four years ago," she said. "Every celestial has been arranged into teams, and the rules are being strictly enforced. Anyone who disobeys is put on probation. The novices are now terrified that they'll become targets for demons if they breathe wrong, so if the goal of the killer was to scare everyone into inaction, it's working."

I swore under my breath. "Maybe they have a point."

As much as she might be on my side, that'd change if I hinted at my suspicions—or Nikolas's, to be more accurate. Nobody would believe any celestial in their right mind would work with a demon, even under coercion or brainwashing. In fact, it'd be a very demon-like strategy to *make* us suspect one another, and it'd further their goal of turning us against each other. The inspector, though—as she'd reminded me, he'd been on the warpath against demons since his former partner had died in the attack on the old guild headquarters. And it'd been an ex-celestial working against us who'd caused the whole debacle. But was that enough of a motive for him to turn against us?

"What does that mean?" she asked. "What's your theory?"

"Er… hypothetically, how seriously do the inspector and his merry band of fanatics think the Divinities take the doctrine? I mean, the rulebook? Could one of them burn someone's eyes out as punishment for some sin?"

"The Divinities? Nobody knows how they work. Hypothetically, they might be responsible for anything, but murdering their own celestials? *That's* your theory?"

"Don't sound so disappointed in me," I said. "You just said the inspector and his minions are going down the victim blaming road. Also, setting someone on fire like that looks more of an angelic than a demonic punishment. I've *seen* demon fire."

"You think someone's passing down divine judgement on the recruits?" Scepticism tinged her voice.

"They'll burn the sin out of you," I said. "That's what the first victim said. And, *all will fall* was written on the walls. Someone is using the doctrine against the celestials. What if that's what it's all meant to be—an imitation of celestial fire? Arch-demons are fallen angels, after all."

"There's more proof of a demonic presence than a divine one, Devi," she said. "If it were an arch-demon, we'd be looking at war, not murder."

"Sounds like the inspector wants a war already."

"Yes, it does." She paused. "I don't need to remind you not to intervene at the guild, do I? I can't stop you while I'm on bed rest, Devi. Don't do anything rash."

"I'll try not to." She didn't need to know what Nikolas and I planned to do tonight. If I'd already been kicked off the case, I might as well make my last exit from the guild a memorable one.

I heated a microwavable meal and then turned the kitchen into a miniature lab to brew up the aura vision potion again. I wouldn't drink it until just before we left. Seeing my newly darkened aura once was bad enough. *Demonglass. I can travel through demonglass.* Too bad I didn't have any to hand to practise my new ability on. As far as I knew, even the guild didn't. It was an ingredient in summonings, so warlocks would have a small supply. Not that I should even be thinking about experimenting with a new power I hadn't wanted in the first place. It wouldn't help me here. No—unfortunately, to get into the guild, not to mention to get out again, I had to rely on Nikolas's shadow power.

My demon mark didn't fade when I scrubbed at it in the shower. It was a reflection of my angel mark, even the same arrowhead symbol, but pointing towards me rather than away. *How is this possible?* The Divinities chose their soldiers, but I'd never heard of the arch-demons marking humans to act as their soldiers in a similar manner. There were more than enough demons to fight on their side. Was I part of their new plan to make a move against the celestials? A weapon? As long as I didn't know who had put the mark on me, everything was cast in doubt.

The war was changing. A war I'd never been involved in, not directly. If this world was their target, the whole of mankind might be collateral damage.

As I was towelling my hair dry, there was a knock on my door. I frowned. Nikolas couldn't be here. He didn't even know where I lived.

I opened the door to find a grinning Rachel on my flat doorstep.

"Hey!" she said. "I heard you need some new shoes."

"How'd you know my address?" I asked. "Nikolas?"

"He'll be here soon," she said. "We figured it'd be easier than meeting at the guild. There are teams of celestials in most public places tonight."

"Hope that means there won't be as many of them around the guild."

"I have these." She held up a pair of leather boots. "They're magical."

"Really?" I took the boots from her, turning them over in my hands. Looked like normal black leather to me. "What, can I fly? Or turn invisible?"

"No," she said. "But you can climb walls. Like Spider-Man."

"You watch Marvel movies?"

"Obviously. I don't live under a rock." She bounded past me into the living room, examining my souvenir collection. It was probably kind of sad that I kept relics from my time as a globe-trotting Grade Three celestial soldier all over my flat, but they made for good stories. Rachel picked up each wooden animal and shook each plastic snow-globe, a grin on her face.

I perched on the sofa to change into the new shoes, which fitted surprisingly well considering I'd never given her my shoe size. My feet barely made a sound as I walked across the hardwood floor. Comfortable, practical—and damned useful, if I was going to be breaking and entering later tonight.

Rachel put down a carved wooden elephant I'd bought in Kenya. "Nice place," she commented. "Cosy. Thought you'd have weapons everywhere."

"The guild stores all weapons on its premises," I said. "I don't need to carry my sword on me, anyway." Though if this demonic mark kept developing, would I even be able to access my celestial weapon anymore?

"So where does the sword go when you don't use it?" asked Rachel.

"It's stored in a sort of pocket dimension I can access anywhere. Using this." I tapped the mark on my left wrist. "We're allowed to carry weapons, technically, but it gives us the element of surprise."

"Neat," she said. "Invisible swords are cool. But I'm jealous of your demonglass hopping power."

"Nikolas told you?"

"I'll keep quiet," she said. "Wouldn't want any of the others finding out. That dimension's a nasty place."

"No shit." And to think I'd once thought kleptomaniac lizard demons were the worst it had to offer. I doubted Dienes would be pleased if I told him—not that I planned to. He was a self-confessed blabbermouth, and besides, I wasn't quite sure I believed it myself. For all the wild theories I'd thrown at Clover, I didn't believe it was a coincidence that I'd developed the ability to cross dimensions right as someone with a similar ability was murdering people.

Another knock heralded Nikolas's arrival.

"Who told you my address?" I asked, upon opening the door to allow him inside the flat.

"Javos."

"Great. Even the celestials don't know where I live."

"I take it you haven't spoken to them." He joined Rachel in the living room. I was glad I'd cleaned it fairly recently.

"I spoke to a friend of mine who retired years ago," I said. "They suddenly rehired her, and she managed to get injured chasing a demon. Not related to the case, but they've officially lost their minds. Dragging every retired soldier back means more people will get hurt needlessly."

"As I suspected, they're panicking," said Nikolas, eying a painting on the wall of the Northern Lights.

"Hopefully enough not to notice us sneaking in and out of their guild," said Rachel. "I'm excited. I've never been there before."

"You can't come in," I said. "You know both of you would set the anti-demon alarms off, right?"

"Relax," said Rachel. "I'm just coming to watch your backs in the shadow realm."

Let's hope Nikolas's brother stays far away. "All right, but be careful."

"I'm the one who should be telling *you* that. Niko told me about the arch-demon." She bounded off the sofa. "I can't believe you stabbed Azurial, too. Are you trying to set a record for the number of warlocks you can piss off in a short space of time?"

"Only the ones who try to kill me," I said. "Is there anything Nikolas *didn't* tell you?"

"I only told Rachel and Javos," Nikolas said. "Specifically, about the arch-demon and your mark. But others will recognise it now it's manifested."

"Honestly, I don't have room in my head to worry about that tonight," I said. "Just how does this castle of yours overlap with the guild?"

"More or less exactly, but the inhabitants of the castle are mostly warlocks or demon kin. So we'll have to avoid those areas if you don't want to invite unwelcome questions." He placed a tablet on the table, and switched it on. A map of the guild filled the screen. He tapped the screen and a second image replaced the first—an unfamiliar outline of a large building. The castle. "I can send you the images, but I think you'd be best to memorise what you can before going in there."

"I only need to know part of it." I tapped the screen. The guild was familiar enough that I knew every entrance and shortcut, but the castle was an unknown. "The bodies will likely be in the morgue by now. That's underground."

"You'll have to cross over upstairs," he said. "The castle's catacombs aren't the sort of place you want to go into at night."

"Got it." I nodded. "I cross over, walk downstairs into the morgue, look around, come back up..." I flicked the screen onto the second image, trying to memorise the sections I needed. If I crossed at the upper left corridor, I'd materialise in the middle of a wall. I didn't want to find out the hard way what would happen to my body in the process.

"I'll wait in the castle," he said. "Then I'll come over when we meet at our designated spot. I can create a small opening to keep an eye on you at any time without being seen."

"Nice knowing you're spying on me," I said, my nerves spiking. "Right. First stop, the morgue. After that, I need to get inside a locked room in the west wing." I traced the path on the screen, on the castle image. "There's also the Inspector's office, but I sneaked into there once already when I borrowed his props."

"A locked room?" asked Rachel.

"The west wing," I said. "The section nobody below Grade Four is allowed into. It's where they keep anything they don't want the rest of us to see. Info on the arch-demons, and the Divinities themselves."

"Sounds exciting," said Rachel. "So you think someone at the guild's involved in the murders?"

"I don't. He does." I jerked my head at Nikolas.

"The west wing overlaps with one of the castle towers," he said. "We should be okay in there, but I'll be with you for that part anyway."

"Right." I tapped the screen a few more times, to memorise the details. "The guild should be closing up soon."

I checked the time on my phone, and looked up to see Rachel pretending not to look at my wrist. I tugged my sleeve down.

"Did it hurt?" she asked. "I think you're the first marked human I've met."

"Probably the first celestial." As little as I wanted to discuss the subject, it might make the difference between life and death in the demon realm.

"First of a kind," she said. "Weird. But the cool sort of weird. Maybe you'll be the first angel-demon hybrid."

"Bloody hope not," I said.

"That's not possible," said Nikolas. "Celestials aren't actually angels. They're chosen and imbued with celestial magic, and the selection seems to be entirely random. You were ordinary before, correct?"

"Yep. Boring, even. Now look at me talking to warlocks in my own house. I suppose you've always been super special and extraordinary."

"There's no such thing," he said. "Every one of us is unique. I'll say that much for the demon dimensions—they don't encourage conformity."

"Probably because you can't keep more than one of them in the same room without them trying to kill one another," I said. "Also, the guild will be closed for the night by now. I think we should go."

I drank down the aura vision potion, put the anti-warlock trap around my neck, and put on two wristbands to cover the marks. I mostly wore the trap in case Nikolas's brother showed up, but he'd still be recovering from the last time. I was kind of counting on it, really. We had enough enemies, and this trip was risky enough without considering the other inhabitants of the shadow realm.

"Don't worry," Rachel said. "We'll be watching for enemies on the other side. You just concentrate on the break-in."

"We're going to head to the street outside the guild," Nikolas said. "If my geography is accurate, it overlaps with the inside of the castle grounds, so we'll be inside the gates without being detected. I'd rather nobody else in the shadow realm knows about your presence there."

"If they're all like your brother, the feeling's mutual," I said. "So we're walking it?"

"I'm driving." Nikolas led the way to an unremarkable black car parked up against the pavement. A pair of devil horns sat in the window. "Those are Rachel's," he added, when he saw me looking. "We tend to avoid drawing unwanted attention."

"Because you and Javos are boring rule-followers." Rachel bounded into the front seat, leaving me to sit in the back, behind Nikolas. We drove through the darkening streets in near-silence, parking a short distance from the celestial guild. My boots trod lightly on the pavement, like they were almost weightless. I wished I'd had time for a trial run before pelting headlong into danger.

Finally, the familiar shape of the guild appeared. There were guards outside. *That's new.*

Nikolas halted. The shadows closed in around us, and when they receded, it was to reveal a forbidding stone castle blotting out the night sky. Its obsidian slabs were disturbingly similar to the arch-demon's palace, but while his had been built on a rise over a city, this castle stood alone surrounded by wasteland. A tall black wall behind us told me we'd landed inside the castle's first layer of defence. Beyond that, stars studded a night sky of deep blue, like an ocean reflecting constellations bigger and brighter than any I'd seen on Earth. Beautiful, really. Pity I couldn't stop and admire the view.

Nikolas led the way to a small wooden door in the stone exterior. "Whereabouts did you need to go?" he asked in a low voice. "The nearest entrance to the morgue aboveground will be in the left-hand corridor, correct?"

I thought back to the map. "Yeah. Just keep walking this way. If I can't actually cross over downstairs, then the same corridor will do."

I never thought I'd be glad a warlock knew his way around the celestial guild, but his knowledge came in handy now. The dark stone corridor looked nothing like the modern day building that overlapped it, but if I screwed up my eyes, I could envision the corridors of the guild. I counted steps, while Nikolas consulted his map. Though we moved quietly, the eerie atmosphere in the castle brought shivers out on my arms. I wouldn't like to be alone here.

Once he'd found the right point, Nikolas summoned the shadows. The next second, I stood in the dark corridor of the guild. I'd been accurate with my planning, and the stairs to the morgue lay not ten metres away. Perfect.

"I'll be back in five minutes," he whispered in my ear, then the shadows took him away again.

I listened out. No sound came from inside the morgue. Hoping nobody had anticipated that I'd do something this reckless, I crept downstairs, tugging on a pair of gloves. Silence followed, and the smell of brimstone clung to my nostrils. I didn't dare switch on the light, but instead used my celestial mark as a torch, shining it around until I tracked down the third body. Lightly covered with cloth, it moved at my gloved touch.

Like the others, her eyes were burned out, mouth stretched in an expression of utter torment. My palm hovered above her bare arm. Warmth poured from her skin, not searing heat like before. It should be icy cold. She was pretty clearly dead, but apparently demon fire took a while to die down. Had they tried cutting open one of the other victims yet? It seemed the next logical step, but the other bodies didn't appear to be here. And nor did any notes or indication that anyone had come to a conclusion about the deaths.

Flipping her hand over, I looked for a mark like mine, but found nothing. Of course, mine hadn't been activated until I'd touched that pillar. Maybe there wasn't a connection, not one I could prove now they were dead. Squinting in the dark, I focused on my aura vision. Her bright celestial aura was marked with scattered fragments of shadow. Demon magic had pervaded her body. But what sort?

I screwed up my eyes. The swirling pattern in her aura wasn't random. It'd started somewhere. My gaze followed the path of the shadow, which covered her right wrist. My heart lurched. I bent to examine it, and a knocking sound made me jump violently. Tugging down my sleeve to turn off the light, I backed into the shadows. Footsteps passed by above, but nobody came downstairs. I counted seconds, then backed up the stairs, pausing at every step. The guild's corridors were downright sinister at this time of night, and I silently thanked whoever had installed crappy fluorescent lighting rather than those automatic lights a lot of modern buildings had, the type that reacted to movement.

Nearby was a window looking out over the quadrangle. As I watched, a familiar figure passed by. The inspector. Out of everyone here, he was the one I trusted here the least, yet for all his unpleasantness, I didn't see him murdering novices. Or offering them to a demon. He lived for this job. But for some reason, here he was prowling around alone while everyone else was running dangers.

"Need a hand?" Nikolas's voice whispered. "We can tail him."

"How'd you know where I was?" I turned around, not seeing him at first. Then I spotted the shadows move. He'd opened a slither of light above me to look down on the corridor. "Yeah, why not."

He pulled me back into shadow. Total darkness covered us, but we only moved a few steps before the shadows opened a little—revealing the inspector hunched over a computer. I stared at the numbers on the screen.

Well, well. Looked like someone had a little gambling problem. I wonder what the Divinities would say about *that*.

I hovered behind him. Apparently he wasn't going to indicate any proof of working with the demons, so I'd need to look elsewhere. I mean, if stealing our money wasn't bad enough by itself. Prick. But that didn't make him in league with netherworlders.

Shadows flowed over my vision, leaving nothing behind but us.

"Nothing," I whispered. "Except Mr Inspector has a gambling addiction, but the Divinities alone can have him for that."

I stopped as I realised Nikolas had drawn to a halt, staring at the ceiling. "There's someone moving above us," he muttered. "Nobody should be in this part of—"

The darkness shifted above our heads.

"Back so soon, brother?" whispered a voice, and the shadows clamped over Nikolas, swallowing him up.

16

"Nikolas!" I called his name, but the corridor was too dark to see even the shadows. I pulled down my armband, shining celestial light into the rounded eyes of a demon with three rows of teeth.

"Shit," I said.

Teeth snapped at my arm. I jerked back, aiming the beam of light, which fractured off the walls, showing more of them gathering around the stone-walled corridor. *The bastard. He was waiting for us.*

I grabbed my sword, cutting into the creature's chest. It fell, bleeding, not disintegrating as it would back home. This was its home realm, and I was far outnumbered. Nikolas was my only way out. And where was Rachel? *This was a really bad idea.*

I cut down another enemy, my blade the only light in the gloom masking the dark flagstones. The castle probably didn't have electric lighting, but the demons must be able to see in the dark. I couldn't see any further ahead than my blade's glowing edge. What I hadn't anticipated was that without vanishing, the bodies piled up fast. I climbed over them, stabbing everything that came near me, slowly advancing forward.

Light streamed in from somewhere ahead, and I turned a corner. Moonlight flooded the corridor from a wide open window, reflecting from pillars supporting a high ceiling. The clear glass of the pillars reflected the bodies of dead demons, and my own aura—light and shadow. *Demonglass.*

There was a startled scream from the open window ahead, at least one floor above the ground. *Rachel.* I ran towards the window, and stopped, staring out into the night. Rachel struggled in the clawed grip of a demon shaped like a gigantic scaly bat. A vulker demon.

"Put her down," I warned, holding out the sword. I was too high off the ground to make a jump for it, even taking my celestial powers into consideration. I advanced towards the window anyway, calculating whether it was worth the risk to throw the sword at the demon without making it drop her.

A pair of claws grabbed my jacket from behind. Another demon. With a pterodactyl-like screech, it beat its leathery wings, lifting me into the air. I twisted, cursing, trying to stab it, but the sword slid out of my grasp, my stomach plummeting as we dropped out into the night sky.

Cold night air whipped my exposed skin, and the demon's wingbeats carried me into the air. I stopped struggling as the dark castle walls wheeled around below us until we were high enough to see the constellations etched in the sky.

"Put us down!" I shouted. "Or so help me—" I shrieked as we dropped some twenty feet. "Stop it!"

The two beasts flew on, wings beating, ignoring my attempts to break free. We flew over a long stone walkway to a spire-like tower, separated from the rest of the main castle. Rather than the obsidian colour of the castle's stones, it was clear but not transparent, reflecting the coin-like moon and constellations from every angle. A widely open window beckoned, and the two bat demons flew through, tossing us roughly onto the stone flagstones. I landed in a crouch and ran to the window, but stopped immediately. The drop to the walkway below was impossible to jump and survive. And there was no other way out, nor any way back to the castle other than flying. However pretty the stars might be, I didn't want to die here on an alien planet.

"Damn," I said, my teeth chattering. "You okay, Rachel?"

"You should be more concerned for yourself."

Zadok, Niko's brother, appeared from the shadows behind us. His skin still looked like he'd taken a bath in purple paint. My defensive attack had done a stellar job. Sitting down, walking and otherwise moving would be painful for at least a day. But it apparently hadn't stopped him from setting up an ambush.

I couldn't suppress a grin. "How's your new look working out for you?"

"You're going to suffer, celestial," he growled. "You never should have come back."

"Look, don't take this personally, but I don't give a flying fuck about your little grievances now. I'm on a mission, and if you don't mind, Rachel, your brother and I would like to leave for our own dimension. You can save your eternal grudge until we're done saving the world."

"You need to learn some respect," he said quietly. "Nobody mocks the son of an arch-demon and lives."

"I couldn't care less if you were the son of Divinity. Where's Nikolas?"

He smiled. He had the same even white teeth as his brother did, but far more malice and cruelty in his expression. "I left him in the shadow place. If he can find his way out before one of you dies, you might get lucky. But I wouldn't count on it."

"Have you been murdering celestials in our realm?" I asked.

"What?" He blinked, a modicum of surprise entering his expression. "Aside from you?"

"That's a no, then." I sighed. "I'm on a murder investigation. I don't have time to get kidnapped by a pretentious warlock with an ego problem. If you don't mind—"

"I *do* mind," he growled. "You humiliated me."

"Technically, it was your brother who shot you in the face with lightning," I said. "If you can survive that, you'll get over the rash."

"It's more than a rash," he said through gritted teeth. "And you won't get any more information about me, celestial."

So much for getting him to admit his weakness. But I didn't need to permanently kill him. Just incapacitate him long enough to get us out.

Shadows blurred around Rachel, throwing her into the air. She screamed, and a shadowy figure caught her, tossing her to a second shadow-man in the corner. Zadok had created more shadow clones, apparently. I lunged forwards, but the dark figure threw her towards the window, another one catching her at the last second. The message was clear—if I attacked, they'd toss her out into the night.

The shadowy figure whirled around and threw Rachel at me. Her feet caught me in the face, and warm blood filled my mouth where I'd bit my tongue. Before I could pull her out of harm's way, the shadows snatched her into the air again.

"Put me down, you bastard!" she yelled.

I spun around, but Zadok had disappeared into the shadows himself. He must still be in the room somewhere. *Damn. If I can find him, I can stop him.*

"Show yourself!" I yelled.

Laughter spiralled around me, echoing. *Where the hell is he?* He must be here, but the entire room was covered in shadow, save for the window open onto the night sky. To track him, I needed a clue. Even my celestial light—*wait.*

I pulled off my wristband, letting the light grow brighter until my whole arm was ablaze. His own shadows were immune to celestial light, but regular shadows would disappear when I turned the light up to max.

Light bloomed, filling the room—everywhere but the far corner. *Gotcha.*

I jumped. Celestial light fuelled me, and I flew in a perfect arc, slamming into the solid shadow. He appeared, snarling in anger, arms over his blistered face as a shield.

"The shadows take you," he growled. "Bitch."

"Devil!" Rachel yelled.

The shadows pulled back, revealing her dangling out the window over the walkway. I took one step—and they let go.

I didn't stop to think. Fuelled by celestial power, I leaped after her. Cold air rushed past, and my hand snagged her jacket—the demon-marked hand. The celestial-marked one grabbed the windowsill. I hung there, gasping. Pain wrenched my shoulder where I held her.

"The shoes..." she whispered. "You should have let me go. The shoes—it won't hurt when you land. Jump—"

Claws dug into my back, lifting me into the air. Another vulker demon. Twisting, gripping Rachel's jacket hard, I wriggled free, hoping those magical shoes worked as well as she claimed.

We dropped through the air, landing on the walkway with a thud. The impact should have broken my legs, but Rachel's miracle boots must have absorbed the landing. Across the walkway was the rest of the castle... but the path was barred.

Three scorpion-like venos demons stood on the walkway, side by side. Scorpion tails waved behind them, equipped with deadly stingers. Insect-like hands sprouted along their bodies, and they had at least four too many legs. Apparently Zadok had high-end guards for his warlock hideout. Crap.

I conjured celestial light to my hand, bright as I could make it. While the creatures were momentarily blinded, I whipped out my blade. The sword sliced off a scorpion's stinger, but one of its flailing legs knocked me off my feet. Scrambling to stop myself from sliding off the walkway's edge, I collided with a wall of shadow. *Zadok.* Before I could strike, shadows wrapped around my arms, tying them behind my back.

"You will die slowly for humiliating me, celestial," his voice purred in my ear.

The shadows pushed me over the walkway's edge, my legs flailing in the air. Below, water surged. A moat of thick dark water. The shadows slipped, and I kicked at the air, trying desperately to connect with the bridge's side. The boots stuck, and I pulled myself free of the shadows, leaping back onto the walkway. I landed in front of the tower, which gleamed with reflected light.

The shadows reformed in front of me, and Zadok's hand reached out, throwing me into the air. I hit the tower's side. My elbows struck solid glass—demonglass—but a weightless sensation crashed over me almost immediately. *How? I'm not falling—*

Too startled to yell, I kept falling until my knees hit the floor. Darkness surrounded me once again, and stuffy air filled my lungs. In the space of a second, I'd gone from a bitterly cold night to a warm... cupboard?

Wait. The warlock's tower... it was made of demonglass, and Zadok had thrown me into it. Had my ability kicked in again? Where *was* I?

My head spun with vertigo, and my elbow smacked against something hard. Wood—a door. A small space, judging by the closeness of the wall behind me. Definitely a cupboard or similar, barely large enough to contain a person. I pushed the door. Locked.

I might have escaped Zadok, but I didn't even know which realm I'd ended up on. I'd thought I could only travel between the arch-demon's realm and Earth. Instead, I'd managed to get myself locked in a cupboard on an unknown planet.

Taking in deep breaths, I braced myself, then shoved with my elbow. My hand lit up with celestial light, showing the cramped interior of a small wooden space, backed with demonglass.

Switching the light to max, I aimed it at the lock, willing it to break. *Break, damn you.*

Resistance sizzled against my palm. Magic... of a very particular kind.

Celestial.

I was in the storeroom at the guild. *Demonglass...* someone had put a sheet of demonglass in a cupboard there. I must be in the forbidden part of the guild. Calling for help would get me arrested. Nikolas and Rachel couldn't follow me if they didn't know I was here. Unless I went back to find them, through the glass, but I didn't know how I'd transported myself to this exact spot.

I threw myself against the door with all my strength, grabbing my sword as I did so.

The blade sliced through the locks, and I fell through the door, catching myself at the last second. I really had ended up at the guild, somewhere in the west wing. *Well, shit.*

I grabbed my phone, snapped a couple of pictures, and hesitated before sending them to Gav. There was no good reason to keep demonglass—a restricted substance—in a hidden room with no explanation. Unless they had a good story, someone would be in trouble.

An alarm sounded. I'd tripped the security system. Lucky

I wouldn't stick around to see the fallout. Sword still in hand, I threw myself through the demonglass again.

My phone buzzed with a response, but I was already falling through smoke. The next second, my feet touched down outside the tower. Bits of dead demon indicated Rachel had been busy, but there was no sign of her—or Zadok.

I frowned. Wait. The west wing of the guild didn't line up with this part of the castle. The tower clearly belonged to Nikolas's brother, and besides, I remembered enough of the map to know I wasn't anywhere near the spot where the guild's storerooms and the castle overlapped. So did I not need to be in the same place to use the demonglass? That was different to Nikolas's power.

Maybe I can transport myself anywhere from here. Including wherever Nikolas is.

I turned to face the sheer glass surface and pressed my hands to it again. *Rachel and Nikolas,* I thought clearly. I didn't know if my thoughts could affect where I ended up, but short of running through and hoping for the best, I might as well fall back on my celestial training. Belief was central to accessing our power. If there was demonglass anywhere else in the castle, theoretically, I should be able to reach it.

The glass turned transparent, revealing the pillared hall we'd been in before Rachel had been taken. In front, Nikolas and Rachel stood back to back, surrounded by scorpion-tailed venos demons.

All right, then.

The glass swallowed me up, and the next second, I tumbled out of the pillar beside them.

Rachel's eyes widened. "How in seven hells did you do that?"

"Thought I'd drop in and help out." I grabbed my sword, and stabbed the nearest venos demon in the mouth. Blood splattered the ground, along with demon venom. "Where's your delightful brother?"

"I incapacitated him." Nikolas regarded me for a brief moment. "You're full of surprises, aren't you?"

"Apparently."

Lightning crackled from his hands, spearing another demon. My blade found another target, cutting it down, and I ducked under another's stinger. I slid underneath its feet, slicing into its lower back. It fell in two halves, still twitching. *Ugh.* With another slice, I cut off its head. A second immediately took its place.

I leaped onto its back, sinking my celestial blade into its skull. Rachel was locked in battle with another, while three had Nikolas backed into a corner. I ran to one of them, severing its stinger. "Need help?"

"No," he said, black lightning arching from his fingertips and striking the three scorpion demons down simultaneously. "Zadok must have left the gates open all day to allow this many demons in."

"Probably because of me." I sliced another scorpion demon in two, my celestial blade gleaming with blackened blood.

"I'm still lost on *how* you got here, Devina," commented Nikolas. "I wasn't aware Rachel's shoes could make you walk through solid objects."

Rachel screamed. Nikolas and I moved at the same time, bearing down on the scorpion demon at her feet. It was dead, but Rachel had fallen, bleeding from her arm.

Nikolas stepped in. "The venom got her," he hissed. "It'll be fatal if I don't heal her, but we need to get somewhere safe. The castle isn't. He brought all his minions in."

"Well, if you're going to cross over, do it quickly," I told him. "The guild's about to be overrun."

"How exactly do you know that?" He looked at me, dark

red hair gleaming in the moonlight, streaks of demon blood on his face.

"Because I found proof there's something wrong at the guild and alerted them."

He cut me a sharp look, lifting her in his arms. *It's not like I could have known this would happen.* We should never have come into this realm, and heaven knew the proof itself was shaky at best. Keeping demonglass hidden away didn't necessarily mean foul play, and the inspector wouldn't take kindly to accusations of treachery. But I hoped Gav would have the sense to look into the issue without anyone getting killed. He, at least, had authorisation to be in the hidden parts of the guild. I wasn't supposed to be near the place at all, and definitely not with two warlocks—one severely injured—in tow.

"We can't escape through this dimension," Nikolas said. "There are too many wild demons waiting outside the castle gates."

"Shit." I took a step back, thinking hard. The guild wouldn't hesitate to take them down, but maybe I could engineer a diversion. It wouldn't be the first time I'd done it. "All right. Cross over now. I'll divert their attention."

Bye, bye, freedom. It was nice knowing you.

17

When the shadows faded, sirens rang in my ears, over and over. The celestial guild's emergency alarms.

"Intruders!" bellowed the inspector's voice from across the quadrangle. Dizzy from the abrupt change of scenery, I pinpointed our location as the corridor just down from the morgue.

"Shit, they're quick on the uptake." My phone buzzed, and I grabbed it from my pocket. *If you're still at the guild, run,* the message said. Great advice there, Gav.

"This way." I pointed. "The back exit's through there. I take it you can use your ability on the guards?"

"Yes, I can," he said. "But not higher level celestials."

"Don't worry," I said. "I'll distract them. I have more of an alibi than you do."

Nikolas gave me a hard look. "If you're wrong—"

"I'll deal. Go. Now."

And he did. I'd consider how in hell I'd got to the point where I was bossing around warlocks when I got out of this situation. I looked wildly around for an obstacle, but short of stripping naked and sprinting through the quadrangle, I hadn't the faintest clue how to draw attention away from —*wait. The shoes.*

I ran around the corner to the stairs to the upper floor, took them three at a time, and swung into the nearest empty room. Normally I wouldn't jump out a window without checking what was below, but normally I wasn't wearing gravity-defying shoes. I shoved the window as widely open as it would go, climbed out, and was halfway to the roof before shouts came from below. *Go on. Look at me, not the warlocks. Look right past them.*

I climbed around the roof, not even bothering to hide. The boots' grip was sure, and besides, the more attention I drew away from the back corridor, the better. I trusted Nikolas would have the common sense to wait until the coast was somewhat clearer before sprinting towards the back gates—and hopefully the guards on duty wouldn't put up a fight before he hypnotised them.

"Hey!" I shouted, my voice carrying out into the night. "Hey—help!"

Saying goodbye to dignity, I faked tumbling down the sloping roof, before dangling dramatically over the quadrangle. Several torchlights shone up at me—celestial torchlights, that is.

"What in seven hells—" someone broke off. "It's her. Devi Lawson."

"Really, I had no idea." I leaned too far and fell off the roof.

For the second time that night, I flailed my arms against empty air, screaming at the top of my lungs. I crashed into a bush, careful to land on my feet. I thought it was an Oscar-worthy performance, but I didn't get so much as a clap.

"Miss Devina Lawson!" The inspector parted the crowd immediately, an expression of utter fury on his face.

"All right." I held up my hands. "You caught me."

"Give me one good reason not to lock you up," he said.

"I'm here on guild business," I said. "You know why I was here. You shut me out of the damned investigation."

"Then you'll know by now we've been raiding suspect houses all day, and my novices helped bring the possible culprits to jail."

"What?" I forgot all about my excuses. "You caught the killer?"

Not bloody likely. More like he'd ordered the novices to haul in any possible scapegoat. Which meant preternaturals. The jail was on the east side of the guild, and I hadn't thought to check there because I'd assumed they still thought Nikolas and I were the suspects. But if they'd locked anyone up, I'd bet my newly acquired boots it wasn't the actual killer.

"A number of warlocks have abilities similar to the killer's," he told me.

"You *locked* up warlocks? Please tell me you knew they were actually guilty first."

He eyed me coldly. "Unfortunately for you, you're not responsible for whoever the guild decides to arrest."

"Damn right I'm not." I brushed grass from my knees, my hands shaking. Nikolas should have got away by now. "So you don't need me. Clearly, I'm *not* the killer."

"Whether you are or not, you're trespassing."

A dozen novices stared at me, not speaking. Nobody came to my defence. They were too scared of the inspector.

"I'm here because I'd like to know who the killer is," I said. "And you refused to let me help investigate, despite *hiring* me to do so. Who are these suspects?"

"One suspect remains at large," said the inspector. "That warlock you claimed to have *interrogated.* It seems he has the ability to hide in another dimension. Is he watching us right now?"

"I wouldn't know," I said.

"Then find out," he said. "If you don't bring that warlock in by midday tomorrow, you *will* be arrested—both of you."

He's actually letting me go? I'd expected an ultimatum, but I'd thought I'd get jail time first. I couldn't let freedom slip between my fingers, so I faked a bored expression. "All right, I'll bring you the warlock. If I can catch him, which I sincerely doubt. Since, as you pointed out yourself, he's probably hiding in another dimension laughing at us." It wasn't like he could read my mind, but I still tensed inwardly as the inspector scanned my face. Apparently finding the right balance of disdain and annoyance he expected from me, he waved a hand impatiently.

"We have interrogations to run," he said. "Novices, kindly escort her from the premises."

Two novices stepped in to obey. He'd apparently taken over from Mr Roth entirely, and I'd seen no signs of Gav at all.

Bad Haircut Sammy approached me. "C'mon, you troublemaking bitch," he said, grabbing my arm.

I yanked it out of reach. "I can walk myself to the doors, thanks. Unless someone wants to explain why you suddenly have a new boss and nobody else has any authority?"

The two younger novices ignored my questions, wearing expressions of nervous terror. I'd bet the inspector had terrorised them more thoroughly than the murders had.

Sammy kept up a stream of taunts, which I ignored. He probably wanted to bait me into a fight, one I didn't have the energy for. I blanked him all the way to the exit, until he grabbed my arm before I could saunter out the door.

"I said, you're the real criminal here," he said, leaning close to my ear.

"Believe it if you like." I shrugged. "You're a long way from my first priority here, dog breath."

I left him spluttering and strode away as fast as I dared. Once I was out of sight of the front entrance, I circled the guild from the side, seeing no signs of the two warlocks. Had to mean they'd got away, right? I wished I'd got Nikolas's mobile phone number. It was the more logical development in a relationship to the ability to transport myself into his home dimension.

Relationship? I was definitely losing it. If I didn't hand Nikolas over tomorrow… I'd been right all along. Both sides were setting me up to take the fall.

Divinities above, what a fucking night. On top of that, I couldn't follow Nikolas home without risking being tailed by the inspector's novices. It wasn't late enough that the pubs had closed yet, so I was tempted to grab a drink to soothe my frazzled nerves. But going into a preternatural district after the narrow escape I'd had would be very unwise. *Bloody guild.* I needed actual tangible proof to bring to them, but Gav hadn't said he'd show my messages to anyone, and he hadn't been at the guild at all. Unless he'd left before I'd come back.

I took the train, having the misfortune to end up in the same compartment as a group of drunken tourists, all of whom decided to snap photos of me. I got off several stops early and made for the high street. I needed to tell Javos his people had been arrested, and I couldn't think of anywhere else to look for Nikolas at this time of night that wouldn't lead to me being ambushed.

When I turned into Prince Street, I made for the Harpy's Nest. Before I could open the door, the shadows moved, and Nikolas appeared before me.

"I thought I'd find you where you're not supposed to be," he said.

"Speak for yourself." I gestured at the receding shadows. "Is Rachel okay?"

"Yes, I managed to get her to Javos."

"Good. But I should warn you, they've given me an ulti-matum: bring you in tomorrow, or get locked in jail. I didn't have any other way of contacting you, but I didn't really expect to find you here anyway."

"That can be dealt with." He took my phone from my hand, where I had Gav's message still open. "Who's this from?"

"My old mentor. The guy I sent the proof to. Apparently it wasn't good enough for the guild." I heaved a sigh. "Not that I actually heard from him afterwards. The inspector's deposed everyone else in charge."

"Well, you can reach me at this number when I'm in this dimension." His fingertips raced across the screen.

"No cross-dimensional messaging, huh. I always wondered how that worked."

"Demons have alternative means of communication." He handed my phone back to me, his fingertips lightly brushing against mine. My chest warmed. I didn't hand my number out to just anyone, even if we had survived several near-brushes with death alongside each other.

Even if my freedom entirely depended on him.

"The proof," he said. "What were those pictures of?"

"Just demonglass in a hidden cupboard. I tripped the alarm before I got a good look around. Nikolas, *how* are you planning to get out of this one? If they catch us, we'll end up in jail with the other warlocks."

"*What* other warlocks?" said a growling voice.

Javos approached us. *Oh shit. He didn't know.*

"What did you do?" he growled. Power burned in his eyes like an oncoming tornado. "Tell me what you did, celestial."

I raised my hands. "Not me. The guild locked a few people up on suspicion of being involved in the recent murders. They didn't tell me who. I'm not working for them any longer."

Javos let out a low growl. His huge body loomed over me, and he seemed *bigger*, somehow, filling the whole street with his huge presence—horned head, slavering jaws, hands built to crush. The street lights flickered and went out, and deadly silence filled the space where laughter and background noise from the pubs had been. As though he'd hit the mute button on the world.

Terror froze my limbs. I had nothing in my hands but my phone. He'd kill me before he listened to reason.

My phone buzzed with a new message, and he halted, frowning. *Wait.* My fingers skimmed the touch screen, loading the classical music I'd downloaded earlier. Then I upped the volume.

As Javos prepared to charge, music blared from my phone. He growled, shaking his head, his petrifying aura receding. The street lights flickered back on. My legs swayed, but I managed to stay on my feet. *That was a close call.*

Javos turned his back and stormed back into the pub. I breathed out shakily. "Just what I needed—another warlock who wants me dead."

"You handled that well," Nikolas commented. "I've never seen him calm down so fast."

"Are you joking?" I fought to rein in my temper. "Is everything a game to you? The celestials want a war, and at this rate, they'll get one. Several of your people are locked up in jail, and they want me to hand you over to them, too. What the hell am I supposed to do? We're backed into a corner."

"Then we'll think of a plan." He rested a hand on my shoulder. Warmth radiated from his skin to mine, almost making me forget I still wore the anti-warlock trap. "I'd suggest you go home and rest. Try not to use that ability of yours again."

"I don't have any demonglass. Unless ..." I trailed off. "Wait. I think I know how to catch the killer."

His brows rose. "How, exactly?"

"It's obvious." So obvious, I should have realised the instant I'd fallen through that pillar. "My ability—I can go *anywhere*, as long as there's demonglass. All I have to do is keep hopping around the city until I find the place the demons are being summoned. Since there are so few places with demonglass in this dimension, I'll know pretty quickly if it's definitely the guild or not. But I don't think they summoned the demon there."

His jaw tightened. "It's risky. For one thing, you'll be transporting yourself into the hands of the enemy, in all likelihood. You've had quite enough excitement tonight already."

"Oh, this is pretty standard for me." He still hadn't removed his hand. And though he was nowhere near my demon mark, an electric shiver ran up both my arms. Oh no. I wasn't actually attracted to the guy, was I?

"The second issue," said Nikolas, "is that I don't actually have any demonglass myself. It's all at Javos's house."

"Oh. Shit."

"Exactly," he said. "So if you don't have another plan—"

My phone started to ring.

Seeing it was Gav, I sighed in relief. "Thank the Divinities for that. Gav, I need—"

"Devina," said a stranger's voice—it took me a minute to place it as Mr Roth's. The former man in charge, before the inspector stepped in. "I'm going to need you to come to the guild, now."

That wasn't good. "What are you doing with Gav's phone? He's at home."

An icy feeling had begun to spread through me. *No. Please—*

"We found his body two streets from the guild. He was alone."

The words buzzed together like static, as though our

connection was fading out. But I could hear perfectly fine. My mind just didn't want to accept what I heard.

He couldn't be dead.

He's not a new recruit, thought the part of me not blank with shock. *He wasn't even out in the field.*

In fact... the only thing that could have possibly made him a target were the messages I'd sent him. The pictures.

"Devina!" said Mr Roth, sharply. "Did you hear what I said?"

"No," I said numbly. "No. It can't be him."

"Did you two speak to one another today? Apparently, the last phone conversation he had was with you."

"We just exchanged a few messages. I sent him pictures of my findings when I was investigating—"

"You mean, trespassing. You don't have an alibi. Where are you?"

"Walking home." Shit a brick. I was nowhere near the guild, but they'd reach my house before I did. And if I handed myself in, I'd never find out what had happened to him.

I sent him those photos.

An image exploded into my head—Gav screaming, eyes burning with fire.

I gripped my phone hard, trying to anchor myself in the present. "Please. I need to see him, but I'm not coming to the guild if you're going to lock me away. I wanted to find the killer."

"That was an order, Celestial Devina."

I gripped the phone hard. "I didn't do it," I said. "The phone you're using has photo evidence on it. Check it. Please—"

A beeping tone told me he'd hung up.

"You bastard." I threw my phone to the ground, tears burning my eyes. Gav hadn't deserved to die. And if I hadn't sent him those photos—if I'd swallowed my pride and gone straight to the head of the guild…

You'd still be locked up. The inspector has it in for you, and he's suspected you from the start.

I bent down to retrieve my phone. Luckily, its protective casing had stopped it from breaking. Swallowing hard, I turned to Nikolas. His expression was almost sympathetic, which made things worse. I felt more emptiness than grief, like I'd been hollowed out by sheer exhaustion.

"It's over," I said quietly. "Gav is dead, and they blame me for it. I can't go home. I can't go anywhere. And I think it's my fault the demons got him in the first place." *Just like Rory.*

His hand rested on my arm. "You can stay at the warlocks' headquarters tonight. They won't find you there."

I shook my head insistently. "No way. Isn't that Javos's place? The guy just nearly killed me."

"His powers are switched off, and he won't attack you," Nikolas said. "It's safer than my place, if the guild really is keeping tabs on you."

"You'd better be right." I rubbed my eyes. "Also, we're grounded in this realm until your brother calms down. I get the impression he won't forget about us overnight."

I didn't even have space in my head to worry about the dude with the army of demons. I'd be inclined to believe Nikolas's brother was behind all this crap, but he didn't even know we were investigating a murder until I'd told him. Despite the futility of winning a fight against the guild, I wished I *had* found incriminating evidence. The pictures on Gav's phone weren't enough.

And now they've killed him for it.

Even in my mind, I didn't know if I meant the demons or the guild.

Nikolas and I walked down the street in silence until he stopped beside his car, which he must have moved from near the celestial guild. If not for Rachel's shoes, I'd have killer blisters by now, so I sank into the passenger seat with relief. He drove in silence, which I was grateful for. My thoughts were a tempest and only exhaustion kept me from breaking down in rage and grief.

Finally, we stopped outside a large brick house behind a high fence. After getting out of the car, Nikolas pressed a hand to the wooden gate much like celestials did when entering our guild. It opened with barely a sound, though the hum of magic permeated the air, suggesting protective spells were on the gates.

Inside the house, a dark hallway led to carpeted stairs. Upstairs, Nikolas pushed open a wooden door, revealing a small bedroom.

"One of the guest rooms," he said. "There's nobody here but Rachel and me, but I'd advise you not to go wandering around the house on your own. I'll talk to Javos in the morning. Get some rest."

And the demonglass? I was too tired to make a desperate attempt to find the killer now. I'd end up in even worse trouble, and besides, I didn't even have a plan. Not yet. Gav's death ate a hole in my chest, tearing open the wound of losing Rory. I didn't say a word more to Nikolas, and he left in silence.

A sob caught in my lungs, and I sank onto the bed, pressing a fist to my mouth.

I won't break. I won't surrender. I'll make them pay.

18

The smell of brimstone greeted me, tickling my nostrils. I inched my eyes open, frowning around at the small unfamiliar room. I'd draped mud and brimstone all over the bed covers and the floor, which explained the smell. And then it hit me: I was a fugitive. I had nothing but the clothes on my back and my phone. I picked it up. Dead battery. Great. Did warlocks keep iPhone chargers? If Javos was in as bad a mood as last night, my source of music to calm him down was gone.

I brushed my hair out of my face, catching sight of my reflection in the small mirror above the bedside table. My eyes were puffy, there was a growing bruise on my cheekbone I didn't remember receiving, and my hair was tangled. My body ached all over, and I apparently hadn't remembered to use the en-suite bathroom to shower before I'd crashed, sucked under by the crushing weight of grief. With Gav dead, I had no reasons remaining to catch the killer, except to save my own skin. But the black mark on my right wrist told me I was doomed to flee from the celestials no matter what. My future was as blank as it'd been when I'd turned my back on the celestials, and my freedom dangled from the hands of a half-demon who'd nearly trampled me into the pavement last night. Maybe that's why I felt so calm about my oncoming demise. From rock bottom, you could only look up.

There was a knock on my door, and I walked to answer it, hoping it wasn't Javos.

Nikolas stood outside, dressed casually in jeans and a plain T-shirt that showed off his muscled arms. He also held a pile of fresh clothes. "These are Rachel's old clothes. They should fit you."

"Thanks." I took them from him. "Is she okay?"

"She's here, but recovering. She doesn't have regenerative abilities, so it takes a little longer for her to heal compared to some other warlocks."

"Must come in handy," I said. "Do you have anywhere I can charge my phone? I'll bet the celestials have been hounding me all night."

There was a clock on the wall I hadn't noticed, which told me it was ten in the morning. I'd slept heavily, worn down by the events of the last few days.

"Not to worry," Nikolas said. "Give me your phone and I'll recharge it. If anything else had happened, I'd know."

I hesitated before handing it over. It wasn't like I had any options left. "And Javos?"

"He wishes to speak with you."

I raised an eyebrow. "I assume he's going to apologise for nearly smiting me last night?"

"I doubt he remembers," said Nikolas. "When his power kicks in, he often forgets himself entirely. I'm glad you were able to subdue him."

"Me too. Believe me."

I took a quick shower and changed into the jeans and T-shirt Nikolas had brought. The shirt—white, embossed with red devil horns—hung loosely to my knees, but that was apparently the style. I replaced my wristbands, hiding both celestial and demon marks, and surveyed my reflection. Marginally better. The aura vision potion had worn off by now, but I didn't need a potion to know what I looked like to them.

Maybe I was better off throwing my lot in with the warlocks instead.

I turned right once I left the room and followed the sound of voices down the carpeted stairs. A door led into a kitchen, where the great hulking form of Javos covered one entire side of the table and appeared to be devouring a dead demon's leg. Not a human one, anyway. *Ugh.*

"Coffee?" he asked, in a deceptively polite voice.

"Er… thanks." I sat down as far from the bloodstained meat as possible. "Do you have… normal food here?"

"Of course," said Nikolas from behind me. "Javos has select tastes. But a number of warlocks frequent the guild. Not humans, though. I can't say we've ever had one of those here."

"Yay." I accepted a mug of steaming hot coffee and a plate of toast from him. "I'm honoured."

"I should think so," rumbled Javos.

Ah, crap. Apparently my brain-to-mouth filter had disappeared somewhere in the middle of the night. Considering the relentless shitstorm the universe had unleashed on my life, I wasn't doing too badly, but I'd never imagined eating toast in the kitchen with a pair of warlocks, one of whom had a human-sized leg dangling from his mouth. I nibbled toast in awkward silence before Nikolas handed me my phone back.

"How'd you charge it already?"

"I have many talents."

I raised an eyebrow at him. "Please tell me you didn't zap

it with demon lightning. I have evidence stored on that phone."

"Relax. I just used one of our specially enhanced chargers," he said. "By evidence, you mean the photographs of the guild?"

Javos dropped the demon leg. "I do hope the guild doesn't mistreat their prisoners."

Slowly, I inched my chair back from the table, ready to sprint if he exploded in anger again. "They don't normally *have* prisoners. Inspector Deacon's running the show and has everyone dancing to his tune. I'm sure he'll be open to negotiation."

There was more chance of *me* getting a pardon from the guild than the warlocks, but anyone with half a brain could guess that. The inspector didn't see the warlocks as human.

Nikolas put down his coffee mug. "What we need to discuss right now is Devi's new ability to travel through demonglass. The repercussions for us—and for this new demon case, too—might be potentially catastrophic. No human has ever had such a power before."

Javos looked at me. "Your new talent is bound to get you into a lot of trouble if you don't learn to discipline yourself and use it sparingly."

"I didn't plan to make a habit of it," I said. "I was kind of being chased by angry demons and an evil warlock at the time."

"So Nikolas tells me," he said. "You can pass from this realm to others, and you also appear to be able to move around within the same dimension using the glass, which is almost unheard of. Just where did you get this ability?"

"Apparently, I was marked with it," I said. "Unfortunately, the demon who marked me is possibly linked to the murders. But I don't know for sure. This potential evidence from the guild throws all my other theories out the window. They have demonglass in their secret storeroom."

"And did you see other evidence of a demon summoning?" asked Javos.

"No," I said. "Also, there's no way anyone could have actually let a demon loose in the guild. There are too many wards in there. Someone would have noticed. But if demonglass is needed for the summoning, that limits the possible locations. So I figured I could maybe use my ability to track them down. I don't have a ton of options."

"Nikolas mentioned there was another death last night," he said. "He said you were planning to do something reckless. Are you prepared to deal with a nest of demons?"

"Yes," I said, looking him in the eyes. "The guild wants me to hand Nikolas over to them, or get locked in jail. I don't know if they're guilty or not, but my mentor died right after I sent him potentially incriminating evidence of the guild's involvement. So I don't know what to believe. The fact that they killed Gav—it broke the pattern. Not only was there more than a day between his murder and the one before, he wasn't even a novice. Whoever killed him wanted to get to me."

"That suggests the guild was involved, for certain," said Javos. "This inspector figure."

"He has a gambling addiction," I said. "But we didn't find any evidence he's the one working with the demons. And Gav's body was found two streets from the guild, not in the building."

But one thing was certain—his death wasn't random. Someone knew I was investigating, and had intentionally targeted someone I cared for. That was reason enough not to walk away from this.

"Show me the photos," Javos said.

I loaded up the last message I'd sent Gav, without looking

at it. I didn't have time to stop and grieve. Catching his killer before the guild found me was paramount.

The warlock took the phone in his huge hand. "Either he sent the message to the guild and they took him out—in which case, we can expect an attack—or a demon saw it. Either might be true."

"I know," I said. "It's still a toss-up whether the guild just *look* guilty. The fact that all three of us have reason to hate them doesn't help, to be honest. I think it's almost designed to make it look that way—the victim burns from the inside out, like how our own celestial light works against nether-worlders. But I saw the body of the last victim, and the place the aura changed was around her right hand. There." I held up my wrist, where the mark was hidden under my wrist-band. "You couldn't see my mark to begin with, but it was there."

"Are you certain that's what you saw?" asked Nikolas. "I haven't seen any demon marks on a person, but if it's along the same lines as a celestial mark—you all wear the mark on your left wrist?"

"Yeah," I said. "So maybe demon marks are the same. It might not even be the same demon either. But the victims… it's the only way I can see someone killing them without laying a hand on them. The mark's invisible until it's trig-gered. With me, it gave me powers. But if the person being tested is a low-ranked novice…"

"Then their body rejects the change and it consumes them," said Javos, handing me my phone back. "It's not a bad theory, Devina, but it leaves out the crucial question of who summoned the demon, for that purpose. And why."

I closed down the message from Gav and found two from Fiona asking where I was. I composed a quick response warning her not to leave the flat, and sent it. Hopefully she'd heed my warning and the guild wouldn't make her life difficult. I looked up at the others. "Just warning my friend to lie low. I need to fix this. The demonglass will take me directly to the enemy, whoever they are. It's the one plan the guild can't stop."

"How exactly do you control where the glass takes you?" asked Nikolas. "You did so at least once before, right?"

"I just pictured where I wanted to travel to," I said. "There's one way to know for certain. I have to test it."

"Without being caught?" asked Nikolas. "We have yet to establish whether you can take other people along with you. If not, then you'd be transporting yourself into the hands of an unknown enemy with no backup."

"If it's like your power, then she'll have to train it," said Javos. "But we have only one full sheet of functioning demonglass hooked up to a power source. The summoner must be using something similar. The power drains out of the glass over time, so it would need a demonic energy source to keep it functioning. If the demon is indeed hiding in another dimension, the source would need to stay active."

"Right." I nodded. "There's not a lot we can do if it *is* the guild, because they'll arrest me the moment I show up there."

"Not if their attention is elsewhere," said Javos. "I'll go to speak to the guild. I imagine my arrival would cause enough of a stir to draw their attention away from the storeroom long enough for you to remove or break the glass, correct?"

"Technically, yes, but I don't think—"

"All the weapons you need are within reach," said Nikolas. "You can escape through the glass again if there's an ambush waiting."

"It's too risky," I said. "Besides, I need someone to wait on the other side of the glass if it all goes to shit. There's a chance I might come through with the entire guild on my tail."

"They won't be able to follow you." Javos got to his feet.

"And I've left my people for long enough. Make the decision, Devina. If you do decide to proceed, allow me fifteen minutes to divert their attention."

He swept out of the room, leaving the remains of the demon leg on the table. I swivelled to look at Nikolas. "Doesn't take orders well, does he? I really hope he doesn't declare war on them."

"He has more sense than that," said Nikolas. "The demonglass is ready, if you're sure."

"You know I'm not," I said. "I realise we nearly died last night anyway, but it's people's lives we're gambling with here. And it's personal now. They're after people close to me." Guilt twisted through my chest. "I'm worried about my neighbour, Fiona. She's human, but I wouldn't put it past them to target her, too."

"Humans cannot be demon marked in the same way you are," he said. "But that's all the more reason to make a decision. I don't like the idea of you risking your life by going through the demonglass alone, but I'm unlikely to be able to follow you."

"Never thought I'd be glad to have power better than yours."

"Oh, better, is it?" He arched a brow. "Maybe if we survive this, we can test that theory."

I shrugged. "Honestly, I need all the hope I can get at this point. Where's this glass?"

"In the back room." He rose to his feet, beckoning me through a door on the kitchen's other side. "Are you absolutely certain?"

"I'm certain I have no choice." I took in a breath. "If I get trapped on the other side, or if their demon is there... I don't even have my warlock-repellent. It expired. And they might have broken my doors down by now." Fiona hadn't responded to my message, and I hoped the guild would leave her alone. She wasn't a celestial, so they wouldn't have a reason to hurt her. Attacking humans reflected badly on the guild's image. If they hadn't thoroughly trounced their own reputation already.

His gaze dropped to my right hand. "I wouldn't normally tell you this without the proper training and instruction, but that mark of yours contains demonic essence. It ought to act against anything celestial—and other demons, too. Certainly other preternaturals. Just showing the mark will trigger a reaction."

"Let's hope it doesn't make them want to kill me." I followed him through the door, down a short corridor, where he unlocked another room. It was set up like a store cupboard containing a lot of boxes and not much else. Except for the sheet of clear glass at the back, identical to the one at the guild. I approached it, half expecting to see my own reflection, but it showed nothing but the wall behind. I reached out a hand, and hesitated.

Nikolas stepped to my side. His hand slid down my cheek, deliberately, raising goosebumps. He smelled of heat and brimstone, fire and wind—a force too strong to contain, too wild to tame. Pity I couldn't drag him through the glass with me, and unleash all that power on the guild.

"What do you reckon?" he said, in a low purr. "Since you're no longer wearing your inconvenient trap, do you want a kiss for luck?"

"I don't need luck, I need a miracle," I responded.

But I didn't step back as his lips hovered over mine. And perhaps it was because of my imminent arrest or death, but I kissed him back. What the hell. I was on my *way* to hell, one way or another. Might as well have something good to remember when I went up in flames. In a wild rush of desperation, I crushed my mouth to his, committing every detail to memory—the smell of brimstone, the scent of magic, the touch of his hand on my cheek.

Then he stepped back, gave me a nod, and indicated the glass. I walked towards it before I lost my nerve. When I pressed my palms to the surface, the view of a dark room appeared. The guild must be empty, or distracted by Javos's diversion.

Here goes nothing.

The glass turned transparent, and I stepped through.

19

I turned around, pulling down the wristband on my left arm. A mirror-sized patch of demonglass covered the back wall. Despite the darkness, the room seemed larger than the cupboard-sized room at the guild. Had they moved the glass? Or was I somewhere else entirely? The room smelled strongly of brimstone, with a coppery tang. *Blood.* But I hadn't got the falling sensation as I did when I'd crossed through dimensions, so I must still be on Earth.

Tentatively, I stepped forward, my shin colliding with a solid edge. Ow. My celestial light illuminated a large object blocking my way, almost knee-height. I felt my way along its rectangular shape. A heavy wooden box, maybe. And another one lay beside it on the hardwood floor. I carefully stepped between them, the light in my hand growing. The room was bigger than I'd thought, and contained a dozen wooden boxes, all more or less identical. A door stood at the other end of the room, which had no windows. What kind of weird setup was this?

Light in hand, I knelt beside the nearest box. The lid

slightly overhung the top of its rectangular shape, and the smell of blood came from inside it.

Oh shit. They were coffins. I'd transported myself into a vampire's nest.

If it were night time, I'd be in real trouble, but they'd sleep until sundown if left undisturbed. At least they weren't immune to celestial light, but what the hell were a bunch of vampires doing here?

I turned away to the demonglass wall. Some power must be fuelling it, for the glass to keep functioning when its guards were asleep. Sure enough, a number of fist-sized stones outlined the glass. Bloodstones. As well as a source of energy for vampires, they also worked as a source in demonic summonings, if a rare one. The stones must have kept the glass tuned into the demonic home dimension, before I'd messed it up by coming here. Nobody came into a vampire's nest during the day. It was the perfect hiding place, and even a team of celestials couldn't disarm and subdue an entire room of angry vampires. Not without risking a massacre. And if the vamps lost control, carnage would follow.

But… the guild wasn't the enemy at all. And I'd sent Javos there, potentially to start a war. I switched my phone to silent mode, then sent Nikolas a quick message. Why hadn't I considered that other preternaturals might have been involved before? Louise's boyfriend had been one of the undead. And the client with the stolen bloodstone… had he been involved, too? He might be an innocent—but it'd been a demon which had stolen it. From Pandemonium, the city ruled by an arch-demon of fire.

I knelt down and examined the bloodstones. I needed to disrupt the circuit powering the demonglass, before one of them woke up. Vampires slept like the dead, but they might smell my human blood or hear my heart hammering against my chest. Power pulsed through each stone, and rather than the pale red of normal bloodstones, they were jet black. The same colour as a demon's aura. *That's new.* And worrying as hell.

I felt my way around the trap and disconnected one of the stones. Its darkness continued to pulse, but the demonglass immediately began to dull. The stone hummed in my hand. I shoved it into my pocket and reached for the next one.

A slithering noise came from behind me.

My shoulders stiffened. Swivelling round, I bumped into a tall, solid figure.

Vampire.

He smelled cold, like empty tunnels. His eyes—half-open—were jet black. The only thing more dangerous than an awake vampire was a half-awake one. He probably didn't even register me, only that I smelled like a human. If his buddies woke up, they'd devour me in bloodlust without even opening their eyes.

Swallowing hard, I stepped to the side. The vampire turned that way, too. I sidestepped, and he moved along with me, his hand latching onto my shoulder.

I slammed my elbow into his ribs. Pain shot up my arm, but I brought my knee up hard, eyes watering with pain. He didn't seem to feel it. His fingertips dug into my shoulder, yanking me towards him.

Squirming away, desperate to avoid those fangs piercing my neck, I thrust the still-vibrating bloodstone against him. Demonic energy wasn't deadly to vampires, but it was bound to give him a shock.

His body jerked back, his eyes opening a little, and I wrenched his hand from my shoulder. I ducked around him and ran for the glass. A marble-white hand shot out and threw me to the ground. The vampire's eyes remained half-open, zombie-like, but he moved freakishly fast. I rolled to the side, behind a coffin, gripping the bloodstone tight. If I ran for the door, there was a very good chance I'd run into more enemies on the other side, assuming it wasn't locked. But he was between me and the glass, and with the bloodstone gone, it'd shut down soon. *Okay, the door, then.*

I was on my feet in a second, but the vampire caught me by the arm and flung me into the air. I flipped over and landed on another coffin. The lid slid free and a second vampire sat blearily up. "Robert, stop that," he mumbled.

"Now you've done it," I said through gritted teeth. As the first vampire stalked towards me, I climbed over the coffin. The second vamp mumbled something unintelligible. I dodged out of his line of sight, catching the blood-crazed eyes of the first vampire again.

He leaped like a jungle cat, crashing into me. I hit the wall, pinned beneath his solid form. Freeing one hand, I jabbed a finger into his eyeball. The vampire screamed, and I took my chance to switch on the light, directly into his face.

He moaned, leaning out of reach, hands twitching. I quickly turned off the light, hoping nobody else had been roused by its brightness, and sprinted to the door.

My hands scrambled for the handle. As I'd feared, it was locked—from the other side. I rammed my shoulder against it, hard. The first vamp groaned, writhing on the floor.

"What are you?" slurred the second guy, stumbling towards me. "Why are we awake?"

"You're sleepwalking," I improvised. "Get back in your coffin. I'm not really here. You're dreaming."

"Smells human," said the second one. "Human..." His eyes opened a little. "Why is a human here?"

"Not human." I flashed my demon mark, improvising.

"I'm a demon. I came through your summoning trap by accident."

"You smell good."

Ew. "Yeah, great. Can I go, now? I'm needed at the Great Arch-Demon Themedes's palace."

"You're with him?" asked the second vampire.

"Yes," I said. "He wouldn't like it if you hurt me. My blood tastes terrible anyway." Vampires didn't like warlock blood, I knew already—and Nikolas had said my mark would repel or attract some other demons. Would it affect vampires, too? I pushed the wristband up, entirely exposing the black mark for the vampires to see. "I'm on a mission, and I came here by accident. I have his mark. See?"

"You have his mark," slurred the vampire. "That's not his… that's not his mark. Intruder!"

His voice rose to a shout. Heads popped up in the other coffins, and I gave up on the door, sprinting to the demonglass.

I didn't make it more than a metre. My knees hit the wooden edge of a coffin as a very much awake vampire yanked me on top of him.

"Did he send us human prey?" he purred, teeth grazing my arm through the sleeve. I elbowed him in the face, climbing off the coffin, but more lay between me and the demonglass.

"It's been too long," groaned another one, fingers grasping at my ankles. "Demon blood tastes foul."

Demon blood. They were in the service of the arch-demon, for sure. And the bloodstones—were they infused with *demon* energy?

The vampire grabbed for me again. I kicked him away, my gaze snagging on the demonglass. It'd turned dull, the battery dying out. *Oh fuck.* The only way out was the locked door. So much for not causing a scene.

I yanked my left armband down fully, engulfing the room in blinding celestial light. Shrill screams came from the vampires, but their hands stopped grabbing for me. Once again, I slammed against the door, which barely rattled. Cursing, I kicked it, hard. *Wait. I can climb.*

I ran up the wall, and my feet stuck like velcro held me in place. *Thanks for that, Rachel.* I kept the light turned up to max, taking advantage of the confusion to grab my sword. Light glided up my arm, and its familiar weight settled in my hands.

I hung from the joint between wall and ceiling, holding the sword as a shield. A vampire got too close, and I severed his hand. He yelled, high and loud, and the others did, too. The light was painful to look at for a regular human. To a half-awake vampire during the day, it was unbearable. *Keep making noise,* I thought at them. The more of a racket they made, the more likely it was that someone would come and unlock the door. I was more than content to hang around on the ceiling all day, at least until one of them calmed down enough to interrogate.

"So," I said, "as long as we're at a stalemate, can one of you please explain to me why we're locked in a room with a demonic summoning trap?"

"Only if *you* explain how you got in." One of the vampires stalked towards me. The celestial light gleaming from my hand made his pale skin glow—another marble statue, too beautiful and deadly to be real. If any of them bit me, I wouldn't turn into one of them, but if I got bitten too many times, I'd be infected with venom that would put me under their thrall until they drank me dry. I hoped these boots didn't have a time limit on them.

"I got in through the glass," I told them.

"You're a celestial," spat the vampire. "You stole something of ours."

"The bloodstone?" I asked. "No, I'm not giving it back. Did the demons give it you? Is that why you're working with them?"

"The demons offer a better world than the celestials ever could," said the vampire in front. Something was slightly off about his dead-eyed stare. The others, too. Now their eyes were fully open, I could see every one of them had the same weird dark irises. Vampires' pupils were dilated when they were blood-crazed, but I had the sense there was worse wrong with these ones. What had the demons done to ensure their loyalty?

"You'll die if the demons take this realm," I said. "But you killed someone I care about." I pointed the blade at him. "If you touch my sword, you burn. Tell me… which of you will it be? Who gave the order to murder my mentor?"

"You'll all die the same." The vampire below me slammed his iron-like fists into the wall. *Now they're trying to shake me loose?*

I waved my sword down at them. "Last chance," I said. "I'm planning on bringing as many of you bastards down with me as possible, one way or another. Whose bright idea was it to set up the demonglass?"

"The great arch-demon," growled the vampire. "It's time for you to die, celestial."

My boots lost their grip as the vampires hit the wall again. I flipped over, sword pointed downwards, and vampires darted out of my way to avoid the blade. I spun it in a circle, whipping the celestial blade through the air to hit anything that came near. The sword point sank into flesh, and the vampire I'd hit screamed in fury, a hissing noise rising from his marble skin as the celestial light burned him. One touch and he burst into white flames. Nothing was more deadly to vampires than the light of heaven.

Light blazed around me, the magic forming a halo that stopped them from touching me. Temporarily. Like my boots, it'd blaze out within less than a minute… unless I took them all out in the next few seconds.

Challenge accepted.

20

I decapitated the first vampire to lunge at me, sweeping low to catch a second one who'd tried to grab my legs. Keeping the light on max power meant I burnt out faster, but it also blinded them. I cut three vampires down, dancing lightly over the coffins, until I was nose to nose with the first one who'd woken. He bared his sharpened canines at me. "I'm looking forward to tasting you, human."

I stuck the blade in his chest. He snarled, writhing, his body glowing as the light consumed him from the inside out. His eyes burned bright, blazing, and I froze, still gripping the sword.

He slumped down, dead. Like the fires of heaven or hell had extinguished what remained of the life inside him.

Three vampires stirred amongst the dead, and I ran for the door, sliding my celestial blade between door and wall. Before I could shove the door again, one of them grabbed my leg.

"I'm gonna tear you to pieces," he growled.

I threw my weight against him, and we toppled through the door. Kicking him down, I lurched forwards, only to hit the floor again as he grabbed my ankle. I slammed the heel of my boot into his face as hard as I could. Even with his abnormally tough skin, he screwed his face up against the impact, and I took the opportunity to break free and run into the hallway. Now I was out of that damned room, I could figure my way around better. First step: find the nearest window.

The vampire lurched after me, bleeding from his nose where I'd kicked him, but not weakened. I ran, and he slammed into my back, sending us both crashing into the floor. I thrust my elbows back, bruising them against his rock-hard chest. His teeth grazed my neck, nearly breaking the skin.

I wrenched my celestial-marked hand free and turned the power up, flooding the hall with blinding light. He roared in rage, but didn't let go. I squirmed away from his teeth, waving my hand beside his face. His teeth brushed against my palm. *Wait.* Inspired, I tore my other hand free and waved it underneath his teeth. If demon blood tasted as foul as he'd said, what would the mark taste like?

He turned his head away. "Get that mark gone."

I crawled free, darting through the nearest door into a living room. The windows were boarded up from the outside. So much for Plan B. I snatched up a wooden chair and hurled it at the window. Glass shattered, but the boards held together. I climbed onto the windowsill and grabbed my sword again, thrusting it into the gap between the boards.

The vampire's arm locked around my neck, and I lost my balance, crashing on top of him.

"You'll pay for this," he growled.

"You really shouldn't... stand so close to the window." Hot blood trickled down my face. I hoped the wound was shallow.

"We can make you forget, if you like," he whispered,

leaning over me from behind. "We can drink the light out of you. You'll become one of us, one of the undying."

"No thanks." I twisted around, holding my blade between me and him. His eyes gleamed, partly with bloodlust, partly with that strange darkness as the others'. "What did the demons do to you?"

Blood dripped from his nose. "We are infused with the power of hell. We'll burn the sin out of you."

I recoiled. "You—you're consuming demon blood? I thought it was deadly to you."

"It depends what type." His obsidian eyes glimmered with bloodlust. "Demon energy makes us stronger. Soon we will walk in the day as well as the night."

Shit. I'd been looking for a *demon* mark. But vampire wounds sealed within seconds. If the vampires really had some kind of demon magic, biting their victims was the easiest way to spread the virus. And if the demon magic ended up inside a celestial…

"You infected them," I said. "Even Louise."

He laughed. "He didn't mean to kill her, believe it or not. He didn't realise there was a deadly side effect to our bite. He was one of the first to try the demonic energy. And *you*, celestial… I wonder if you will burn the same?"

His teeth grazed my ear, and my elbow snapped back into his sternum. Pain spiked to my wrist and I snatched it away, spinning into a kick that barely winded him. There were few ways to keep vampires down—except the obvious.

I jumped at the shattered frame of the window, kicking at one of the wooden planks shutting out the sunlight. A thin beam came through, and I stood directly in its path. "If you touch me," I told the vampire, "you'll die."

The vamp halted, hissing between his teeth. "Soon I need not fear the sunlight, celestial."

"You'll still burn," I said. "And it'll be as painful as divine judgement for your crimes. If you want me to let you go, tell me which demon's behind this."

He lunged, and I moved, too. My sword impaled him before his teeth could pierce my neck, and his lifeless body collapsed on top of me, still burning. I crawled out from underneath him and walked into the corridor.

"If there's anyone still alive in here," I said, "tell me who you're working for and I'll spare your lives."

Silence followed. Swearing under my breath, I stalked back to the open door to the coffin room.

A vampire slammed into me, landing right on my sword. Once again, light burned in front of my eyes. At the same time, the front door flew back on its hinges, and two people ran into the hall.

"Devi!" shouted Rachel. "Get back, vampire, or you're dead."

"He already is." I spun to face her—and Nikolas, who stood at her side, wielding palms of black lightning. "You're a little late. But there's one witness still alive in here. They're summoning the demons on someone's orders."

"Who do I need to kill?" He stalked to the open door beside me.

"Nobody," I said. "There's one survivor, maybe more. None of the others gave me adequate answers as to who's calling the shots here. But it's definitely someone working with the arch-demon. It's that dimension, for sure. Their demonglass linked there."

I found the light switch, and turned it on. Bodies lay draped over the coffins, still smoking where I'd burned them with celestial flames. None appeared to be alive. I turned back to him. "There was one alive. He must have run off, but he can't go outside with the sun up."

"He must still be in here," Rachel said, running for the

stairs at the corridor's end. Nikolas, meanwhile, tried one of the other doors.

"Locked," he said.

"That's the main demon summoning room." I jerked my head over my shoulder. "The person in charge should be reported, but the other vamps are dead. There were never demon marks involved. It was vampire venom—spiked with demon energy."

Once bitten, all the victims would have to do was summon their celestial light—say, if they saw a demon—and they'd die. It was a deceptively easy way to kill without leaving a demonic trace behind at all.

Nikolas turned to look at me properly. Heat flushed my cheeks at the memory of our kiss—part of me had thought we'd never see one another again, and hadn't accounted for the awkward aftermath.

"They're being bribed, I think," I said, looking away. "They get the blood of their victims *and* demon energy out of the deal, and the venom takes care of the rest. But if they've already bitten anyone else, they can't use their celestial power. If they do…"

"It reacts." He nodded. "All right. I'll inform the leader of the vampires. She'll question the survivors. She takes threats to the vampire code seriously, and biting celestials definitely counts as violating the code."

"And then some," I said. "I took out one bloodstone and killed the demonglass, but we need to remove the others."

"Yes, we do," he said, sweeping into the room. "You killed all of them yourself?"

"Yeah. They woke up when I dismantled the demonglass. I used my sword to break the door down."

"If I'd known the situation was that dire, I'd have been here in a heartbeat." His hand brushed against mine, and I stilled, feeling vaguely ridiculous when he took the bloodstone. "Did any of the vampires say who they summoned?"

"No. They died first." I turned away to search for the other bloodstones, picking two of them up. "This isn't the work of a single vamp. They must have volunteered, but I don't know if they all did. Apparently Louise's vampire boyfriend didn't know he'd kill her when he bit her."

Lightning flashed from Nikolas's hands, and the bloodstone exploded into a million pieces.

"Er…" I stared at him. "That can't be reused, right?"

"No," he said, reaching out a hand for the others. Lightning sparked between his fingertips, changing colour from white to blue, to jet black yet strangely luminous. The same colour as his aura. I watched, slightly mesmerised, and the snap of the bloodstones breaking brought my attention to the demonglass.

"Are you going to break that, too?"

"It's defunct. I'll send someone in to remove it later. The important thing is establishing if the vampires bit anyone else. A mass death of celestials might push your boss over the edge."

I grimaced. "Yeah. I know. The vamps are dead, so it's not like they can confess. If it's been over twenty-four hours, the venom has fully spread. But it still doesn't explain how the victims kept appearing miles away from where they were supposed to be."

"No." His brow furrowed. "I don't think we were supposed to find out the vampires were behind this at all."

I shook my head. "Vampires wouldn't have been our first conclusion, not when we were fixated on the other details. Anyway, we need to warn the guild. Have you heard from Javos since he went there?"

"No."

"Shit," I said, another possibility striking me. "I just

thought. There *is* a demon who can appear and reappear pretty much anywhere in the city if he's summoned."

I'd met Dienes the night of the murder. *He* was from that dimension.

He's been going back and forth between dimensions for weeks. And he'd known about the bloodstones…

"I think," I said quietly, "I know who their messenger is."

21

Nikolas looked at me expectantly. I took in a breath, and told him my brief history with Dienes. The demon who'd helped me, even when the price I offered was low. I'd known he was as conniving as the rest of them, but I'd never have connected him to a murder plot.

"I don't think he's innocent, but he's probably been coerced," I said. "You know what that world is like."

"I do," he said. "However, a lesser demon wouldn't have had the ability to throw those humans around the city."

"But I'll bet he's the one who let them know who the targets were. I *told* him I was investigating the murder. It wasn't connected to what happened two years ago at all."

"Two years ago?"

"I'll explain later." My mind whirled. "I have to summon the bastard. He can confirm who's behind the attacks."

"Do it now," said Nikolas. "The other vampires will be sleeping, and even I don't have the authority to wake their leader. We need to find this demonic killer."

The arch-demon. Or someone from that realm. This room wasn't a great place for a demonic summoning, but the familiarity might help my case. I shone celestial light onto the wall, forming a pentagram shape. The whole room already stank of that dimension.

"Hey, Dienes," I said, as the horned demon appeared. "Recognise this place?"

He looked up, then side to side, as though searching for a way out. "Shit."

"Tell me, you bastard," I growled. "Tell me who you're working for or I'll burn you in celestial light. Is it the arch-demon?"

He yelped as I shone the light in his eyes. "Not him— another bears his power, his fire."

"Don't give me crap," I told him. "Who is the demon that keeps hopping in and out of this dimension? You weren't behind it."

His eyes closed. "You met him. Azurial…"

"Him?" I said in disbelief. "But I killed him."

Crap. He was a warlock… or as Nikolas said, a demigod. The child of an arch-demon. And I remembered too clearly what'd happened when Nikolas had shot his brother with lightning. He'd been back on his feet within a day.

He must have known.

"Azurial steals more of his master's power every day, celestial. He can already cross realms without assistance."

"And drag celestials back into his own realm." My words dropped from my mouth like heavy stones. "So he can throw them wherever he likes, and leave the rest of us to pick up the pieces. That's his plan."

There was no rhyme or reason to the murders at all. Just the acts of a mad demigod stealing the power of his arch-demon sire and using it to cause chaos in this dimension.

"And his endgame?" asked Nikolas.

He shook his head, eyes screwed up in pain. "I don't know. I'm only the messenger."

"Yeah, you're disposable," I said, ignoring his pleading look. "Both to him and to us. How does he track the victims down?"

"Through… the fire."

"What fire? The victims burst into flames after seeing him, right?"

"Not that fire. Inside you… the flame."

My celestial flame? He's planning to use our *magic?*

"He can travel through celestial fire as well?"

He nodded quickly.

"But he still can't actually materialise in this dimension," Nikolas said. "That's why he needed to use a proxy."

"He plans to," said Dienes, shifting inside the pentagram. "Get me out—ow, that hurts."

"I don't give a crap. You were complicit in murdering people, Dienes, and threatening my friends. Tell me what he's planning."

He breathed shallowly. "I can't—"

I moved the celestial light so it burned his arm. He yelled in pain, smacking against the pentagram's boundary.

"Tell. Me. A demon killed Gav, my friend. You *knew* that."

He shook his head frantically. "No. He must have figured out how far you'd progressed in your investigation. I never wished to harm you, Devina, but I was offered a price I couldn't refuse. If the arch-demon dies, so does the city of Pandemonium. We need a new leader before he expires."

"You should have thought of that before you fucked with me," I told him. "Because I won't just kill your demon boss— I'll burn your whole city to the ground."

Anger rolled through me, bright as celestial fire.

Nikolas spoke before I could break the pentagram and wring his neck. "Did I hear you say he's taking power away from his father?"

"He will be the next ruler of Pandemonium, so he needs

the power of an arch-demon," said Dienes. "But before then, he'll come here. He's coming for the celestials. If you don't hide, this world will burn around you."

The door slammed off the wall behind us, and two vampires ran in.

"Celestial," one of them shouted. "You murdered our entire nest."

He darted forwards, impossibly fast, as though the coffins and bodies on the floor weren't there at all. I drew my sword, and at my side, Dienes vanished into the pentagram.

I'm not done with you, you traitorous little worm.

Nikolas advanced on the vampire with black lightning dancing from his palms, but the bloodsuckers barely staggered when hit with his lightning attacks. Though he moved quickly and was probably immune to vampire venom, I didn't have that luxury.

The first vampire and I circled one another. My blade swiped high and low, and I pursued him across the coffins. The tip caught his arm, slowing him, and I thrust it into his chest. I didn't quite hit the heart, but it didn't matter. The celestial light set him ablaze.

Nikolas blasted the second vampire in the chest with lightning, his dark aura blazing. The vampire flew into the air, hit the wall, and slid down into a heap. He turned to me, eying the dead bloodsucker at my feet.

"So that's how you knew the true method by which they killed the victims," he said. "I should have guessed."

"I've not killed many vampires before now, but that's no excuse," I said. "I just didn't think you could *do* that to celestials."

The vampire who Nikolas had hit groaned a little, and tried to climb to his feet.

Nikolas got there first, grabbing him by the scruff of his neck and pinning him to the wall.

"Talk," he told the vampire. "Whose idea was it to collude with demons?"

"His." He jerked his head at the dead vampire next to me.

Nikolas cursed under his breath. "He must have been offered a hell of an incentive to work with the demons."

"Hell is kind of their speciality," I said.

Lightning sizzled from Nikolas's fingertips, and the vampire's head caught fire. He crumpled, screaming shrilly, until he dissolved into ashes.

"I have the distinct impression they weren't alone," Nikolas said. "Rachel's being unusually quiet."

"They didn't get her, did they?"

"She'd have made more noise if they had." Nikolas stalked towards the door, power crackling in his hands. Every hair on my body stood on end and power trembled through my very bones.

"You might want to stand outside for this part," he called over his shoulder. "Rachel, come out."

Lightning surged from his hands, and cracks began to appear in the ceiling.

"Wait!" I hurried after him. "What if there are innocent people in here? Or another stash of demon traps?"

"I'd sense them if there were," he said. "Besides, only vampires are affected by daylight, and no vampire in here is an innocent."

Lightning struck the door, blasting it off its hinges. Daylight flooded the hallway, and the vampire poking his head out of the next room recoiled in terror. Rachel kicked him aside, covered in blood, but didn't look hurt. She bounded past outside, as more lightning bolts struck holes in the walls and ceiling. I took Nikolas's advice and sprinted through the gap where the door had been.

Not a moment too soon. The walls *dissolved* in black lightning, leaving a gaping hole opening outside. Screams came from the vampires inside the house. Nikolas walked out, throwing another handful of lightning over his shoulder. The roof disintegrated, prompting more screams. Faces appeared in the windows of the neighbouring houses. Humans. The vampire nest was hidden amongst ordinary people.

The screaming continued. "Nice going there," I told Nikolas. "Not that they didn't deserve it, but a house of dying vampires might just draw a little attention."

"That's why we need to move."

He took off, and I followed, breaking into a sprint. Warlocks might not be as fast as vampires, but I was still out of breath by the time we left the vampire's screams behind and returned to a more familiar area, near the warlocks' house.

"Javos is still at the guild, right?" I asked. "Shit. I *have* to tell them, even if they lock me up. They're still searching for me as it is. But… I think Azurial's planning a direct attack on them next. He tracks them using fire—celestial fire. I doubt they'll believe me, but they're the biggest source of celestial energy in the city, and Dienes will have run off to tell him that we destroyed his vampire nest. He'll be angry. I don't know the guy, but he seemed a little hot-tempered."

"That's putting it mildly," Rachel said. "But we don't want him here in this realm. We need to figure out how to stop him. You'd think his arch-demon father would have put a stop to him."

"He's not exactly all there, is he?" I pulled out my phone first, typing a message to everyone at the guild via their universal email link. Not everyone bothered to check their messages, but I hoped someone would have the sense to. As a last resort, I sent a message to Gav's phone again, telling whoever held it that a direct attack on the guild was immi-nent, and that the demon was using the celestials themselves as the conduit. If Azurial was stealing power directly from his arch-demon father, he'd be able to materialise fully in no time at all.

My phone started ringing before I'd finished the message. I hit send and answered—"Fiona?" I asked. "What's—"

The sound of a voicemail tone sounded in my ear. Then—

"Devi!" she screamed. "Help me. A demon's in the flat. Now. I'm hiding. I thought you—"

Her voice cut off. So did the voicemail. The timer said it'd been sent several minutes ago.

I stared at the phone, then at Nikolas. "Azurial has Fiona. My friend… she has nothing to do with this."

Fury blazed through my nerves. Not content with murdering my mentor, the demon had decided to kidnap my one ordinary human friend. Clover was incapacitated. And I had nobody left to rely on… except the two warlocks at my side.

A deafening scream came from down the road. Nikolas flashed me a grim look, and we ran.

22

Nikolas and Rachel overtook me in seconds, even with my celestial power switched on. My feet pounded on the pavement, as the warlocks' guild drew closer.

The gates lay open, the defences switched off. My heart plummeted at the smell of brimstone. I took one step towards the gates, and a venos demon leaped out, stinger swinging wildly. I jerked out the way of the scorpion demon's deadly venom, grabbing my sword. Someone must have destroyed the house's defences while we were gone.

Venom splattered the ground, narrowly missing my new shoes. My sword sank into its tail, severing the deadly stinger. The scorpion swung around, its tiny mouth opening and revealing pointed teeth dripping with even more venom. Yay. Gotta love defence mechanisms. Blood pumped from its severed stinger, and it spat venom at me. I jumped, swinging my blade, and decapitated it.

"Nikolas!" I shouted, running to the doors. "Are you in here?"

No sound responded. The door hung off its hinges, and

silence blanketed the house. I walked into the hallway, seeing more demon blood and venom on the walls. How'd they broken into the guild? Was the fire demon here?

A human-sized body slammed into me, pinning me to the ground. Teeth pierced my hand to the bone and I screamed aloud, pushing at the impossibly hard weight on me. A vampire. He'd *bitten* me.

Shock numbed me, slowed down time to a trickle of seconds. My body went limp, then a surge of adrenaline ignited my nerves. The vampire's cold, strong hands pushed me into the carpet like I was a fly in a net. My hand throbbed, and I could almost feel my pounding heart hurrying the venom's flow around my bloodstream. Slowing my instincts. Hastening my impending death.

His teeth grazed my neck. I tried to lunge forward but barely managed to free my trapped hand. My demon's mark was exposed, pulsing dark. I had nothing left to lose at this point.

I shoved my demon marked hand into his mouth.

The vampire's teeth bit down. I yelled again, agony spreading from my right hand to my arm. The vampire gagged and lurched away from me, spitting blood onto the carpet. Gasping, I staggered to my feet. Both my hands were torn open at the palm, making it impossible to hold a weapon even if I had one.

I backed out of the hall. *I'm dead.* My celestial light reacted immediately to an enemy's presence. If the demon did show up, I'd catch on fire like the other victims before I could even land a punch. Of all the pointless ways to die. And Nikolas was nowhere to be seen. I didn't really want him to have to watch me catch on fire, but some ridiculous part of me had hoped we'd get more out of this little misadventure than a single kiss.

I stopped, scrambling for my phone. My hand stung with

pain, but the wounds had already begun to close. Vampire wounds were self-healing, even on celestials. Had anyone at the guild known it was possible to die in such a way from demon-infected vampire venom? Surely if they did, someone would have guessed the cause of the deaths sooner. But when Rory had died—not only had we not run into any vampires, the guild had outright dismissed my reports and refused to accept them as truth.

Now I might die in the same way he had, after all.

I opened my contacts and found Nikolas's number.

"Where the hell are you?" I yelled. "I'm dying down here, you arse."

No answer. I swore and skipped to the next number—Javos's. Not like I had anything to lose.

"Devina," said a deep voice.

"Javos?" I said, not having expected an answer. "I need to know if there's an antidote for vampire bites infected with demonic energy. Otherwise I'm dead. It's how they're killing the victims. The venom reacts with our celestial magic and—"

"Stop babbling. You have a demon's mark, which makes you immune to most demon diseases."

Oh. I breathed out. "Thank the Divinities for that," I said, thankful Nikolas hadn't witnessed my minor meltdown. "Nikolas and Rachel are missing. We were attacked at your house. And I know who the killer is. Azurial."

There was a short pause. "His mark wasn't on the bodies."

"No, the victims died from vampire bites infected with demon energy. But he's calling the shots, and he has my friend captive. Do you know where—?"

My phone flew from my hand as the vampire slammed into me again, and we collided with the wall. Apparently he'd recovered from sinking his teeth into my demon mark. I twisted around, no longer afraid of his bite. His eyes had the same weird tint as the others who'd been infected. How'd he even got into the house, anyway? He'd die in the sunlight, so he must have got in another way. And there were no traces of any demons in the street. So they'd been summoned inside…

There was only one place they could have come from.

I elbowed the vampire in the side, then punched him in the nose. Pulling myself to my feet, I ran through the kitchen, down the hall to the room with the demonglass.

The sheet of glass blazed bright, and the smell of brimstone filled the room. Around the glass lay shattered pieces of stone. Ingredients to make a portal.

"You didn't," I whispered.

Nikolas had gone to ambush the fire demon himself. Didn't explain the vampire, but maybe he and the demons had got loose when Nikolas had left the portal open. But why? To stop Azurial targeting the celestials… or to stop him attacking me?

The vampire swooped in behind me. I hadn't asked whether summoning my celestial blade would still have adverse side effects with my newfound vampire infection, but right now, I didn't need it. I kicked the vampire viciously in the side, and held up my demon marked wrist. The wounds had sealed entirely.

Without looking back, I jumped through the glass.

Fire engulfed my body, roaring flames filling my vision. The humming in my ears turned to screaming. A scream I'd heard in my nightmares for weeks—for months. So real, it might have come from right beside me.

"Rory!" I shouted.

His face burst into life before my eyes—eyes burning, mouth stretched open in terror. I grabbed his hand and dropped it, smoke pouring from my own hands as though I'd brought divine judgement on both of us.

Only now, I remembered exactly what that judgement had looked like.

We'd been tracking a demon in Cornwall, which had involved a lot of crawling through caves in search of the beast we'd been sent to kill. After we'd tracked it through a cave full of lesser demons, we'd found where it'd presumably been summoned—a room containing an active pentagram. Before I could shut it down, the demon had grabbed me. The last thing I'd heard was Rory screaming my name before the demon yanked me through the portal.

I fell through fire, crashing onto burnt earth. The world was a wasteland, smoke rising from the barren ground, nobody and nothing around but the demon before me.

The true form of a Grade Three demon was a terror to behold. I didn't recall the entire fight. Just the desperation— the clash of teeth on sword, and the grim knowledge that I was going to die here, in a realm that wasn't mine.

When the demon lay dying at my feet, I turned my gaze to the burning sky. I kicked its body away, retracing my steps to where it'd pulled me through. I'd been doomed the moment the demon had dragged me along for the ride. But now the adrenaline of the fight had begun to wear off, the cold grip of panic ensnared me. I was stranded on an alien world with no way back to the other side.

In a panic, I'd appealed to the Divinities for help. "Get me out! Please."

I held out my hand, baring the celestial mark, and turned the power up to max. Light flared around me, washing over the barren wasteland. A beacon to heaven, if such a place existed here or in any realm. Wherever the Divinities were based, I didn't know if they could see me here. I was willing to try anything to get out.

The Divinities had performed exactly one miracle for me in my life, and I hadn't expected an answer. But my right wrist had stung with sudden pain like a wasp had landed on me. My skin tingled all over, and the light continued to burn, like white flames.

Then it faded, and a pentagram lay in its place. My hand stung like crazy, but someone had answered my prayers. Apparently the Divinities weren't quite dead in this realm after all.

I stepped into the pentagram, which ignited around me. First came a second round of white light. Then, fire. Agonising, torturing flames licking up my arms, burning my sleeves, scorching my exposed skin.

I fell out of the demon's dimension, the flames disappearing, my knees hitting the floor. The fire was gone... but someone was still screaming.

Rory. He screamed and screamed, fire pouring from his hands, his eyes melting in their sockets.

That should be me, I'd thought, watching him in stunned disbelief.

I'd stood helplessly as he died, thinking I was to blame. Thinking a demon had answered my call, and I'd pay the price for bargaining with hell. And somehow... I'd ended up marked. Because in one thing, I'd been right.

Whoever had answered my call wasn't a Divinity at all.

In the present, the fire died, and I landed in front of the same pillar I'd used to transport myself out of this realm. I expected to see the arch-demon in his antechamber, tormenting Fiona, Nikolas, or Rachel. But nobody appeared to be around. Blood pooled on the floor, the signs of a struggle. But my celestial power hadn't killed me. I was immune to vampire venom, and apparently that meant I wouldn't burst into flames either. Unless I ran into a certain fire demon, of course.

Someone groaned at my feet. Apparently the vampire had followed me. Big mistake.

"It's your lucky day." I pulled him to his feet by the scruff of his neck. "Tell me where your master is."

"Right here, celestial," said a voice, speaking in Higher Chthonic.

I whirled around. The demigod Azurial appeared in front of the demonglass, a man shaped in flames, larger than the last time I'd seen him. How much of the arch-demon's power had he stolen? I had the suspicion he could melt my blades with no effort. Demon fire couldn't be extinguished by water. Only magic, if anything at all. Arch-demons could ignite whole cities in a single breath.

"So it was you," I said. "I'm disappointed. You didn't put up much of a fight last time."

"Last time was different."

"Sure it was." I rolled my eyes at him. "What exactly do you want from this? I mean, if it's world domination you're after, you might have tried a little harder. Or were you too scared to target anyone other than novices and a retired celestial? Pathetic."

"Scared?" he said, his form flickering with orange flames. "I told my vampires to target anyone they could. The aim was to sow chaos amongst your ranks, and it looks as though I succeeded."

"I caused more chaos than you did by climbing on the roof," I said. "Nice try, but the reason everyone panicked was because they thought they were up against an enemy who was actually threatening. You, on the other hand, have the personality of a wet shoe."

Flames surged, reaching for me. I dodged behind his pet vampire, who crawled away with a hoarse scream.

"Where'd you get *him*, anyway?" I asked. "Doesn't seem like a fair trade-off getting a bunch of vampires to help you when they burst into flames so easily."

"I needed them to subdue my father, celestial. If it hadn't

taken me so long to work out his weakness, I could have deposed the weakened old fool and taken this city for my own." Flames surged high to the ceiling. Still didn't come close to the arch-demon's power, but if he'd stolen his magic…

"I don't give a fuck," I shouted over the crackle of flames. "I don't even care what happens to this shithole dimension, to be honest. But you'd better tell me what you did with Fiona."

My blade appeared in my hands. Celestial fire tingled up my left arm, and demon power burned at my right.

"Your friend is irrelevant," he said. "I didn't need her, but the celestials sent to arrest her got a nasty surprise. More of them will burn before this is over. As will you, Devina."

The flames moved forwards, and the vampire screamed as they burned him to ashes.

23

Flames smacked into me, sending me flying back into the pillar. In the split second before I hit it, I willed my body to pass through the demonglass.

I fell from the ceiling, directly on top of the fire demon. He moved at the last second, hissing in fury as the celestial blade caught him across the back. There was no demon the blade couldn't kill, but I'd never run up against its limits before, and if he really did have the power of an arch-demon… nobody but a true Divinity could kill one. And I'd bet there wasn't one coming to save us. We were on our own. I needed to find Themedes and set him free, before Azurial absorbed all his power.

My blade sung, smacking off a shimmering edge. Azurial conjured a sword of his own, made of rippling flames.

"How did you do that, celestial?" he bellowed.

He doesn't know. Obviously. Even I hadn't known about my ability to travel through demonglass. But this whole palace was made of it.

You're in trouble now.

"I'm full of surprises." I dropped through the floor,

dodging his flaming sword, and cut him again. My blade didn't break his fiery skin. *Okay. Time to set the arch-demon free, then.* If I freed his demon boss before he died, then maybe I'd stand a chance in hell of stopping the apocalypse after all. Like Nikolas, Azurial could regenerate after death, so killing him wouldn't stop him—not unless I took down his power source first.

I leaped through the demonglass and landed in a wide hallway. The unbearable stench of brimstone filled the place, and two vampires spun around, fangs gleaming.

With dizzying speed, one of them grabbed me by the throat and hurled me into the wall. I passed through it, falling through the ceiling and crashing into him from above. He fell with a choked yell as I sank my blade underneath his ribs.

His neighbour lunged at me, but I raised my sword, cutting his throat. The sound of thundering footsteps came from ahead. I readied my sword as another vampire sprinted into the hall, but before I could strike, Rachel leaped over my head, sinking a stake into the vampire's chest.

"Nice of you to drop in," she said.

"Nice of *you* to tell me where you were going." I was almost certain Nikolas wouldn't have wanted his little sister coming into the fiery hell dimension, but she'd probably followed him. "Where's the arch-demon? He has my human friend captive here somewhere."

"I dunno where she is, but Themedes is through there." She pointed ahead. "With a bunch of demons guarding him."

"Well, I need to kill that arch-demon before Azurial absorbs all his power, or let them duke it out and preferably destroy this place in the process."

She winced. "This city… there are innocent people down there." She took in a breath. "This is my dimension, Devina. It's my home."

A thunderous wave of footsteps rolled through the hall, followed by a horde of venos demons. Rachel snarled at them.

"I'm not gonna get hit again." Her jaw unhinged, hands elongating into claws, and fur sprouted all over her body. She ran forwards and three sets of teeth snapped down, severing scorpion stingers and tails. *Okay. Now I get why she can't use her real form back on Earth.*

I cut down another scorpion with my sword, urgency driving me forward. Fiona—she had to be somewhere in the palace, but so was the arch-demon. Not to mention Azurial, who'd find me eventually. It wasn't like I had a map of the place.

Lightning speared the demonglass floor, announcing Nikolas's presence. He grabbed two scorpions and snapped their necks, clearing the way forward. His dark aura roiled around him, appearing like a pair of shadowy wings. *Whoa.* I'd thought Rachel's form was scary, but Nikolas was closer to going full-on demigod than I'd ever seen him. Lightning sizzled from his hands and struck down three scorpion demons at once.

With the path clear, I sprinted through a pair of open doors into a hall. Heat brushed against me, the familiar echo of the arch-demon's aura—but muted compared to the fire demon who was surely tearing the place apart to find me.

Then I spotted him. Themedes lay on the floor, not moving. *Is he dead?* I ran to his side, crouching down. Carefully, I lifted his arm, which flopped limply. So did his wings, which appeared much smaller. His form was more human-sized than the demonic being he'd confronted me as before.

"He's trapped in that form," said Rachel from behind me. "He can't wake up as long as his son keeps leaching off his power. I can't set him free." Her normal-sounding voice came through the demon's ferocious-looking mouth, setting off an unsettling wave of chills down my spine. But perhaps killing the arch-demon wasn't Azurial's plan. As long as the arch-demon lived, so would his magic. Perhaps he wanted to keep him imprisoned forever, feeding on his flames as he ruled in his place.

"He's bleeding you dry!" I slapped the arch-demon's face. "Wake up."

No response came, not so much as a flicker of his eyelids. I punched him again, shaking him violently, but I might as well have shaken a doll. Drawing back, I punched him in the nose with all my might. Blood spurted, but not a sound escaped him. A second later, the wound began to heal before my eyes. He still had enough of his power left to regenerate, but not enough to wake up.

A crackling noise sounded. I dropped the arch-demon and sprang to my feet, faced with a wall of fire. Flames had sprung up in a box, caging me and the arch-demon inside it.

Then a terrible scream came from above. *Human.* I looked up to see a cage hovering overhead, containing…

"Fiona!" I yelled. "Put her down, you scumbag."

The fire demon appeared as an outline in the flames, an ugly leer on his face. "It's getting hot in here," he remarked. "I wonder if that power of yours will let you save her from the flames, or will you let her burn, like you did your partner?"

"You fucking dare—"

"Help!" Fiona clung to the cage bars, eyes bulging with fear. "You're no Divinity, you lying bastard!"

Oh, boy.

The cage bars opened, releasing her above the flames. Fiona shrieked, legs tumbling, and began to fall.

I jumped through the demonglass floor. The cage wasn't made of glass but the ceiling was, and I plummeted down directly above. My legs slammed into the metal and I half fell, mentally thanking Rachel again for the shoes' grip. I caught Fiona's arm and held onto her, pulling her back into the cage. Below, all I could see were roaring flames.

"Hang on to me!" I told her as she gripped my arm for balance.

"What the hell is this?" Fiona screamed in my ear. "What're you mixed up in, Devi?"

"I'll explain later. Hold onto my back." I hauled her onto my shoulders, already tallying up how many nights of shitty movies I owed her for putting up with this crap. Quickly, I jumped onto the cage's top, careful not to drop her, and touched the demonglass ceiling. *Please let me take both of us through.*

Fiona screamed in my ear, gripping my upper arms, and we fell into nothingness. The crackle of flames vanished, to be replaced by the room of the warlocks' house.

"Sorry," I said, scrambling to my feet. "I'd have taken you to the celestial guild, but there's a demon wanting to attack them right now. Open all the windows in case any vampires come back."

"Have you lost your mind?" She sat on the floor, staring at the glass. "You can walk through walls now. Are *you* a Divinity?"

"Definitely not. I'm really sorry about this, but I have to go kill a mad fire demon."

I jumped through the glass again, aiming for the entrance to the hall containing the arch-demon. Flames leaped in front of me, but the arch-demon lay where he had before. Even the crackling flames hadn't woken him up. Was he sedated? *Wait a second.* Azurial had *told* me how he'd subdued his father. Vampire venom. There was no cure... not for humans. But my demon mark had reacted against the vampires' venom before.

Quickly, I ran my celestial blade over the mark on my right wrist, and pressed it to his mouth. His teeth clamped down and I yelped, not expecting such a violent response. Demons didn't normally drink human blood, but it *was* an energy source, though not a potent one. He gripped me hard, teeth piercing through the skin of my palm.

"What are you doing?" screamed Azurial's voice. He appeared in the flames again, surveying me as I struggled against his father's grip.

"Trying not to die." I managed to wrench my hand free, blood dripping from my wrist. But the arch-demon slumped back onto his knees, his gaze sliding out of focus. Pain pulsed from my demon mark. Unlike a vampire's bite, the wound wouldn't seal, and from the dizziness encroaching on my vision, he'd drained me of too much blood. Out of the corner of my eye, I saw Nikolas and Rachel surrounded by a wall of flame, keeping them from getting to me.

Azurial faced me, lined in fire. The smokeless flames stung my eyes, filling my mouth with the taste of brimstone.

"You're terrified of the flames," he whispered. "Aren't you? I know who you are. I looked into your history, celestial."

"Who hasn't by this point?" I didn't have the energy left to be afraid. With blood streaming from my right hand, I raised my left one and called my own celestial fire, blasting it at him. Before he could retaliate, I leaped through the demon-glass floor.

I landed beside the two demons as Azurial's flames enclosed Themedes. The arch-demon screamed, arms flailing, trying to put out the fire. *He's trying to kill him after all?* But even in that state, he'd heal no matter what suffering Azurial inflicted on him—no matter how much of his magic he drained.

Which left me with a single choice.

I reached for the arch-demon, biting back a cry of pain as the flames surged over my hands. Grabbing his wrists, I pulled him with me through the floor. To the only place I could think of.

The flames died the instant we landed on the walkway outside Zadok's tower. The arch-demon fell sprawling onto his face, nearly tipping over the edge. I grabbed his arm and gasped in pain. I'd immersed my hands in the fire, and the skin of both hands and arms was blistered. Eyes stinging, I staggered to my feet.

"Don't move," I told the arch-demon. "There's a long way down from here. I had to cut off his power source."

The arch-demon looked blearily up at me. He looked startlingly human—except for the wings, which splayed behind him, majestic even in his weakened state. "Where am I?"

"I wouldn't go into that tower," I said. "I'll send Nikolas after you."

I ran—okay, more hobbled—towards the tower's demon-glass wall again, drawing my sword as I did so.

And I willed myself to land directly beneath Azurial, blade held out to pierce him through the heart.

The wall turned transparent, and I leaped upwards. The blade sank through flesh, through fire. Azurial struggled, falling onto his back, wings splayed out. The flames didn't die, but it'd use a significant amount of power to regenerate. More than he could afford to spare, with his power source now temporarily in another dimension.

I smelled burning flesh, my whole body screaming with pain, but the celestial blade engulfed us both. I gritted my teeth, holding him down. Sapped of his strength, he shrank, the flames receding until nothing remained but a human-shaped, hairless man with shrivelled leathery wings.

I let go of the sword, falling onto my back. My skin felt like it was on fire, and my head swam, but I clung to consciousness by sheer willpower. Azurial collapsed, seemingly dead, and Nikolas descended on him—my vision was blurry, but he looked like he had wings of his own, shadowy ones. Azurial raised his head with a final cry, and his body dissolved like a vampire caught in sunlight, turning to ashes.

Someone grabbed my arm, prompting a yell of pain.

"Sorry, Devi," said Rachel, leaning over me. Her face turned human again, flickering before my eyes. "Ow. I can get you some healing salve, but this is gonna be rough."

"Not as bad as the trouble the arch-demon's in." I lifted my head, willing my body to stand. "He's—at Zadok's tower. Get Niko—"

"I'm on it," said Nikolas's voice, but I was slipping away.

"Good," I mumbled. "Crisis averted."

Then I passed out.

24

There were a few people I wouldn't mind having at my side while I was on bed rest in the hospital. Bad Haircut Sammy wasn't one of them.

"I didn't set a demon loose in the guild," I told him wearily for the tenth time. "I sent you that message so you'd get the hell out before a fire demon could materialise on top of you. There were witnesses."

Since the only non-warlock witness was Fiona, the poor girl had been bombarded with questions by both the warlocks and the celestials, and the occasional member of the human law enforcement as well. I felt bad for her, but my severe burns made it a little difficult to hold conversation for the first couple of days of my recovery. At least Nikolas had taken me to a human hospital rather than the celestial guild's infirmary.

"Your messages make no sense," he said. "Neither do any of the crackpot theories you've been throwing around since you butted into our investigation."

"I was invited," I said. "Not my problem if your inspector

dude didn't like it. Where is he, anyway? I assume it must be important if he sent you in his place."

"He's busy, of course," he said. "Running the guild is hard work."

"Considering he's not meant to be in charge in the first place, and illegally locked up a group of innocent warlocks, I imagine he's neck-deep in paperwork."

His silence told me I was right on the mark. I couldn't suppress a grin. I wished Gav was around to see this. At least Clover had been discharged with no side effects. And Fiona, too. Rachel came to visit me disguised as several different people a day, which I appreciated. But I hadn't seen Nikolas yet. I assumed he was dealing with the arch-demon I'd dropped outside his brother's tower. I hadn't wanted to leave such a dire situation unsupervised, but the hospital flat-out refused to let me leave until my arms healed up.

"How'd you get burnt anyway?" Sammy asked.

"I killed a fire demon. Demigod." I tried to shrug. "You know the story. It doesn't matter to me either way."

He narrowed his eyes at me. "You always thought you were better than the rest of us. You and that partner of yours. Was it the same demon who killed him?"

I gave him a blistering glare. "I'm pretty heavily drugged right now, so I'm not entirely responsible if I end up punching your lights out. Just a warning."

He took a step back. "You're a liar, Devina," he said. "Everyone knows your story's a bullshit cover-up for you and those warlocks."

"Did someone say warlocks?" A girl with a shock of red hair bounded into the room. "Hey, Devi. I brought you cookies. Who's this?"

"Sammy, meet Rachel. She can turn into a creature with three sets of teeth."

Sammy jumped sideways. "Warlock!"

"I'm allowed in as a visitor," she said. "You, on the other hand, aren't. If I'm thinking of the right Sammy, there are a few warlocks who want to have words with you."

He paled and backed further away. I frowned at him. "Wait, *you're* the one who got those warlocks arrested? What did you do, hand over a random list of names pulled up from a google search?"

"Something like that," said Rachel. "Don't worry. We've all done foolish things in our quest to gain power."

Her hand flickered, momentarily replaced with a long claw. Sammy took one look at her and bolted.

I laughed. "Seriously? He's been hiding in here all day because he's scared of the warlocks?"

"Apparently." She shook her head. "I don't understand humans."

"Nor me, half the time." I took the bag of cookies from her, fumbling with the bandages. Not being able to use my hands was a nuisance, but at least my demon mark was hidden, for now. "They have the real story. It's up to them whether they choose to believe it or not."

"It'll be okay," said Rachel. "The human newspapers printed your story, and a huge interview with Fiona. The majority of people know the killer got caught."

"What we don't know is if anyone else was bitten," I said. "The side effects won't go away even though he's dead."

"Er, Devi, he's not actually dead."

"Crap. He regenerated?"

"Not before Niko and I shoved him in a prison cell. His power's totally drained, though. He won't be attacking anyone soon."

"Good." I closed my eyes. "I can't help the celestials if they don't listen to the warning. And we've no idea how many other vampires might have been infected. We only destroyed one nest of them."

Others might have had the same idea. After all, Azurial's death might have cleared up the murders, but not what'd happened to Rory. As far as I'd known at the time, he'd never been bitten by a vampire. But now I knew I wasn't to blame, I felt a sense of peace I hadn't since long before his death. I'd been so numb with disbelief when the celestials had disbelieved my report that I'd gradually forgotten the details of our mission, but we'd spent hours crawling through demon caves on our path to tracking the beast we'd been sent after on that fatal day. Now I knew how little it took for the demon energy to fatally spread through a victim, any one of the demons we'd run into might have been responsible.

Of course, it didn't bode well for the celestials, knowing the demons had found a weakness in their divine strength. And I'd bet Azurial was only the first to exploit it.

"The authorities know about those dodgy bloodstones by now," Rachel said. "After he let the warlocks out of jail, Javos went to see the vampire sires and terrified them. I don't think they'll be a problem for a while."

"Unlike the inspector," I said. "Is he even still at the guild, or hiding?"

"I think he left early this morning. Or sneaked out. He's not very popular there at the moment. Someone exposed his dodgy dealings with the guild's money…"

"Ha." I grinned. "Finally. I don't think he was actually working with a demon, but… did anyone have an explanation for that demonglass?"

"I haven't spoken to them," said Rachel. "They don't like warlocks."

"They're not fond of me, either," I said. "We'll get over it."

With the inspector on the guild's shit list, I'd be able to have a proper talk with them after I'd recovered. Didn't mean they'd ever *like* the warlocks, but if everyone would stop trying to kill one another for five minutes, it'd make my life a hell of a lot easier.

————

I wasn't naive enough to think the brief peace would last. Wounds were too raw, and even with the killer caught, inflamed tensions didn't die down easily. Some of the more astute celestials noted that the body of the demon responsible had never showed up, and it wasn't like any of them could verify it without going into the other dimension themselves. It'd be up to the high council to evaluate the evidence, and I was already dreading having to recount the whole thing, my own involvement, minus any references to using the demonglass *or* my mark. I needed to manufacture a cover story for the guild's superiors before then. Rachel and Nikolas might help, but the guild would trust even my word over a warlock's.

After a week, I had my first meeting with Mr Roth. My arms were still bandaged to the elbows, though my celestial mark still activated the guild's doors. Whether my demon mark functioned, too, remained to be seen. The bandages certainly attracted enough stares in the lobby. I pointedly avoided looking at everyone. If things went my way, I'd never see any of them again.

I made for the office which had once been Gav's, then the inspector's, and now—who knew. One glance at the demon almanac on the desk, of all things, made tears spring to my eyes. I blinked them away and planted myself in the seat opposite Mr Roth like I owned the place.

"Before you ask how I'm doing," I said, "I was having a great time recovering before I got dragged here and paraded in front of everyone like a circus freak. Why not meet with me somewhere else?"

He frowned at me. "You want to use a different room?"

"Never mind," I said. "Just get this over with. Am I getting arrested or not?"

"Of course not. Your actions—rash though they might be—saved lives."

"That makes the way you treated my best friend worth it, then," I said. "Don't think I haven't heard about your people showing up at Fiona's flat. She's human, and got dragged into this by accident."

"I never sent anyone to her flat," he said, sounding tired. "I can't control every celestial, and those who followed the inspector's lead are... restless. Not all of them believe your story."

"I figured that much out when they sneaked into the hospital to gloat at me," I said. "Never mind them. I just want reassurance that you'll leave me, and the warlocks, alone. You're free to pester the vampires if you want, but don't make it my problem."

"I wanted to offer you your old position back, Devina."

"You're probably expecting me to give you the benefit of the doubt," I said. "Seeing as I broke into your headquarters, broke the law several times, and caused chaos across three dimensions."

His brows drew together, and he opened his mouth to speak.

I got there first. "Unfortunately for you, your inspector accused me of multiple murders on no evidence, refused to listen, and let his little grudge against the local warlocks hide what was really going on. I've no intention whatsoever of working here again, in a consulting capacity or otherwise. If you manage to get yourself into another mess, go and hire someone else."

His jaw dropped. "Devina Lawson."

"You know, you'd get along better if you didn't act as

though you're above everyone else because you were chosen by the Divinities. Because I don't think they give any more of a crap about us than the demons do. Tossing blame around won't help if they decide to attack our dimension again." I had no doubt they would. The passing of an arch-demon wouldn't be without its side effects. Even if he was likely still alive, his time was limited.

"I wish you'd reconsider—"

"Don't," I said, lifting my bandaged hands. "I wouldn't have ended up like this if your people had listened to reason. And I'd really like to know what that demonglass in your storeroom is doing there."

He blinked. "What demonglass?"

"Don't pull that one on me. Why do you think I sent pictures of it to Gav? Where's his phone?"

He looked around. "I don't know. The inspector had it—"

"And have you been in the west wing lately?"

"Devina, I don't see how this is relevant to—"

"There's a sheet of demonglass hidden in there. I'll send you the pictures, but if one of your people is talking to demons, I have no interest whatsoever in cleaning up your mess."

He shook his head. "I regret what happened to you, Devina. I wish it could have been handled differently."

"Welcome to the club." I pushed to my feet. "I'll see myself out."

I'd said my part, and the guild had nothing more to offer me. Just bad memories, tinged with regret. I never had confirmed the same demon virus had killed Rory, but anything was possible. Even a celestial with the mark of a demon.

I found Clover waiting outside the front doors.

"I take it you said no?" she asked.

"You knew, did you?" I rolled my eyes at her. "Honestly, I

don't know why he even asked. He must have known I won't come near this place again. Not with an invite anyway."

"I suspected," she said. "So are you going back to your old job?"

Considering the trail of vampire corpses I'd left behind me, they probably wouldn't want to hire me anytime soon. As for the humans… it depended how many had closely followed the news. Or saw the latest pictures on DivinityWatch.

"Maybe," I said. "I need to speak to the warlocks."

"They're not in jail anymore," she said. "But I suppose your warlock friend told you."

"Yeah, she did," I said. Probably, she meant Nikolas, but again… I'd seen no sign of him. Not since I'd given him an arch-demon to lock up in his home dimension. Considering the trouble I'd caused, he and Javos probably wanted to avoid me for a bit. "And the celestials who were bitten?"

"Isolated and kept under watch," she said. "The inspector might have handled things badly, but putting the novices into groups did make it easier to figure out who was affected. Only three novices are known to have been bitten, and we're working on a cure for the venom."

"Just as long as they don't run into any demons." I grimaced. "As for the inspector, one halfway decent idea doesn't change the fact that he nearly started a war. I'm not forgetting who enabled that, and who tried to get me thrown in jail."

"No, you'd be wise not to." Clover paused. "I'd advise you to be careful who you let into your circle, Devina." Her gaze briefly went to my right hand, then to my face again, too fast for me to be certain she'd looked at the demon mark. *Does she know?* The question hovered on the tip of my tongue, but even now, I didn't trust the guild not to have had me followed. And I didn't trust them, end of. Not just because I wouldn't forget what they'd done, but because there was plainly someone here interested in covering their tracks. Missing demonglass, Gav's stolen phone… and the reminder that I'd never truly figured out how Rory had died. I might not have caused it, intentionally or not, but who knew for sure what'd happened while I was in that demon dimension?

"I'll be careful," I told her, and walked away.

I hadn't reached the end of the road before I saw the shadows move out of the corner of my eye. Pausing, I glanced to the side. "That's not very subtle of you."

The shadows peeled back, revealing Nikolas. His gaze immediately dropped to my arms. "I hoped you wouldn't suffer lasting damage. Unfortunately, the hospital lies right over a demon-infested crater in my own realm, so I was unable to stop in and check on you."

"I thought you were busy," I said. "With your new guest."

A shadow passed over his face. "Yes. His power's mostly gone, but he's imprisoned safely in the castle. He probably won't live very long. Pandemonium will be facing a lot of changes soon."

I shrugged. "That's their problem. I take it our fiery friend won't rise again and cause trouble?"

"Not if I have anything to do with it. I didn't know you could take others with you when you travel through dimensions. Did you?"

"No. I was improvising."

"I wouldn't have thought of it," he said. "Moving demons between dimensions is generally not advisable, but I think in Themedes's case, his power isn't strong enough to make a significant difference. However, Devi, I'd prefer it if you asked my permission in future before bringing undesirable characters into my castle."

"Not like I planned to make a habit of it, believe me." I held up my bandaged hands. "I'm not sure what else I can do with the mark, but there's one person—a friend at the guild —who might have guessed. She won't tell anyone."

She doesn't trust the guild. And the demonglass? That was a major red flag if I ever saw one. Someone was up to no good in the guild. But not the killer. Thank the Divinities for that.

"Javos will need to know," he said. "It's required. You might be the only person we know of with a demon's mark, but everyone we train is logged in case accidents happen."

"You seem awfully convinced I'll let you train me."

"It's in your interests to." His expression was serious. "If you can't tell me who gave you the mark, then it's possible they will come for you in future, whoever they are. You'll have to be ready."

"You still don't trust me." I watched his face for clues, finding none.

"I don't trust the arch-demons," he corrected. "I'd rather know if someone planned to step in and claim you. I was just starting to like you."

His answer caught me off guard. "Only just? I'm disappointed."

A smile curled his lip. "You're something else entirely, Devi, and I'd like it very much if you told me what you know. Everything you say to me will be confidential."

I screwed my eyes closed, then opened them again. "My partner, the one who died," I said slowly. "I... wasn't exactly in this dimension when it happened."

I told him. I admitted that I'd prayed to the Divinity who'd saved me for help, only to find Rory dying on the other side of the portal.

"I thought I did it, somehow," I said, not looking at Nikolas. "I thought I'd somehow transferred the curse over to him, or accidentally brought down divine judgement on both of us. The celestial training taught me that, and obviously I wasn't going to *tell* them. So I took the coward's way out. Until these deaths. I thought I was cursed."

"Not cursed," said Nikolas. "Unlucky, certainly. Demons don't answer prayers, generally. Not a celestial's either."

"Yeah, well. The vampires seemed to recognise the demon whose mark is on me. Unfortunately, they're all dead."

"I might be able to answer that question," said Nikolas. "The mark is unmistakeably from an arch-demon, not one I've seen before, but there's only one way an arch-demon can be created."

"Because the Divinity who gave me my celestial powers is no longer an angel," I said. "They fell."

He gave me a brief nod. "Yes. I suspect that's the case. You couldn't have known. Netherworld alone does."

"But what does that mean for the other celestials?" I asked. "I can't have been the only one converted by that particular Divinity."

"That," he said, "depends on whether you were considering going back to work for them or not."

"Have you been spying on the guild?"

"It was obvious, Devina. They're trying to save face. But my offer is still open. Work with Javos and me. You'll need to train your demonic power if you don't want anyone taking advantage. News of your exploits has doubtless travelled by now."

"Yeah, I figured. What sort of work would it be?"

"Whatever needs doing. I think it's best that we keep you away from arch-demons in future, but considering the only one we're in contact with is locked up in my castle, that shouldn't be an issue."

The guild hadn't been my home for a long time. Maybe it never had been. No other celestial would ever accept a mark from hell, but the demon mark didn't have to be a sign of condemnation. Not if I didn't want it to be. One mark from the Divinities. One from the demons. Whichever choice I made, whatever cause I fought for, I'd do so on my own terms.

"All right," I said. "Don't speak too soon, though. I have a reputation."

"I'm sure you'll give Javos a run for his money." He paused for a moment. "Now, I've checked my brother is safely ensconced in his tower, and there happens to be an impressive light display happening in the shadow realm right now. Want to come and watch?"

I hesitated. "No demons?"

"Absolutely none. They don't like the daylight."

"Then okay. Sure."

Shadows closed in around us, then faded, and the cold air of the shadow realm rushed in. Before me was a sky striped in purple, still etched with stars.

I turned to Nikolas. "I didn't know this place looked like that during the day."

He pointed. "Watch."

A star detached itself from the constellation, falling down. Another followed, leaving a glittering trail behind, and another, etching themselves on my vision. I thought I'd seen it all, but the demon world proved me wrong.

"How did you know I'd like this?" I asked.

"I had a hunch." He took a step closer to me, and I let him, my bandaged hands held loosely at my sides.

"You were right," I admitted. "But I reckon you wanted to prove this realm isn't all bad. If you forget the swarm demons, your brother, and the arch-demon you have locked up here."

A smile tugged at his mouth. "Yes, I suppose I did."

"All right. You win this round."

I tilted back my head to watch the last star fall with a trail of light, over the wasteland of the demon's realm.

ABOUT THE AUTHOR

Emma is the New York Times and USA Today Bestselling author of the Changeling Chronicles urban fantasy series.

Emma spent her childhood creating imaginary worlds to compensate for a disappointingly average reality, so it was probably inevitable that she ended up writing fantasy novels. When she's not immersed in her own fictional universes, Emma can be found with her head in a book or wandering around the world in search of adventure.

Find out more about Emma's books at
www.emmaladams.com.

www.ingramcontent.com/pod-product-compliance
Lightning Source LLC
Chambersburg PA
CBHW020756190726
48285CB00006B/2053